"I Won't Do It Again!"

Steve shouted. "I *can't* do it again!"

"Can't do *what?*" Kitty shouted back.

He faced her across the room, his face grim in the dim light. "I can't let what happened between us happen again. I will not allow you to seduce me again."

"But I wasn't," Kitty breathed. "I wasn't trying to seduce you!"

"You don't *have* to try!" he said bitterly. "You don't have to try at all."

LUCY HAMILTON
is the mother of a young daughter and writes in her spare time. She looks forward to "translating a lifelong affection for books into a new career."

Dear Reader:

Silhouette has always tried to give you exactly what you want. When you asked for increased realism, deeper characterization and greater length, we brought you Silhouette Special Editions. When you asked for increased sensuality, we brought you Silhouette Desire. Now you ask for books with the length and depth of Special Editions, the sensuality of Desire, but with something else besides, something that no one else offers. Now we bring you SILHOUETTE INTIMATE MOMENTS, true romance novels, longer than the usual, with all the depth that length requires. More sensuous than the usual, with characters whose maturity matches that sensuality. Books with the ingredient no one else has tapped: excitement.

There is an electricity between two people in love that makes everything they do magic, larger than life—and this is what we bring you in SILHOUETTE INTIMATE MOMENTS. Look for them this May, wherever you buy books.

These books are for the woman who wants more than she has ever had before. These books are for you. As always, we look forward to your comments and suggestions. You can write to me at the address below:

Karen Solem
Editor-in-Chief
Silhouette Books
P.O. Box 769
New York, N.Y. 10019

LUCY HAMILTON
All's Fair

Silhouette Special Edition
Published by Silhouette Books New York
America's Publisher of Contemporary Romance

Other Silhouette Books by Lucy Hamilton

A Woman's Place

SILHOUETTE BOOKS, a Simon & Schuster Division of
GULF & WESTERN CORPORATION
1230 Avenue of the Americas, New York, N.Y. 10020

ISBN: 0-671-53592-7

First Silhouette Books printing May, 1983

10 9 8 7 6 5 4 3 2 1

Map by Ray Lundgren

America's Publisher of Contemporary Romance

Printed in the U.S.A.

*With all my thanks to Thomas C. Hemmer
for the technical assistance which made
this book possible; to Dorothy Linton
for her hard work and invaluable suggestions; to Lynne, who thought writing was a
good idea in the first place; and to
Dennis for his love and support.*

All's Fair

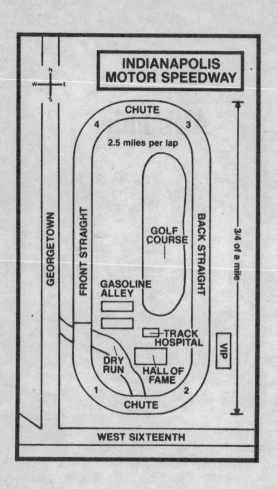

Chapter One

"This is it," Jack Hampson said, addressing his troops like a general before a battle. "We've all done a helluva lot of hard work in the last few months, and tomorrow is the moment of truth." He ran a gentle finger along the side of the low-slung, scarlet race car, then looked back at his crew.

"Steve will arrive from Europe tomorrow. He'll stop by to see the car, and all of you, then the next day he'll take the car out for a run. Tomorrow we'll fill him in on the modifications we've made in last year's design. Kitty," he nodded to the chassis engineer, the only woman in the room, "your big job tomorrow will be to give Steve all the details of the changes in the chassis. I'll fill him in on the engine."

Petite, raven-haired Kitty Gordon nodded and made a brief note on the clipboard balanced on her knee, while Jack gave some last-minute instructions to the mechanics. "That's it then," he concluded. "We're all through here, so—take the rest of the day off!"

Like children let out of school early, the crew gave an exuberant cheer and scrambled to leave for home, while Jack watched with the genial smile of the benevolent dictator he was. After the months of work they had all put in on this race car, the seven-day weeks of fourteen-hour days, the moment of truth, as Jack had said, was indeed upon them.

The next day was the opening day of practice at the Indianapolis Motor Speedway, and a moment of truth for all the racing teams entered, Kitty mused, collecting her purse and briefcase and sending a general "Good night" around the garage before leaving. It would indeed be a moment of truth for her, in more ways than one.

She had been a member of Steve Duncan's racing team for four months now, since she had received her degree in automotive engineering the previous January, and in that time she had done her best to justify Jack's decision to hire her. This job had been an opportunity she couldn't pass up, a chance to work with the acknowledged elite of automotive specialists.

The Indianapolis 500 was far more than just a car race. It was a piece of history, an *event*, and a showcase for the ultimate in automotive design, construction and driving skill. Since childhood, Kitty had dreamed of being part of this race. As a twenty-three-year-old engineering graduate, she had viewed the offer of the job of chassis engineer on a racing team as her dream come true. Even the prospect of working with Steve Duncan could not dampen her enthusiasm.

At least it hadn't dampened her enthusiasm until today. She swung her car, an old but meticulously restored Ford Mustang, into her garage and walked quickly to her back door to let herself into her small, bright kitchen. Without pausing there, she continued to the bathroom to strip off her work clothes and step into the shower. Today, when Jack had begun to talk about Steve's arrival tomorrow, the reality of her decision had suddenly come home to her in a rush. She was committed to working with him, working closely with him, from May 1, tomorrow, until the race was run on Memorial Day, and now that the moment was at hand she could no longer deny the tension, almost fear, that the thought of seeing him again aroused.

She leaned against the tiles, letting the water drum on her shoulders, and raised one dripping hand. It was trembling, and Kitty's lips twisted in a humorless smile. So much for her undampened enthusiasm.

Showered, wrapped in a terry robe and carrying a tuna-fish sandwich and a glass of iced tea, she dropped onto the living-room sofa, curling her legs beneath her and gazing sightlessly at the evening news on television. She took a bite of her sandwich and munched absently on it, but her thoughts were far from her supper.

The time had come for her to face Steve Duncan again, the time that had seemed so far off when she began working on the crew last January. Then she had comforted herself with the thought that the inevitable confrontation was months away. As the months dwindled to weeks and the weeks to days, she had avoided thinking of his arrival at all, but now it was upon her, and she had no idea how to deal with it.

It had all happened so long ago, seven years ago, and she had tried, really tried, to bury the memories. They were pushed deep down within her, but they were always there, ready to pop out, gibbering and sneering, if she lowered her mental guard for even an instant. She had played with fire, and in the way of these things she had been burned and left with scars she could never erase. However painful and humiliating, the memories were there, the events of the past shaping the woman she was today from the sixteen-year-old she had been.

Knowing she would see him again the next day brought it all back. Tiredly Kitty leaned her head back against the cushions, her eyes falling closed as time slipped away, taking her back to the summer she turned sixteen. She had idolized Steve since she was five years old, when he and his family had moved into the house next door, but as she reached her teens, her childish hero worship had changed into something much more complex.

The summer when she was sixteen, Steve was twenty-five and in the Army. When her brother John, Steve's age and his longtime best friend, came running into the kitchen one evening to tell Kitty and their widower father that Steve was coming to Indianapolis for a long weekend, she had concealed her leaping sense of elation beneath a calm surface.

Steve was coming! He would be staying next door in his parents' house, empty for the summer while they vacationed in Michigan, and she would insist that John bring him over for all his meals. He'd see, he would finally see, that she wasn't a little girl anymore. She'd *make* him see that she was a woman now, and she'd show him that she loved him. After that . . .

"After that" had been vague in her teen-age mind, far too vague, as it had turned out. At the time she hadn't thought about anything more than the plans that had kept her busy until the Friday of Steve's arrival. That morning found her hurriedly washing her father's car, anxious to complete the task before lunchtime so that she could shower and change into the new scarlet sundress that was laid out on her bed. The evening meal was already prepared and waiting to be popped into the oven, so that she could greet Steve at the door when he came for dinner, cool and unruffled, the perfect hostess. She dwelt on that image of herself, cool and sophisticated, serving a delectable meal to an awe-struck Steve, and bent to scrub the hubcaps. Her hair was caught back in a ponytail, and she was dressed for grubby work in brief, cutoff jeans, a T-shirt that had been a good fit last year, but was now too snug for her newly blossoming body, and ancient sneakers with holes in the toes.

From her position in the driveway, screened from a view of the street by the house and some shrubbery, she heard a car pull up to the curb and the slam of a door. John had told her he was coming home for lunch, and she called to him as she dumped her bucket of soapy water out on the drive.

"John, your lunch is in the refrigerator, but before you go in, would you turn on the hose for me?"

"Be glad to."

"Thanks a—" Her voice died away as she straightened, hose in hand, and saw who had replied.

"Steve? Steve!" she shrieked happily, and forgetting all pretense of sophistication, dropped the hose and sprinted around the car to hurl herself into his outstretched arms. They closed around her and he swung her in a circle before lowering her feet to the ground and stepping back, holding her shoulders and smiling down into her upturned face.

He was so handsome that he took her breath away. Fully a foot taller than Kitty's five feet one inch, he had the kind of classic all-American good looks that were used to sell everything from hot dogs to expensive cars. Thick, straight, wheat-blond hair fell onto his forehead above clear gray eyes, a straight nose with slightly flaring nostrils and a finely chiseled mouth with a firm upper lip and a slightly fuller, more sensual lower lip. High cheekbones, a square jaw and a deep tan completed the picture, and Kitty gazed at him with something approaching awe.

"You're prettier than ever, Kitten," he said, and caught her to him again for a brief hug. When he released her, she could only stare foolishly up at him for a moment, tingling all over from the feel of his hard body against her. Recovering herself and belatedly remembering her plans to be cool, *soignée* and mature, she wiped the silly, beaming grin off her face and replaced it with the friendly but casual smile she had practiced in front of the bathroom mirror for days.

"Why, thank you, Steve," she replied in a well-modulated voice that drew a faint narrowing of the eyes from him. "What a nice compliment. Would you like to have lunch with us? John should be home any minute."

"I'd like that very much, Kitty." Steve accepted with more than a hint of amusement in his voice and eyes. "I'll take my suitcase in and change. Will ten minutes be OK?"

Kitty agreed that ten minutes would be acceptable and watched him stride across to his front steps, turning away hastily when he glanced back at her as he fitted his key in the lock.

Damn and double damn! It was all going wrong! She was dressed like a slob in her ratty T-shirt, rattier shorts and absolutely disgusting tennies with holes in the toes; she didn't have any makeup on, and her hair was in a ponytail, of all the dumb, juvenile hairstyles in the world, and she was washing a *car!* Sophisticated women *never* washed cars! She gave the outdoor tap a vicious twist and turned the hose on the car. If she got it rinsed off fast enough, maybe she could change before lunch.

She certainly rinsed it quickly, with the tap full open; Niagara Falls wouldn't have washed the soap away much faster. But even as she turned the tap off and jumbled the hose hurriedly out of the way, not taking time to coil it neatly, John swung his car into the drive.

"Hey!" His shout halted Kitty on her way up the back steps. "Aren't you going to dry it?"

"The sun'll dry it just fine." She trotted up the last few steps. "Steve's here already," she tossed casually over her shoulder, and grinned at John's roar of glee. "He's at his house, if you want to say hi. Lunch will be ready in about ten minutes." And five of those will be spent on me. The door slammed behind her, and she sprinted for the stairs.

She whipped into the bathroom and slammed that door as well, locked it for good measure and bent to wash her face. No need for powder or blush, she had the sort of creamy skin that loved the sun, going gold in the first spring sunshine, and excitement had pinkened her cheeks. A touch of eye shadow, mascara, lip gloss, then she brushed quickly through her hair until it lay, long and straight, like black satin around her shoulders.

"*Kitty!*" John bellowed from the kitchen. "Where's lunch?"

She added a spray of cologne to augment the faint scent of floral soap that lingered from the morning's shower and opened the door to call down the stairs. "I'll be right down!"

A final check in the mirror. Maybe she should change clothes? No, it would look as though she were trying too hard. Plus, John would undoubtedly make some crack about her dressing up and embarrass her to death. She stuck out her tongue at the frayed toes of her sneakers and skipped lightly down the stairs.

She slowed to a deliberately graceful walk outside the kitchen door, and her entrance was as sophisticated as an entrance can be when the person making it is dressed in cutoffs and a too-small T-shirt. Sadly, this effort was wasted, for both men were standing on the back porch, beer cans in hand, roaring with laughter at some shared joke, and they didn't even notice her until she took the pot of soup she had made the day before out of the refrigerator and banged it smartly onto the burner.

At the clang of metal against metal they turned and Kitty smiled sweetly, seething inside. "It will take a few minutes for the soup to heat," she told them. "You two just enjoy your beer." When they did just that, ignoring her completely, her irritation grew, and though it hadn't cooled by the time the soup was bubbling hot and a plate of sandwiches had been set in the center of the neatly laid table, she had at least slipped a mask of composure over it.

They brought their beers in with them and took seats, declining Kitty's offer of iced tea to drink. She ladled their soup into bowls and poured a glass of tea for herself, puttering around before joining them at the table, unaware of Steve's eyes following her as she went about her small tasks, although her mind was filled with his image.

He had changed into tight, well-worn jeans that

molded his slim hips and long, strong legs, and a knit
sport shirt of thin cotton in a deep cream color clung
lovingly to his broad shoulders and the planes of
muscle on his chest. His arms were muscular and
darkly tanned, with a furring of golden hair, and the
hand that lifted his spoon was square and strong with
long, straight fingers.

After several minutes John said something teasing
about her silence, and she looked up, first at him, then
at Steve. John merely looked cheerful as usual, but
when her eyes met Steve's she caught, in the instant
before he could hide it, a fleeting glimpse of something new. She wasn't sure what it was exactly, but it
made her feel sort of warm and tingly, and as she
dropped her eyes to her plate in confusion she could
feel a blush heating her cheeks.

When she looked up again it was at John, who was
watching her with an altered expression as well. The
look in his eyes made her uneasy, composed as it was
of speculation, surprise and a hint of grimness. At
sixteen she hadn't understood that look on his face,
but now, with the increased comprehension of maturity, she knew that he had suddenly seen her through
his friend's eyes.

He had seen the way Steve was watching his little
sister as she moved around the room, and when he
looked back at Kitty he had realized what had put that
look in the other man's eyes.

She was just his little sister, but now he looked and
saw the beauty of her young body: slim, shapely legs,
golden tanned and long for one so petite; tiny waist;
gently rounded hips that moved enchantingly in her
snug denim shorts. He saw the new shapeliness in her
slim arms and the firm young breasts that pressed
against her too-small shirt. He'd always known that

her face was pretty; now he saw the new maturity in
the large, cocoa-brown eyes heavily fringed with dark
lashes, the loss of childish plumpness from the small
face with its high cheekbones and wide brow, and the
provocative fullness of the lower lip with its shine of
berry-pink gloss.

She had only begun to understand what John must
have been feeling as the years passed and she looked
back on that day, remembering how his cheerful
banter had suddenly become forced and how he'd
hurried Steve on his way as soon as the meal was
finished. He'd come back to the kitchen while she was
washing dishes, clearing his throat and shuffling his
feet restlessly before he spoke.

"I know you have to wear old clothes to wash the
car," he said in an oddly nervous voice, "but you've
grown, and that shirt is kind of . . . uh—" He broke
off uneasily, and Kitty glanced down at herself. She
had splashed the front of the shirt, which now clung
wetly to her, making it obvious that she wore no bra.
Flushing, she turned away from her brother's eyes.

"Don't be silly, Johnny," she said, her voice sharpened by embarrassment. "It's just a shirt."

"Yeah, I know, but with Steve around this weekend, maybe you shouldn't—"

"Johnneee—!" Kitty wailed, her face scarlet, and he
grimaced apologetically.

"I just saw the way Steve was watching you," he
went on doggedly. "You know what I mean?"

Kitty nodded silently, her head bent over the
dishes, and after a long moment John left her alone.
She did know what he meant. She had an idea that
John had seen a great deal more than she wanted him
to, and it made her nervous. Johnny would never
understand what she wanted, how she felt.

But there was also the look she had seen in Steve's eyes. It was the way a man looks at a woman, and she had seen it when he looked at her.

At least she thought that was what she had seen. As she sat alone that evening, watching a bad movie on television while John and Steve were out visiting old friends and her father tinkered on his sprint-type race car out in the garage, she wondered if perhaps she'd been mistaken. Steve's treatment of her at dinner had been maddeningly avuncular, despite the scarlet sundress, which emphasized her small waist and left her shoulders bare but for spaghetti straps tied in bows, and he and John had left as soon as the meal was finished.

Suddenly the television was an unbearable annoyance, and she crossed the room to switch it off. She stood in front of the cabinet for a moment, then let her breath out on a long sigh of frustration. Why fight it? She was here, Steve wasn't, and it was silly to sit around, all dressed up, and mope. She might as well go help Dad with the race car, at least that was interesting.

She was back in the garage the next morning, leaning over the car to make minor adjustments in the rate of fuel flow while her father raced the engine, listening to the sputter and roar like a musician tuning his instrument. Kitty was at home here; she'd grown up listening and watching as her father and brother built, modified and tuned the cars a friend of her father's drove in midget- and sprint-car races around the Midwest.

She had begun to help by passing tools when they were needed, and was now a far better mechanic than any of the boys she went to school with, with a particular knowledge of racing cars. Her ambition,

bizarre though it would have seemed to those who did
not know her well, was to study automotive engineering at college and then design race cars.

She opened the valve another tiny fraction at her
father's direction, then peered up from the engine as
she heard a piercing wolf whistle above the engine
noise.

Steve stood in the doorway grinning at them, and
Kitty cursed the malevolent fates that seemed to be
conspiring against her. She hadn't expected to see him
so early in the day, and once again she wore no
makeup, her hair was in one thick plait down her back
and she was dressed in blue jeans and an old blouse
with the sleeves rolled up.

"Come on in, Steve," her father called, "and see
what we've done with this engine."

"Can't!" Steve called back, and gestured at his legs,
bared by a pair of cutoff jeans. "No long pants!"
Frank Gordon nodded his understanding. One hard-
and-fast rule in a racing garage was that no one
entered with their legs uncovered because of the
ever-present danger of burns. Frank shut the engine
off and with Kitty's help pulled a canvas cover over
the car.

"In that case," he said amiably, "we'll come out.
We've been at it long enough for one morning. Can I
offer you a cup of coffee?"

"Thanks, but I just stopped by to see if John wants
to go down to Lake Monroe for the day. Chuck
Caldwell runs a marina there, and he said to bring
John along."

"Well, that's too bad." Frank shook his head
regretfully. "John got called in to work today on some
big contract or other the company just got. He'll be
off around six, though."

Steve frowned at the sidewalk beneath his feet. "I'm afraid that's too late. Chuck said to get there around noon and plan on some sailing and swimming this afternoon, so . . ."

Kitty had stood silently to one side during this exchange, but now Steve looked across at her, and her heart began to pound with slow heavy thumps.

"It's too bad John is busy," he said slowly, "because I wouldn't mind some company on the drive down. Would you like to come along, Kitten?"

Some of the glow of anticipation melted in the face of his indifference, for it was hardly flattering to be considered only one step above an empty seat in the car, and a clear second best to your brother. She drew herself up to her full height, such as it was, and lifted her chin haughtily.

"I don't know," she replied with elaborate indifference. "Dad might need more help on the car."

Frank looked around at her in blank surprise, eyebrows raised, as Steve said, "Well, if you can't go, I guess I'll—"

"*No!*" Kitty interrupted him in sudden panic, and her father's eyebrows climbed even higher at her tone. "I mean . . ." She faltered, flushing under their eyes, her father's surprised but Steve's amused, enjoying her discomfiture. "I mean I'd like to go—if you don't need me, Daddy?"

Steve's eyes were alight with mirth as he turned to Frank, who said dryly, "Of course you can go. I think I can do without you for one day. You just have a good time."

"Thank you, Daddy," she said in a subdued tone belied by the angry glitter in her eyes. "What time should I be ready, Steve?"

He checked his watch. "Actually, if we could leave

right away, we'd get there just about on time. How soon can you be ready?"

"Ten minutes?" Kitty felt that she had given in much too easily, but what could she do? He obviously didn't care a great deal one way or the other, and she'd be an idiot to pass up this chance. At the very least she'd be alone with him for an hour each way on the drive down and back. Somehow she'd make the most of the opportunity.

In even less than the ten minutes allotted to her she had changed into a red sun top and cuffed white shorts that left the slim, tanned length of her legs bare, stuffed a swimsuit and other necessities into a bag, and was waving back at her father as Steve's car pulled away from the curb. The convertible top was down, and Kitty had used a bright red-white-and-blue scarf to tie her hair back at her nape against the wind. It fluttered on her neck as she closed her eyes and let her head drop back against the seat, enjoying the warm sun on her skin, too relaxed to be angry with Steve for his amusement at her expense.

"You look like you could play a jet setter in an advertisement." She could hear the warm undertone of amusement in his voice, but it was not unkind, and she grinned in response.

"I *am* a jet setter, didn't you know that?"

"A jet setter washing a car? No way!"

"*Au contraire,* dahling. Washing cars is all the rage in Paris this year. Better for you than a week at the spa."

"That explains it."

"Explains what?"

"Why they're wearing holey-toed sneakers on the Champs-Elysées."

"You're a nut!" She giggled and sat up, opening her

eyes. They were on West 16th Street, passing the main gate of the Indianapolis Motor Speedway. Like many Hoosiers, Kitty was an avid fan of the Indianapolis 500, not only because she lived in the hometown of the race, but also because of her family's involvement in auto racing. She turned to look at the south end of the Speedway grounds as they passed, though what she could see was mainly the back of the grandstands, then looked back at Steve to find him watching her with a curious expression.

"Are you a race fan?" he asked.

"Of course! How could I not be, with Daddy and John always working on cars?"

"I don't know. I thought you might have outgrown it."

"Oh, *no!*" Kitty replied, astonished at his suggestion. "It's not something you outgrow. Anyway, do you want to know a secret I've never told anyone else?"

"What's that?" He sounded as though he were humoring a child, but Kitty ignored his patronizing tone and went on, her voice low and vibrant with the passionate fervor of youthful ambition.

"I'm going to college to study engineering so that I can design cars, especially race cars, and eventually I'll design a car for the 500. And it'll win!" She gave a little nod for emphasis and sat back, arms folded across her chest. There was a long moment of silence, and then Steve burst into laughter, freezing Kitty into shocked humiliation.

"*You're* going to design a car?" he gasped when he could speak. "Oh, Kitten, I've never seen anyone who looked less like an automotive designer!" He began to chuckle again, and Kitty's icy silence exploded into a furious rush of words.

"What difference does that make?" she snapped. "I don't have to look like a designer, whatever a designer looks like, I only have to *be* one. And I will!" Her voice wobbled and she averted her face, blinking rapidly against the tears that started to her eyes.

"But, Kitten," he said reasonably, "auto racing's a man's field."

"Well, that's just stupid!" She turned back to him, her face flushed with anger. "I already know more about cars, especially racing cars, than any boy I know. Why, I probably know more than you!"

"I doubt that," he said dryly.

"Even so," she conceded, "I like it, I'm good at it, and I'll get better at it. Why should I give it up just because it's a 'man's field'?" she finished with a catch in her voice, and Steve reached over to capture her hand, clenched in a furious fist.

"I'm sorry, Kitten," he said gently. "I shouldn't have laughed at you. You're absolutely right that there's no reason why you should give up your dream. And heaven knows," he added with a hint of humor, "your father and John have given you the background." He gave her hand a final squeeze and released it. "You stick with your dream, Kitten. As a matter of fact, I have a dream, too. Do you want to know what it is?"

"If—if you want to tell me."

"I do." He paused, then smiled. "One of these days, I'm going to drive in the 500."

"Really? Steve, how exciting!"

"I'll tell you what. When I drive in the 500 you can be on my crew."

"Okay," she agreed, going along with the joke.

"There's one problem, though. They don't allow women in the pits."

"They'll have changed that silly rule by then," she

said confidently, and Steve laughed again, friendly laughter this time, not hurtful.

It was strange, almost eerie, the way things had happened. Kitty shifted uneasily on the sofa. It was as though they'd predicted events to come in that silly, teasing conversation, as though they'd seen the future without even being aware of it. Two years after that Steve had driven in his first 500 and finished a very respectable twelfth when his car blew a cylinder near the end of the race. He was now world famous, driving Formula One cars on the Grand Prix circuit most of the year and returning to Indianapolis each May for the 500. The rule barring women from the garage and pit areas at the Speedway had been changed. She had her degree. And she was a member of Steve's crew.

It was a little bit frightening, as though fate or some other powerful, inexorable force were working with their lives, throwing them together again after all the hurt and bitterness.

There had been no shadow of what was to come on that golden Saturday, though, as the drive passed quickly in a highly technical discussion of cars and racing. It wasn't until they drove through the pleasant university town of Bloomington and took the country road toward the lake that she began to feel nervous about meeting Steve's friends. She was so much younger than they were, they might think her gauche, childlike, a bother.

Five hours later Kitty was able to marvel at the fact that she had ever thought she might feel out of place. She had been drawn into the friendly circle and made to feel welcome, and the afternoon she had dreaded had flown by as they sailed and swam.

As she sat in a recliner on the redwood deck at

the rear of the small house, letting the late-afternoon sun dry her brief two-piece swimsuit, she closed her eyes and relaxed with a sigh of utter contentment. Chuck was lighting the charcoal in the barbecue grill on which he would soon cook their dinner, but for now they were all lazy with sun and exertion. Turning away from the grill, he grinned down at the other two: Kitty, petite, very pregnant Maryann, stretched on a recliner like Kitty, and Steve, seated on the deck itself, his back against the rail and his legs stretched out before him.

"What a bunch of deadbeats!" Chuck laughed. "You look like you've all been working overtime!"

"I feel like it," Maryann groaned. "All that exercise—" Chuck's expression changed instantly from amusement to alarm.

"Are you all right, honey?" He dropped down to sit on his heels beside her chair and looked worriedly into her eyes. "Should I call the doctor? I shouldn't have let you do all that swimming—!"

"Hush," his wife commanded, laying her fingers across his lips. "I'm healthy as a horse, and you know it. I'm a little tired, but you'd be tired, too, if you were carrying an extra person around." She patted her stomach affectionately. "Junior and I are just fine, so you stop worrying. OK?"

Chuck nodded in reluctant agreement, and she sat up and kissed him lightly on the nose. "Kitty and I are going to go get the rest of the dinner ready," she announced, "so you two chefs had better get cracking with the steaks. Junior's getting hungry!"

Chuck helped her to her feet, and Kitty rose to follow her hostess inside, saying, "I have a correction for that. Maryann is going to sit quietly in a chair and tell Kitty what to do, and Kitty is going to do it.

Right?" Chuck threw her a grateful glance, which Maryann intercepted with a wry smile.

"I think you two have been conspiring against me, but I'll go along with the program."

"Don't worry, Maryann," Steve called after them. "She does know how to cook!"

"That's good to know, I suppose," said Maryann dryly as the kitchen door swung closed behind them, "but I already had faith in your abilities."

Kitty grinned and Maryann directed her to a guest bedroom where she changed from her nearly dry swimsuit into her shorts and top. When she returned to the kitchen she found Maryann already there, dressed in a full sundress that left her tanned arms bare and flowed flatteringly around her bulky shape. She grinned ruefully at Kitty's neat outfit.

"You look so trim and pulled together, you make me jealous," she said, then looked down at herself and grimaced. "I'm beginning to think I'll never look like anything but a blimp!"

"Nonsense." Kitty pushed her gently toward a chair. "You look lovely, and you'd know it if you watched Chuck watching you. He's so proud he's about to pop!"

Maryann's cheeks pinkened prettily. "Thank you. The pepper is in the cupboard on your right," she added, as Kitty began gathering condiments on a tray. "I was watching you watching Steve." Kitty's head snapped around, the gesture all too revealing, as she realized too late.

Maryann nodded. "I know it's not my place to say anything," she said slowly, her pretty face troubled, "but you're a nice girl, and I'd hate to see you hurt."

"Maryann, you don't understand," Kitty protested, but Maryann interrupted her.

"I'm sorry, Kitty. I know I'm being an interfering

busybody, but you're going to be hurt if you go on the way you are."

"But how . . . ?" Kitty said in a kind of desperate embarrassment.

"How did I know?" Maryann's lips curved in a small smile. "I looked at you."

"Am I that obvious?" Kitty asked, and Maryann shrugged.

"You're very young—and Steve isn't."

Chapter Two

 itty stood rigid, embarrassed, defensive and not a little guilty, for wasn't Maryann, with the best of motives, warning her against the very thing she had been scheming?

"Look, Maryann," she said stiffly, "I know you mean well, but you're wrong. Oh, not about me," she added, as Maryann's eyebrows rose, "I feel as if I've loved Steve all my life, but he doesn't know. He just thinks of me as John's little sister, that's all. I know that, and I know all I can do is worship him from afar. It doesn't matter," she lied reassuringly.

Maryann smiled at her, relieved. "I'm glad you feel that way," she said, and Kitty had to turn away to hide the guilt that must show in her face at deceiving someone who meant well. "If your hero worship were to get out of hand it could hurt both of you."

"Well, Kitty croaked, and cleared her throat, "I don't think you have too much to worry about. I'm just the little kid next door, you know."

She must have sounded bitter, for Maryann rose and laid a gentle hand on her arm. "I'm sorry," she said softly, "for your sake, but I'm afraid it's better this way, for both of you."

"You're probably right," Kitty said quietly, as though she agreed, then picked up the tray she'd filled. "We'd better take this food outside."

"Oh, good heavens, yes!" Maryann exclaimed. "They've probably eaten our steaks by now!"

The meal was delicious, the company cordial, but Kitty felt the weight of Maryann's assessment of the situation balanced against her own desire to be recognized as a woman in Steve's eyes, and found it difficult to relax. As they ate, talked and joked, the sun dropped lower and lower in the west, grew orange, then red, then slipped out of sight. When the first stars pricked the darkening sky Steve looked up at the indigo canopy overhead and struck his forehead theatrically with the heel of his hand.

"What are we doing," he asked them all, "keeping Maryann, and Junior, of course, up so late?" He extended a hand to Kitty and pulled her to her feet. "It's time to go, Kitten."

"Oh, wait just a little bit," Maryann pleaded. "We have a bottle of champagne my parents gave us, real French vintage stuff, that we've sort of been saving for a special occasion. It seems to me that the Army sending Steve off to Europe is pretty special. Come with me, Chuck, and get the wine glasses down." She led him inside, and Steve turned his head slightly to look down at Kitty, still with her hand in his.

A shaft of light slanted from the doorway across the deck several feet away from them, making the darkness in which they stood seem that much deeper. Very gently, so that she was hardly aware of moving, Steve drew her toward him. He had been leaning against the waist-high railing which ran around the deck, and as Kitty moved toward him he half turned so that his back was to the door, his bulk shielding her from the view of anyone inside. Slowly, gently, he took her into his arms, and it seemed that she stopped breathing, that everything stood still save her heart, which thundered in her breast.

His eyes gleamed in the light reflected off the water as they met hers, then dropped to her lips, her face tipped up to his. As his face came nearer her eyes fluttered closed, her body tinglingly aware of his nearness. His arms tightened around her, drawing her between his thighs, the coarse hair rasping provocatively against her legs, and his lips brushed hers lightly, exploring. At the first light touch Kitty melted against him, her hands sliding up over his chest to lock behind his neck as he gathered her pliant body even closer to him.

The kiss, begun so tentatively, changed then, his lips moving against hers in a question she did her inexperienced best to answer.

When he raised his head slightly she opened her eyes to look bemusedly up at him, but he only smiled briefly. One hand came up to caress her cheek, then his thumb slid across her lips to part them a bit, and he murmured, "Kiss me, Kitten. Kiss me back."

His mouth recaptured hers, and now his tongue touched gently where his thumb had been. After the first startled moment Kitty closed her eyes again and let him teach her about kissing, her lips parting softly beneath his, waves of delight washing over her. She had not known she could feel like this, warm and shivery at the same time, and when his warm hand slipped beneath the hem of her top to slide across the silken skin of her waist she clung weakly to him, afraid her legs would no longer support her.

The steel band of his arms tightened around her, lifting her onto her toes so that she was surrounded by the hard strength of his body, his thighs tense against hers, her breasts crushed against the solid wall of his chest, her hands clutching his muscular shoulders for support, her surrender complete. When his lips left hers and his hands pushed her abruptly away she staggered and almost fell, clutching at the railing to support herself while her confused, dilated eyes sought his.

Steve had turned away as he released her to stand between her and the shaft of light slanting out from the doorway. Then she heard the footsteps, the slam of the screen door swinging closed, and Chuck and Maryann appeared carrying a tray of glasses and an imposing green bottle in a plastic bucket full of ice. Kitty glimpsed them over Steve's shoulder as he placed himself between her and the others, screening her from their eyes while she recovered herself.

Gratefully, she leaned against the railing, breathing great gulps of the cool evening air, relaxing as the heat left her cheeks and her heart slowed its frantic beat. With surreptitious hands she tugged her top into place and smoothed her hair, listening with disbelief to Steve bantering casually with Chuck. How did he do it? His kisses and caresses had reduced her to trembling, giddy helplessness, and she could have sworn that he, too, was affected by their lovemaking, but she must have been mistaken. No one could switch their emotions on and off like that. Or could they?

Maybe, she tried to reassure herself, he had been affected, but because he was older, and more experienced, he was better able to conceal it. She stepped from behind him, lightly touching his arm to let him know she'd recovered her composure, and moved into the light.

Maryann was watching her with dismay and a hint of reproof in her face, a look that Kitty met with as much calm as she could muster, though she could feel the telltale warmth in her cheeks. Chuck seemed oblivious to any undercurrents in the atmosphere as a toast was poured and drunk, but Steve watched with a glint of something like amusement as Kitty and Maryann attempted to converse normally. It was a tremendous relief to Kitty and probably, she thought, to Maryann as well, when she and Steve rounded the first curve of the drive and the trees cut off their view of the house.

Kitty felt Steve glance across at her. "Did I detect a note of tension between you and Maryann?"

"Well—a little," she answered carefully, and he laughed under his breath.

"A little, nothing," he said derisively. "You could have cut it with a knife. What was it all about? Aside from the fact that she knew I was kissing you, that is?"

"It wasn't aside from that." Kitty turned slightly in her seat so that she was half facing him and leaning against the door. "It *was* that. She says that you're too old for me, and I'm too young for you."

"Um-hm. She's right, too." Kitty stiffened, but said nothing, and he went on. "I'm nine years older than you. If you were thirty and I were thirty-nine it wouldn't make much difference, but you're only sixteen, you're still in high school, and I'm twenty-five. I've been to college and dropped out, and worked one or two places, and joined the Army." His voice had grown softer until he was almost talking to himself. "And Maryann is absolutely right."

There didn't seem to be anything to say to that, and

Kitty slumped back into her seat, staring blindly out at the dark highway, wishing Maryann had kept out of it and then feeling guilty because she knew the other girl had meant well. It was just that Kitty didn't agree. She was a woman, she *was*, even if she was only sixteen, and she loved Steve. And she wanted him to know it.

The road flowed under the speeding car as they rode in silence, Steve apparently absorbed in his own thoughts and Kitty miserably certain that he would never again kiss her that way, the way a man kisses a woman. Eventually she must have slept, for the next thing she remembered was waking with a start to see that they were in the center of Indianapolis, driving around Monument Circle.

She had slumped down into a remarkably uncomfortable position against the door as she slept, and she pushed herself upright, groaning a little.

"Back with us, again, Sleeping Beauty?" Steve grinned at her groggy face and turned north onto Meridian Street.

"Yes, I think so, but I think I've permanently damaged my neck, sleeping like that." She tried to ease the stiffness and winced again, slowly working the pain out. "I'm sorry I pooped out on you like that. I didn't know I was so tired."

"That's OK. You're cute when you snore."

"I *didn't?*" Kitty gasped in horror, and Steve was unable to suppress the laugh that broke through when he looked at her face.

"No, you didn't," he relented, "but I had to say it just to see you . . . Ouch! No fair hitting the driver!"

Kitty mimed another punch at the hard muscle of his upper arm, then folded her hands demurely in her lap and said in dulcet tones, "You had it coming."

Steve chuckled again. "It's not very late," he said after a moment. "I wanted to take a look at the farm this weekend. Do you mind riding up there with me?"

"Now? Of course not." Kitty allowed herself a secret smile. Things were beginning to work out well for her after all. The farm was not actually worked by Steve's parents, of course, but his father had inherited the land north of Indianapolis from a distant cousin some years earlier. It was leased to the farmer whose land adjoined it. The old farmhouse had been torn down as unsafe years ago, but there was still a patch of trees where the house had stood, a small pond and some outbuildings where the neighboring farmer stored equipment. On a warm summer night, Kitty thought smugly, it would be irresistibly romantic.

And so it was. The pond had originally been located at the bottom of a gently sloping lawn, so that one could sit on the front porch of the house and watch the moon on the water. The house was gone now, but the sweep of soft grass dotted with trees still ran down to the water, and the nearly full moon shimmered across it as Steve pulled the car up the old drive.

He produced a large flashlight from the glove compartment and lit the way for them to walk around the outside of an old barn and two small sheds, looking for loose boards or broken windows. Kitty followed him, stepping cautiously in the deceptive combination of moonlight and pitch-black shadow. She would have liked to hold Steve's hand, but he didn't offer it and she didn't quite dare to reach for him, so she trailed along, fuming at fate.

When they reached the lawn again she knew a moment of agonized certainty that he would get back in the car and take her straight home, but, unbelievably, he stopped in the center of the lawn and sat down. He patted the grass beside him, and Kitty sank down onto the cool blades, drawing her knees up and wrapping her arms around them.

She gazed around her in wonder, distracted for the moment from the man at her side. The moonlight lay in a silver trail across the water, sparkling on gentle ripples. The air was soft and sweet, carrying the perfume of newly cut hay and a hint of summer flowers, vibrant with the trilling of crickets, and as the final magical touch, the trees beyond the water were alive with fireflies that twinkled like fairy lights.

"Isn't it beautiful?" she breathed.

"Beautiful." His voice was very low, with a note of something in it she could not identify, so that she looked over at him in slight surprise. His eyes were on the water, though, his face bland, and without meeting her gaze he flopped back onto the grass, arms above his head.

"Look at the stars."

"Huh?"

He took her hand and pulled her down beside him. "Lie back and look at the stars." Obediently she looked up at the inky sky. "Do you remember how to find the North Star? I taught you when you were in the Girl Scouts."

"Yes, I remember. And it's right over—there!" She finished on a note of triumph, pointing at the star Polaris. "I'm right, aren't I? Aren't I?"

"Oh, yes, you're right." She could hear the smile in his voice.

"Do you know what else I remember?"

"What's that?"

"How, if I begged hard enough, you'd take me to get a hamburger. And an orange freeze."

"Yeah, I remember." He paused. "Would you like a hamburger—and an orange freeze?"

"Now? After that wonderful dinner?"

"No, not now," he said, laughingly exasperated. "How about, say, tomorrow night?"

"I'd love it! If you really mean it, that is?"

She was afraid to believe that he actually wanted to spend time with her, but he replied with casual reassurance, "I wouldn't say it if I didn't mean it. Is it a date?"

"A date," she agreed, and looked up at the stars again. "Isn't it a beautiful night?"

"Beautiful," he answered as before, but when she looked over at him this time he was propped up on one elbow, his eyes on her face, his teeth gleaming briefly in a smile as he leaned toward her.

Her heart seemed to pause as his face drew near, blocking out the moonlight, and his lips touched hers feather-light, brushing across them teasingly. Her lips softened in response, parting gently as he had taught her, and he claimed them in a kiss of sudden fierce intensity. She was frightened, for a moment, of a naked passion she had not before encountered, and her initial response became an instinctive withdrawal.

He felt it and raised his head, a wry smile twisting his mouth as he looked down at her flushed young face.

"I'm too old for you, Kitten," he murmured, and she shook her head in quick denial. "Oh, yes, I am. I scared you just now because I forgot how young you really are."

Kitty's hurt at the first part of that statement was outweighed by her elated realization of the significance of the last bit. She had made him forget her age, so that he had been reacting to the woman he was kissing, not to Kitty the little girl. If she could make him forget once, she could make him forget again.

"I'm not that young," she said softly, and reached

up to stroke his cheek. "I've been growing up a lot lately." Her fingertip trailed across his lower lip, and she raised shy eyes to his, her lips parted slightly as her tongue flicked nervously across them. His eyes followed the innocently provocative gesture, and Kitty heard his sharply indrawn breath before he seized the hand that was against his face, pulling it above her head and holding it there while he claimed her mouth again.

This time no allowance was made for her youth or inexperience, and he plundered the softness of her mouth, forcing her lips apart to savor the sweetness within. Her hesitancy vanished like snow under a spring sun, and response tingled along her veins, her free hand stroking the hard-muscled contours of his back, joined by the other hand when he released it to slide his arms around her. Her slim arms slipped up to twine around his neck as he pulled her body against his, and she shivered with pleasure when he tugged the narrow strap of her sun top off her shoulder, pushing the thin cotton down and following with his lips to find the soft upper curve of her breast.

He tormented her gently, sliding the other strap down and brushing his lips across the delicate pale skin, denying himself, and her, the goal he sought until she moved beneath him, her body arching against his in newly awakened need. Her movements ignited an answering need in him, and he made a low sound deep in his throat as the sun top slipped away and his hands and mouth moved to cup and caress.

Kitty's head was thrown back, her body pressed abandonedly against his, her eyes tightly closed and her breath coming in shaky gasps as she gave herself up to his lovemaking. When he moved away, pulling the top up to cover her, she whimpered in confused protest, her clinging arms tightening around him.

He pulled them away with a short, strained laugh, lightly kissing her forehead before rolling away from her to lie on his back, hands folded beneath his head, the deep breaths that lifted his chest slowing gradually.

"Steve?" Tentatively she reached toward him, turning on her side to look at him, her face uncertain, wary. "Steve, what . . . ?"

"Shhh." He reached out to pull her close, tucking her into the curve of his arm and stroking her hair with a soothing hand. Beneath her ear the heavy thud of his heartbeat slowed and steadied, as did her own, the unfulfilled tension gradually leaving her beneath his gentling touch.

"You are, aren't you?" he said at length, soft amusement coloring his deep voice.

"I'm what?" she whispered.

"Growing up, little Kitten. Growing up."

Suddenly shy, she buried her face in his shoulder and felt him shake gently with laughter. He sat up, pulling her with him, and dropped a light kiss on her forehead.

"Come on, Kitten. It's time to take you home."

Things seemed to be going her way at last on Sunday evening, when she and Steve left for their "date." John and his girlfriend, Pam, had declined to accompany them, and her father was out for the evening, so Steve and Kitty drove away alone.

"Well," he said, turning to her with a grin when the engine had roared to life, "where will it be? The same old place?"

"Where else?" She grinned back. "This *is* a trip down memory lane."

"Anything you say, madame." He swung the car out of the drive. "We'll see if they still taste the same."

They did. The hamburgers, which they ate in the car, were brought by a smartly uniformed carhop and had crispy edges like always; the French fries were shoestring thin, and Kitty's orange freeze, a sort of orange milkshake, was as wonderful as ever and still came with whipped cream and a cherry on top. She saved the cherry for last, retrieving it from the bottom of the paper cup with a long spoon and popping it whole into her mouth, wrinkling her nose at Steve, who was laughing at her fondness for sweets.

"You're still a baby." He grinned and drained the cup of coffee he'd had instead of a milkshake. "You haven't outgrown that sweet tooth."

"You don't have to be a baby to have a sweet tooth. Johnny is crazy about chocolate-chip cookies."

"And so am I, but you're fun to tease, Kitten." She put out her tongue at him, and he laughed again. "I don't want to go in just yet; would you like to ride for a while?"

"Sure," Kitty agreed casually, but her heart began to beat faster, bringing a faint tinge of rose to her cheeks. He drove aimlessly for a time, wandering around the city, past old haunts of his; finally he drew over to the curb opposite the Speedway.

"Were you serious," he asked, "about designing cars?"

"Of course I was!" She paused. "Were you serious about driving them?"

"Yes," he said slowly, quietly. "I'm serious about it."

"But—it's so dangerous," she said faintly. "What if you got hurt, or . . . ?"

He reached a hand over to cup the back of her

neck, gently massaging the suddenly tense muscles there. "I've *been* hurt."

Her head snapped around, eyes raking his face, but he was staring out the windshield at a threatening mass of thunderheads that had been gathering in the southwestern sky for some time. She had the impression that he saw not the black mass of clouds but some dark memory deep within him.

"I've been hurt," he repeated quietly, "and I've seen men die. I nearly died myself, and now I find that it doesn't worry me so much." He must have felt Kitty's soundless gasp, for he looked down at her, and his lips twisted briefly in a wry attempt at a smile. "Don't worry, Kitten, I'm not suicidal; I just don't worry so much about death anymore."

"But we never knew you were hurt. We knew you were sent to Vietnam, but your parents never said—"

"I never told them. It was all over by the time any word could have gotten out. I was in a hospital in Hawaii for a while, but I got my C.O. to tell them I'd been transferred instead of injured. I knew by then that I'd recover, so why worry anyone?"

Why indeed? Kitty couldn't really understand the sort of love that could deny itself comfort when in need in order to spare the pain of others, but she could see that Steve had done what he felt necessary and would do the same again. She could also see that there was a great deal he hadn't told her, but she wouldn't press him with questions. He had already confided something to her that she was sure he had told no one else, and she felt proud and, at the same time, humbled.

A jagged spear of lightning split the clouds, which were now nearly overhead, and was followed by a low roll of thunder. Steve blinked and seemed to see the gathering storm for the first time.

"Sorry about that," he said lightly. "I don't usually bore people with the less fascinating parts of my life history." Another blue-white flash lit the inside of the car with its eerie glow, and he pushed the gear lever into first.

"Anyway, we've been sitting here long enough. We've agreed that one of these days we'll win this race as a team, but if we don't get moving we're going to get caught in that typhoon that's blowing up." Even as he spoke a gust of wind sent leaves and dust swirling down the street in the early darkness and the first fat raindrops hit the car.

"Looks like we'll have to run for it!" he called over the sudden roar as they were engulfed by the storm. The wind-driven sheets of rain thundered on the car's canvas top, making conversation impossible as Steve carefully negotiated rainfilled streets that were turning into small rivers. The deluge was undiminished when he pulled the car into his driveway, and after a moment's hesitation they made a dash for the front porch, Kitty carrying her sandals in her hand.

They bounded up the steps to lean against the house, laughing, gasping and absolutely drenched, while Steve unlocked the door. Kitty stepped onto the small cotton rug just inside the door and stayed there, unwilling to go farther and drip on Mrs. Duncan's polished wood floor. Steve had no such qualms, though, and only stopped halfway across the hall when he realized that she wasn't beside him.

He looked at her in puzzlement. "Come on! Don't you want to get dry?"

"Your mother's floor—I don't want to drip on it."

"Come and get dry before you catch pneumonia, you dope!" Then, as she still hesitated, he said, "Don't worry about the water, it'll wipe up!" He was at her side in three long strides, seized her elbow and dragged her through the house to the stairs and up to the bathroom, where he shoved her through the door and banged it closed behind her.

"Get dry and come downstairs," he called through the door. "I'll fix something to warm you up." Without waiting for an answer he moved away, and over the steady drumming of rain on the window she heard another door close. Slowly she moved away from the door, trembling now with a new and seductive excitement.

This was the chance she had been waiting for, if she had the nerve to take it. Steve had kissed her yesterday, and tonight he had spoken more freely to her about something very important to him than perhaps he had to any other person. He was no longer seeing her as a little girl; tonight she could become a woman for him.

Her hands shook, whether with cold or nerves she could not say, as she peeled off her sopping dress and wrapped a towel around her hair to blot some of the water from it. Wrung out, and then shaken to partially remove the wrinkles, her dress was spread over the shower rod. Her panties were as wet as the dress and received the same treatment. She toweled herself briskly until her skin was warm and dry, then took down the blue terry robe that hung behind the door.

With it in her hand she hesitated, turning slowly to meet her own gaze in the mirror. She reached up and pulled the towel off her head, and her damp hair tumbled in wild disarray around her shoulders. She saw a stranger in the glass; the eyes bright with the fever that pounded through her veins, the mad tangle of hair around naked shoulders, the slim, tanned body with its newly womanly contours were barely recognizable as her own.

Feeling curiously detached, she watched herself pull

the robe on, then comb through her hair, tossing it back and fluffing it with her fingers to speed the drying process. After wrapping the robe around her she tied the belt and folded the sleeves back, then turned, without another glance at the mirror, to go downstairs.

Steve was already there; she could see the light from the kitchen as she crossed the hall. The storm raged undiminished outside, but she could barely hear it above the thunder of her heartbeat as she stepped into the room. Steve was standing at the stove, lifting a pot of coffee off the burner. He was dressed in tight, well-worn jeans and a shirt he had pulled on but not buttoned, and his feet were bare. She said nothing, but she must have made some slight sound, for he looked over his shoulder as she appeared, then set the percolator on the stove and turned to view her properly.

"Very fetching." He grinned. "But are you sure the size is right?" Knee-length on him, the robe almost reached her ankles; the sleeves drooped over her hands despite her efforts to roll them up, and the robe was so bulky that it was impossible to close it tightly in front.

"I *was* afraid that it might be just a tad too small," she replied gravely. "Do you think so?"

"Maybe just a tad." He nodded. "But it'll do in the meantime."

"Actually, it's gorgeous and warm, so long as I don't trip over it or anything." She gathered the folds around her and dropped onto a kitchen chair. "What are you fixing?"

"Irish coffee. If you like coffee, that is?"

"Love it. Daddy says that's what stunted my growth, because I drink so much of it."

He looked her over and laughed with her. "I think

you grew just fine, myself. I'll bet you never had coffee quite like this, but it ought to warm you up just right."

"What's in it?"

"Watch and see." Obediently Kitty watched as he took down two heavy mugs, adding a measure of whiskey to each. "This is really Kentucky coffee, because I don't have any Irish whiskey, so I'm using bourbon, but I won't tell if you won't." Then he added a spoonful of sugar, coffee and finally heavy cream on top. He brought the mugs across to the table and sat down opposite her.

"Cheers."

"Cheers." She touched her mug to his and took a cautious sip, then looked up to see him watching her, a question on his face.

"It's good," she said on a note of faint surprise, which made him laugh. "It really is!"

"Don't sound so surprised. Anyone would think I'd planned to poison you!"

"It's not that at all and you know it, Steven!" she replied with laughing severity. "It's just that—oh!" There was a brilliant flash and a mighty *crack* from overhead, and the lights went out.

"Sit tight for a moment," Steve instructed her. "There should be a match—ah!" The glow of the match briefly illuminated the room, and he reached for a fat candle atop the refrigerator for occasions such as this. The match flame reached his fingers, and he swore and shook it out, then struck another and held it to the candle wick. The flame caught and grew, and the darkness was pushed back by the soft glow that filled the room.

"Is it just us," Kitty wondered from long experience of storms and power outages, "or did the whole neighborhood go?"

Steve drew the curtain aside and looked out. "Looks like the whole street, anyway. All the houses are dark and the streetlights are out. We may be in the dark for a while."

"That's okay. The way I look, darkness is an advantage."

"I don't know." Their eyes met across the candle flame as Steve slid back into his chair. "You don't look so bad to me."

Unable to reply, Kitty dropped her eyes to her mug, grateful for the dim light, which concealed the rush of warmth to her cheeks. She took a nervous sip, then a gulp of her coffee, sputtering slightly as the spirit bit at the back of her throat. He had been absolutely right about the effect of the drink; after several more sips she could feel it sending tendrils of gentle fire along her veins, warming and relaxing her so that she sat back in her chair and smiled across at him, her nervousness forgotten.

He smiled back and she half turned in her chair to lift her feet and rest them on the seat of the chair beside her. The robe fell away from her legs, but it didn't seem to matter, and she leaned forward to rest an elbow on her bent knees.

"This is nice," she told him. "Cozy. Stormy outside, but warm and dry in here." She took another long swallow of her coffee, and this time she didn't sputter as it went down. Steve was watching her when she looked back at him, a slight frown creasing his brow, a small, indulgent smile on his lips. He held her gaze for a moment, then his eyes dropped to her mouth, and lower, and his face changed, went still.

Puzzled, Kitty glanced down and saw that the robe had gapped open as she leaned forward, baring one round breast to his gaze.

"Oops!" She pulled the offending lapel closed and

smiled artlessly at him. "Sorry about that. It's not a very good fit, is it?"

"No, it's not," he said curtly and raised his mug, draining it. Hungrily Kitty watched him, watched the muscles in his throat move as he swallowed, watched the thick mat of golden hair on his chest catch the flicker of candlelight. She raised her mug and drank the last swallows, then reached for his.

"I'll rinse that out," she offered and stood, pausing for a moment as the room swayed around her and then settled back into place.

"You'd better let me do that." Steve was beside her, taking the mugs from her hands as she hesitated. "I think that bourbon may have been a little too much for you."

"Don't be silly." She was in possession of her limbs again after that brief wobble, and she put a hand out to forestall him when he moved to set the mugs on the counter.

Her palm met his chest, and the contact sent a shock of electricity through her. Gently she slid her hand up, fingers tangling in the curling hair. She looked up into his eyes and saw that he felt it, too. There was a hunger there that matched her own, and she swayed closer to him.

"You don't know what you're doing, Kitten." His voice was thick in his throat, and she smiled, knowing with a sure, ageless instinct that at that moment he wanted her more than anything else in the world.

As her hand moved up to caress his neck the overlarge robe slipped off her shoulder, clinging precariously to the swell of her breast. His eyes flicked over her body, then back to her face, and she moved very slightly, almost imperceptibly, closer, but it was enough. Her body brushed against his, and the warm, male smell of him filled her nostrils; the warm, hard strength of him was against her, and his arms came around her almost against his will.

"I said I've been growing up," she whispered.

His breath rasped in his throat as he nuzzled her hair, asking raggedly, "Do you know what you're doing, Kitten? Do you know what I want?"

"Yes," she whispered, and a singing elation filled her.

"And you want . . . ?"

"I want . . . I love you, Steve. I want to love you."

Chapter Three

She was surprised and elated by the violence of his embrace. He crushed her against him, lifting her off her feet and bending her back over his arm to ravage her willing mouth. The fury of the storm howling outside was matched by the storm that raged between them, rendering them deaf and blind to anything but each other. Kitty clung to him and he lifted her to carry her swiftly through the dark house and up the stairs to his bedroom.

Lightning lit the way in intermittent flashes as Steve crossed the room to lay her on the bed, gazing down at her as he shrugged the shirt from his shoulders. The bluish glow highlighted the heavy muscles of his chest and shoulders, then the room went black again, leaving Kitty with Steve's image in her mind. There was a small clink as he unbuckled his belt, and moments later the bed gave beneath his weight as he joined her.

Kitty turned toward him, reaching out in the darkness to twine her arms around his neck as he gathered her against him, his arms closing around her beneath the loose robe, slipping it away so that she was naked against him. He kissed her with a hungry intensity, pressing her back into the pillows, his body half covering hers as his hands explored her, stroking her breasts, flanks, the slim length of her thigh and the soft curve of her hip. She gasped as his mouth left hers to trail a burning path down her neck to the swell of her breast, capturing first one nipple, then the other, teasing the peaks to aching tautness with lips and tongue.

Kitty moved mindlessly, instinctively against him as he kissed and caressed her, her hands twisted into his hair to hold him close, soft whispers of pleasure issuing from her slightly parted lips. His breathing was as ragged as hers, and his heart thundered in his chest beneath her questing hands when he moved to cover her body with his.

With his guidance Kitty moved to accept him, lost in a passion she had never dreamed could exist. There was a fleeting spasm of pain when he took her, passing as quickly as it came, but he had felt her stiffen in his arms for that brief moment.

His lips lifted from hers, and in the sudden, stark brilliance of a lightning flash she saw a look of agonized disbelief on his face. As blackness followed the light he muttered, "Dear God." In sudden panic she knew he was going to leave her, and she couldn't bear it. She reached up and pulled him down to her with a force that was almost angry. Her lips moved against his, her body moved, and he was lost, they were both lost, in an ecstasy that spiraled higher and higher and finally consumed them both.

She clung to him, burrowing her face into the warmth of his shoulder, listening to the thud of his heartbeat as it slowed. His chest lifted in a deep breath that hissed out between his teeth, and the arm around her shoulders slackened.

She made a small sound of protest, tried to hold him, but he took her hands from him and rolled away, coming to his feet beside the bed in the same smooth movement. Above the steady drumming of the rain she heard the rustle of fabric and then the metallic rasp of a zipper.

"Steve?" Her voice was a shaky whisper as his footsteps moved toward the door. "Steve?" she said again, fighting suddenly rising fear, and he paused, turning back to her as the power suddenly returned. The street lights outside dimly illuminated the room, and through the door Steve was silhouetted by a faint glow from somewhere downstairs.

"We'll talk when you've dressed," he said in a flat, cold voice that seemed to freeze Kitty to the heart. He reached down to jerk the sheet up over her naked form, and she lay there, unable to move or think, while he strode to the bathroom, then returned to toss her damp dress and panties onto the bed.

"Come downstairs when you're dressed," he said, still in that stranger's voice, then turned again and left the room.

Clutching the sheet to her breasts, Kitty lay staring blankly after him, sick with dread, until she heard the clink of glassware in the kitchen. Slowly, stiffly, she pulled on her panties and struggled into her damp, crumpled dress, then padded down the stairs and to the kitchen.

She didn't know what had gone wrong, but Steve had changed from a tender, passionate lover to the cold, distant stranger who had left her in his bed, and she had to know why.

He had switched on the ceiling light, and its glare was a harsh contrast to the candlelight that had created such magic for them. He stood with his back to her, wearing only the jeans he had pulled on upstairs, the bourbon bottle and a tumbler on the counter in front of him. As Kitty paused uncertainly in the doorway he poured a liberal measure into the glass, lifted it and regarded the amber depths for a somber moment, then drained it at a gulp.

He replaced the glass on the counter with a sharp clink and turned to face her. There were lines in his face she had never seen before, carved deep in the lean cheeks and scored across his forehead beneath a wayward lock of wheat-colored hair, and his eyes looked tired, old.

"Why?" he asked her wearily. "Just tell me why."

"Wh-what do you mean, why?" She moved into the room, head down, watching her feet like a sulky child, tracing a finger along the edge of the table, always keeping a distance between them. He stood silent for a long moment, then the anger he'd been controlling bubbled up.

"*Why*, damn it! Why this? Why now? Why me?" He smashed his fist down on the counter, and she jumped, looking up at him in sudden fear.

"You set this up, Kitty. You had something like it planned all along, and like the stupid jerk that I am, I walked right into it, and I want to know why!"

He frightened her like this, the barely suppressed violence in him seeming to fill the air around them, and she moved farther away, to the kitchen window, to look out at the steady downpour that had followed the initial violence of the thunderstorm.

"I—I don't know what you mean," she muttered, still staring at the rain, and he gave a short, hard laugh.

"Come off it, Kitty. You had some reason for this! Were you just using me because I was here? Did you decide it was time to 'become a woman,' and was I the means to accomplish it? Thanks a lot, but I don't like being used!"

"That's not the way it was!" she flung at him, stung deeply by his cutting words.

"Then tell me how it was!" he shouted, and she faced him defiantly, her back against the window.

"I wasn't—I wasn't *using* you! I wanted—you were coming home and—and I wanted to show you—to show you that I'm not a little girl anymore. To show you I'm a woman!"

"Good God, look at you!" he exploded, and Kitty was suddenly acutely aware of her damp, crumpled dress and her tangled hair. "You're sixteen, Kitty, not thirty! A beautiful, sexy sixteen, but still only sixteen!" He smashed his fist down on the countertop again.

"You're my best friend's little sister, for God's sake! He trusts me! Your father trusts me! At least, they *did* trust me; they won't now."

"I won't say anything to them!"

"You won't have to say anything to John, he's not stupid. He's been watching me this weekend anyway, but he trusted me because I'm his friend. *Was* his friend," he corrected himself bitterly.

"God, I despise myself! I could see you were flirting, that you wanted a little romance, and you convinced me—I *let* you convince me—that you were

. . . were experienced. And that shouldn't have made any difference anyway!" he snarled at her. "It doesn't matter if you've slept with every boy in your school, you're still only sixteen and you're still John's sister, and it's disgusting that I didn't keep my hands off you!"

He splashed another large measure of bourbon into the glass and tossed it back, then stared across at her, where she stood shocked and silent by the window, his face tired again and sad.

"I can't give you back your virginity, Kitty. I didn't want to take it, but I did and I can't give it back. I'm sorry about that, more sorry than you can know. I just don't understand why it had to be me."

"It had to—it had to be you b-because—" Tears were streaming down her cheeks, and Kitty broke off, gulping down a sob. "It had to be you because I love you!"

"Oh, God, spare me that!" He crossed the room to seize her by the shoulders and shake her. "You don't love me, Kitty; you're too young to love anyone enough to throw yourself away on him."

"But I do love you!' she sobbed. "I love you and I just wanted to make you happy!"

He dropped his hands and pushed her slightly away as he turned back to the bottle. "You picked a hell of a way to go about it!" he said bitterly.

Kitty stared at him, at the broad, brown shoulders, the blond head bent wearily over the glass he had refilled. Pressing a hand to her mouth to stifle a sob, she whirled, flung the door open and ran out into the rain, across the grass to her own back door.

Half blinded by tears and rain, she ran through the kitchen and up the stairs, remembering too late that she was not alone in the house, that John and Pam were in the living room. She dashed into her bedroom and slammed the door as she heard John's shouted "Kitty?" and his heavy footsteps following her. The key was in the lock, but before she could turn it he burst into the room, the force of his entry sending her staggering back from the door.

She saw his hand lift toward the light switch and cried, "No!" but too late. He flicked the switch, light flooded the room and Kitty spun around, head down, shoulders hunched, arms crossed protectively over her breasts.

"Kitty," he said softly, "what's wrong?"

"Nothing—nothing's wrong." She tried to steady her voice, but it wobbled, and her throat was tight with tears. His large hand came down on her shoulder, and she flinched away, but he caught her and held her, turning her slowly around to face him. She kept her head down, but that didn't hide her ruined dress or the shivering that she could not control.

"Kitty, what happened to you?" He took her chin in his fingers and forced her face up to his. "God in heaven, what happened to you?" he shouted, staring in disbelief at her ravaged face, tear-stained and anguished, and the bruised softness of her mouth.

She saw his face change and harden, and she clutched at his arms, babbling frantically. "No, Johnny, it was nothing. I got caught in the rain, that's all. You don't have to—"

"It was Steve, wasn't it?" he asked softly, ignoring her desperate spate of words. "He did this to you." She was truly frightened now, not recognizing her gentle, loving brother in this icily enraged man with murderous eyes.

"Johnny, no! It was nothing! Johnneee—!" She shrieked his name and ran after him as he turned to the door, but he flung her off and thundered downstairs. She stood staring after him, sobbing and shivering, hearing the front door crash open and then fall closed again behind him.

"Kitty? What on earth is the matter?" Pam called from the foot of the stairs. Kitty went to the door, standing with her back to the light as she looked down at Pam's worried face.

"Pam, it's between John and Steve," she said thinly. "Do you mind just letting Johnny tell you whatever he wants to?"

"Of course. Kitty?"

"Yes?"

"Are you OK? Do you need anything?"

"No, I don't need anything." She paused. "I'm going to take a bath. I got caught in the rain."

"All right." Pam nodded and turned toward the living room, but Kitty's soft voice halted her.

"Pam?"

Pam turned to look up at the younger girl. "Yes, Kitty?"

"Thank you for worrying."

The bath was accomplished in a near daze, Kitty going through the motions of washing and drying like an automaton. She pulled on her old chenille robe, ankle-length, faded pink and comforting, in the way a small child's teddy bear is comforting, but tonight it couldn't help, though she wrapped it tightly around her as she sat on her bed and waited for John to come back.

She'd thought she was calm, in control of herself at last, but when she heard the kitchen door slam and John's slow footsteps on the stairs her heart seemed to stop for a painful instant and then resume a heavy, pounding beat. She was staring at her hands, twisting them together in her lap, when the door opened with its usual slight squeak. Slowly she raised her eyes to

John's face, but his expression was shuttered, unread-able.

"What—" Her voice was a cracked whisper, and she cleared her throat nervously. "What happened?"

He looked down at her with a combination of anger, pity and sorrow. "I broke his nose."

"Johnny, *no!*" She flew at him, trying to push past him to go to Steve, who was hurt.

He caught her, holding her just above the elbows in a painful grip. "You're not going over there," he said in a voice of absolute authority.

"But, he's *hurt!*"

"No." He looked down at her anguished face, and his hands on her arms tightened angrily, shaking her. "I broke his nose, Kitty; I didn't kill him." She flinched from the thought, and from the deep rage she felt in him as he added, "I didn't kill him, but I could have."

"No—" she breathed in horror, and he pushed her away with a grimace of disgust.

"No, it wouldn't have been fair, would it?" he snarled at her. "It wouldn't have been fair, because it wasn't his idea. He wasn't chasing you this weekend, you were chasing him, weren't you?" Kitty shrank from the bitter, angry hurt in his voice, his face. She turned away to stand with her back to him, her head bowed and hands clenched tightly in front of her.

"You were chasing him all weekend, and somehow you got him to forget who you are and how old you are, and he did what you'd been begging him to do." He paused to draw a painful breath.

"Why, Kitty? Why did you do it? Why didn't you think about what it would do to you? Or to Dad?" Kitty stiffened, sure that she could never bear the deep hurt that she would see in her father's eyes when he learned of this. She hadn't considered the effect of her actions on those around her, but now she was sickened by the hurt she had so carelessly inflicted.

"I won't tell Dad what happened, Kitty," John said, and she looked over her shoulder at him in surprise, to find him watching her with cold eyes. "Not for your sake, or for Steve's, but because it would hurt Dad too much to know about this.

"You won't see Steve again, Kitty; he's leaving tonight; in fact, he's probably already gone." She looked toward the window that faced Steve's house, then back at John, and he nodded grimly. "I don't expect that this kind of thing will happen again, will it, Kitty?" It wasn't really a question, and she shook her head, mute.

"I'm going to take Pam home." He went to the door, then paused with one hand on the knob to look back at her with cold eyes in a bleak, set face. "I don't know how to forgive either of you." The door closed quietly behind him.

The room had grown dark around Kitty as she sat on the sofa, and now she looked up and blinked, confused for an instant, as though she expected still to be sitting in her old bedroom, wrapped in that chenille robe, frozen and numb with misery.

John had forgiven her in the end, but it had taken a long time for them to rebuild their easy relationship. A long time during which Kitty at first refused all dates and then gained a reputation as untouchable, a sort of snow queen who would accept an invitation to a movie or a party but would flatly rebuff any attempt at even the most innocent lovemaking.

Even without John's warning, she knew she would have led a very different life after that awful night. She had thought she loved Steve, had wanted him to love her, and the nightmarish twist her naïve dreams had taken, the hurt and disillusionment and guilt, had frozen something deep within her. Boys, and later men, pursued her, but as they all discovered sooner or later she simply wasn't interested. And, having discovered that, they either resigned themselves to the status of casual friends or drifted out of her life.

As time passed, the raw wound healed, leaving a scar that was painful if touched, but at least the first agonizing hurt had faded. What had not faded with time was the guilt she felt for having irresponsibly destroyed the friendship John and Steve had shared for more than ten years. To have been the ruin of something so important as a friendship was the most wrongful act of all and one which, however much she might wish to, she could not undo.

She couldn't undo any of it, and she was sorry, so sorry. And tomorrow she would see him for the first time since she had run sobbing from that kitchen seven years ago, and the thought scared her. She rose and gathered her dishes to take them to the kitchen. Nobody likes to confront their past mistakes, and to confront them in the person of a man who knows the worst there is to know about you, and who also has every reason to hate you . . . Yes, she was uneasy, edgy, scared.

But seven years had passed, and they said that time heals all wounds. If some of the pain had faded for her, perhaps it had for him as well. She couldn't very well expect him to have forgotten, but maybe, just maybe, he had forgiven. Probably all she would have to face the next day was a bit of initial awkwardness between them, nothing more. Nothing at all.

Steve Duncan looked up disinterestedly from his newspaper as the transcontinental jet rolled to a stop the next afternoon. The enclosed walkway snaked toward it like some huge, prehistoric beast, meeting the side of the plane with a muffled *thunk,* and Steve returned to his *New York Times* and its assessment of the dismal state of the economy. He remained seated, buried in his newspaper, as the other first-class passengers, and then the coach passengers, filed past him, glancing curiously at his bent head.

When the plane was empty and, he hoped, the arrival lounge in the terminal crowded enough for him to slip through unnoticed, he collected a pigskin briefcase and a beautifully tailored jacket in supple chocolate suede and made his way off the plane. The terminal was satisfactorily congested, and he skirted the crush, keeping his face slightly averted from the man and woman he had immediately identified as reporters.

"Steve? Steve!" He glanced in quick irritation at the portly, fortyish man who was calling to him. Three quick strides carried him to the Amtex public relations representative who waited, grinning, unaware of Steve's anger.

"Shut up, will you, Haskell?" Steve growled as he took the older man's elbow and pulled him toward the baggage claim area. "There are at least two reporters back there, and I do not intend to talk to them right now."

"But don't you think it might be good PR to talk to them?"

"Depends on what you consider good PR," Steve said dryly, and Haskell looked at him in faint alarm.

"What do you mean?"

"Look, Haskell," Steve said tiredly, reaching out to yank his suitcase off the turntable, "I've been on planes for what feels like a week; I've been dodging reporters the entire trip, and after the one who caught me in London, the next person who sticks a micro-phone in my face is asking for a rap in the mouth.

"I appreciate the fact that you have a job to do, and . . ." He raised a hand to forestall the protest he could see Haskell was about to make. ". . . and I understand that I have certain PR obligations to Amtex as my sponsor, but not today."

"You do realize that I have to set up press appear-ances, that Amtex can't afford to invest the money in your car and have you refuse them?" Haskell trotted beside him as they left the terminal.

"I know, I know." Steve waved a silencing hand as he slid into the big, comfortable car, complete with driver, that Amtex had provided for his use. "Just don't bother me with it today, OK?"

"We'll try not to *bother* you any more than we have to," Haskell said defensively. "But we have several appearances scheduled for the month, and if there's an opportunity for you to . . ."

The car slid away from the terminal, and Steve tuned Haskell out. The last thing he intended to do was memorize a PR schedule. If he had an appearance to make, Haskell would no doubt be around to remind him of it. The only thing he was concerned about was what he would find at the Speedway.

Jack Hampson, who had been his crew chief for the last five years, had sent him a fat packet of informa-tion on changes in the car, the crew members and anything else he thought Steve might be interested in. Most of it had been fairly straightforward, but the personnel list had left him puzzled. Well, not really puzzled, but intrigued.

When he read through the list of crew members he'd nodded in recognition of all but two of the names. The new crew members were a mechanic named Rick White and the chassis engineer, who was listed as K. Gordon. Pure coincidence, of course, but that, added to the nostalgia he experienced every spring on his return to Indianapolis, had brought Kitty to mind again.

Little Kitty. He had often wondered what kind of woman she had grown to be. She was twenty-three now. If she went on the way she'd been headed all that time ago, he thought cynically, she'd be a wild one, all right. Maybe he was being unjust, though; that experience might have taught her a lesson.

It had certainly taught him one. He smiled wryly to himself, running the knuckle of his index finger along his nose in a reflective gesture, feeling the slight bump that marred its once-perfect straight line. John had broken it, with his first powerful punch. Steve had been standing in the kitchen where Kitty had left him, drinking, when the door flew open.

John just walked in, growled, "You filthy bastard," and broke his nose. He got in a few more punches, too, before he stopped. Steve hadn't fought back, just tried to ward off John's blows until John had stopped hitting him. In a strange way Steve had felt he didn't have the right to fight back, that he deserved it for what he'd done to John's sister, whatever the provocation, and he'd just stood there, blood running from his broken nose, fending off John's fists as best he could.

They had had a very uncomfortable conversation, and when John "suggested" that he might leave that night he had had little choice but to agree. Holding a towel to his nose, he'd collected his things and thrown them into the car, stopped at a hospital emergency room to have his nose fixed and then stayed the night at a motel on the other side of town, knowing Kitty wouldn't find him there even if she tried.

Oh, he'd learned a lesson all right. In the years

since, he hadn't been near a woman who didn't make it very clear from the start that she knew the score.

He glanced out the window and saw that they were approaching the main entrance of the track. They turned north, off West 16th Street, through the gates. He caught a glimpse of the sign, INDIANAPOLIS MOTOR SPEEDWAY, and the curious emblem, a tire with wings, which always amused him, before they headed down through a short tunnel under the track and turned left past the Speedway Museum, built of Indiana limestone that gleamed white in the spring sun. A service road took them diagonally across the southwest corner of the infield to the garage area, the famous Gasoline Alley.

"I'll take your luggage to the hotel, Mr. Duncan." The driver pulled to a stop near the entrance to the garages. "When should I come back for you?"

Steve grimaced. "As far as I'm concerned, you can take a two-week vacation with pay, starting this afternoon." Haskell looked at him in surprise tinged lightly with shock, and with exaggerated patience Steve explained, "I keep a car in Indianapolis. It was delivered to the hotel today. I'll get a lift from somebody when I'm through here today, and I don't need or want to be chauffeured anywhere until the first day of qualifications. OK?"

"But Amtex is paying for it. They won't appreciate—"

"*They* don't really need to know about it, do they?"

"No-o-o, I guess not." Haskell could see that passing this news along to the Amtex headquarters would cause him nothing but trouble, but it still went against the grain to conceal something from the company. However, what they didn't know wouldn't hurt them, and they'd already paid for the car, and of course Duncan might decide to use it after all. . . .

Steve watched with dry amusement the expressions chasing one another across Haskell's face. The man should never play poker, he was ridiculously easy to read. Seeing that Haskell had reached the right conclusion, Steve looked over at the driver, who was watching them with one arm draped along the seat back.

"That's it, then." He nodded to the young chauffeur. "Take two weeks, then get me here in time for the time trials." He paused, then added, "The name's Steve."

"Les Morris." They shook hands over the back of the front seat, and Steve looked out the window at the teeming mass of spectators, track officials and racing-team members swirling around the car, all part of the opening-day excitement.

"Welcome to Indianapolis," he said dryly, "city of peace and quiet. Come on, Haskell. Let's see if we can find my crew in this madhouse." He pushed the door open and slid out of the car. "See you in two weeks, Les." The driver lifted his hand in a salute and began easing the car back toward the gate as Steve strode away, weaving through the crowd, paying no attention to whether Haskell was following. If the man couldn't keep up, maybe he should find a new line of work. Steve didn't much care for PR people anyway, and felt no compulsion to make their lives easier.

He saw it when he was forced to pause in his quick progress by a gaggle of teen-age girls standing in the middle of the road, talking and giggling while the other spectators struggled to make their way around. Muttering to himself about teen-agers, and girls in particular, Steve glanced around, working his way through the crush, and there it was, not twenty yards away.

Brightly painted, bristling with antennas of all sizes and shapes, it was unmistakably a television remote van, and it was just as unmistakably disgorging a remote crew. He swore under his breath and walked faster, dropping his head in an effort to avoid recognition. He had almost reached the gate when Haskell caught up with him, puffing and pink-faced, and tugged at his sleeve.

"Did you see the TV crew?"

"Yes, I did, damn it to hell." Steve pulled away from Haskell's hand and took out his wallet as he neared the gate. Standing beneath a huge banner reading GASOLINE ALLEY was a burly security guard.

"Good to see you, Mr. Duncan." He glanced at the plastic identification badge Steve extracted from his wallet, then jerked his head toward the thronged Alley behind him. "Go on in, Mr. Duncan. Think you're gonna win it this year?" He grinned and Steve grinned back.

"I'm sure gonna try." Steve clipped the badge to his shirt pocket. Haskell had finally located his own badge and held it out to the guard, who had turned away for a moment to speak to a spectator.

"Mr. Duncan! Steve! Steve Duncan!" Steve looked around and swore harshly under his breath again. The television crew, led by a tall, thin woman with a hard face and improbably red hair, was bearing down on him at a run. Steve turned to melt away into the crowd, but Haskell held him back with a surprisingly firm grip.

"Let me go, you—" Steve muttered, but Haskell stood firm.

"They've *seen* you. What can it hurt to talk to them?"

"I told you how I feel about it."

"And I reminded you of your obligation to

Amtex." Steve glared down at Haskell, but the PR man didn't flinch, and a glimmer of grudging respect crossed Steve's face. So Haskell wasn't quite the cream puff he seemed. That would make it harder for Steve to duck his press meetings, but he liked Haskell better for it. His face still held a trace of a wry smile when the lady reporter and her cameraman caught up to them.

"Mr. Duncan—Steve—I'm Maribeth Sharpe of Headline News, and I'd like to talk to you, if I may?" Steve nodded acquiescence and she turned, dropping her well-modulated on-camera voice to snarl at her cameraman, "For God's sake, get it right this time, Bill! And don't cut me out of the picture! Do you think you can manage that?"

The unfortunate Bill, who wore the sad-eyed look of a much-abused hound, nodded mutely, and Maribeth Sharpe turned back to Steve.

"Now, Mr. Duncan, or may I call you Steve?" she asked in sugary tones, and he nodded again, amused at the Jekyll and Hyde transformation. "Steve, then. When did you arrive in Indianapolis?"

"An hour ago." A crowd was beginning to gather around them, drawn by the TV camera and the now-recognized Steve. He autographed a cap for a small boy who thrust it at him, then moved through the gate to escape the spectators, Haskell and Ms. Sharpe moving with him.

"What are your plans now that you've arrived?" She held the microphone in front of him as they walked, and Bill trotted frantically beside them, striving to keep both faces in his picture.

"To see my car. To see my crew. Meet the new members." Maribeth Sharpe looked a little less sunny as Steve answered her in the laconic, deliberately uninformative manner he adopted with the press.

"Do you have any social plans, Steve?" She laid rather pointed emphasis on the word "social," and Steve's smile became wry.

"Nope."

Ms. Sharpe was becoming annoyed now; it showed in the lines of displeasure that suddenly made her look every one of her forty years and in the venomous glare she aimed at Steve as he calmly walked away from her, waving and calling greetings to friends as he passed.

He was aware of her anger but didn't care. He was back at the Speedway, and he wanted a few minutes to soak up the sights and sounds and smells before that harpy caught up with him again. He didn't stop to talk to anyone, only called greetings and lifted a hand in salute as he passed, but these men understood. They knew he was eager to see the car, the crew, to begin his preparations for the last Sunday in May; they felt the same urgency.

He looked around him, tasting the familiarity of it all: the long, low shedlike buildings that housed the garages, one for each entry; the drivers, mechanics and assorted others who thronged the alley between; the sounds of cars and people, a sputter and roar from nearby, the more distant whine of cars on the track; and the smell of the place, oil and fuel and men and machines, and something indefinable that was the Speedway.

It was a heady combination, one which told him he was home again. As he neared garage number 38, he saw the door burst open to send Jack Hampson hurtling out to meet him.

"Steve!" Jack shouted happily, pounding him on the back. "How the hell are you?" Steve returned the greeting with a couple of thumps on Jack's broad back and grinned down at him as they walked toward the garage. Fifty, balding and burly, Jack was several inches shorter than Steve, with a stocky, powerful build and a cheerful, sunburned face, punctuated by a fat cigar clenched in his teeth. The cigar was never lit, for smoking was not permitted around fuel, but he was never seen without it.

He was talking around the cigar now, yet somehow it remained in the corner of his mouth as he spoke in a rapid staccato, trying to fit four months' worth of information into five minutes.

They had almost reached the garage when Maribeth Sharpe caught up with them. "Mr. Duncan, can you introduce me to this gentleman?" Her grip on his arm was surprisingly firm in marked contrast to the dulcet voice, and the glint of steel in her eyes gave her away. This big, dumb race-car driver wasn't going to make a fool of her again. Steve might have tried, though, to shrug her off and ignore her, had he not seen Haskell's equally determined face behind her.

"This is Jack Hampson, my crew chief." With outward good grace he gave in, but he groaned inwardly when she asked to meet the crew. The boys wouldn't pass up an opportunity to be on TV and they'd all spend half the afternoon standing around out here playing at stardom.

He was at least partly right. Jack beckoned the crew members out into the afternoon sunshine to be introduced, and they shuffled, smiled and mugged a little as Maribeth Sharpe spoke briefly to them, her remarks somehow managing to combine a surface admiration with a less-obvious disdain for these "mechanics." The crew seemed not to notice, but Jack obviously did, and his hostility began to show in his tone.

"Jimmy Miller," he pulled a redheaded, freckle-faced youth forward, "the youngest member of the crew. And—" he looked behind him into the garage. "Come on out!" He beckoned the laggard and a petite figure emerged from the shadowy depths of the garage, dressed, as were the others, in jeans and a scarlet, short-sleeved shirt with DUNCAN and the Amtex corporation logo appliquéd on the back, but filling this "uniform" in a very feminine way.

"Our chassis engineer," Jack announced. "Katharine Gordon."

Chapter Four

Steve was glad the camera was on Kitty and not on him in that first moment, for he was aware that his face must have shown some flicker of surprise before he schooled his features into indifference again. So it was her after all. He hadn't really thought it was possible, but here she was, older of course, dressed for work, but with the prettiness that had been the promise of beauty at sixteen become the thing itself at twenty-three.

Well, well. Little Kitty. He folded his arms and let his heavy lids shield his eyes as he watched her dueling with the redoubtable Ms. Sharpe.

To Kitty it all seemed unreal. She was standing in the bright May sunshine, replying carefully to this awful woman's snidely pointed questions, and all the time Steve was standing not five feet away. She was amazed at her own outward composure when somewhere inside her was an emotional volcano. She couldn't let that show, though, and in a way the sneering reporter helped.

When Jack had presented her the reporter had stared for an instant in pure surprise, then burst into laughter. "Do pardon me," she said sweetly when she was in control of herself again, "but are you the crew's mascot, Miss—ah—?"

"Gordon," Kitty said coolly. "And as Jack told you, Miss—ah—Ship, I am the chassis specialist." The reporter's rather thin lips had tightened at Kitty's deliberate mistaking of her name, and her eyes were hard above the television smile.

"Sharpe," she corrected. "Chassis specialist—is that another name for the person who polishes the car?"

"No, it isn't. The chassis specialist designs the chassis of the car and sees that it is built to his or her specifications."

"And you designed the car?" Disbelief dripped from every word, and Kitty controlled her rising anger with difficulty.

"Not the car, ma'am," she said, underlining the other woman's age with that polite pronoun. "I designed the *chassis* for the car."

"I see." Ms. Sharpe looked around for Steve, realizing that her star had been out of the picture for too long. "And have you met Mr. Duncan yet? Steve!" She waved him closer, and he sauntered over, still with that cynical, slightly amused smile.

"We've met," he said blandly. "How are you, Kitty?"

"Fine, thanks. It's good to see you, Steve."

His only reply to that was a brief nod; then his

attention returned to Ms. Sharpe, whose face had come alight when she realized that they were not strangers.

"So you two know each other?" she cooed. "How convenient for you! Now I understand how you come to be working on the crew, Miss—ah—" She hesitated over Kitty's name again, and Jack stepped forward, bristling, into the breach.

"You don't understand anything!" he growled. "Steve didn't even know I'd hired Kitty here," he dropped an arm protectively onto her shoulders, "before today. I'll have you know that *I* do the hiring of the crew, and I took on the best damned chassis engineer I could find when I hired her."

At that point Ms. Sharpe gave up. This whole thing had been a fiasco from the start, what with that close-mouthed driver, the hostile crew chief, that little snip of a girl. She only hoped she'd be able to edit it down to a minute or two that presented Maribeth Sharpe in a good light.

Kitty watched her leave with some relief. She had been interviewed often enough in the past weeks, for a woman was a rarity as a working crew member, and she had no objections to discussing her work. Ms. Sharpe was interested in another sort of story, though, and Kitty had no intention of being used as fodder for someone's shabby gossip mill.

Jack ushered Steve into the garage with the ceremonial panache due a crown prince, and Kitty trailed after them with the rest of the crew, her eyes on his golden head above Jack's balding pate. She'd really tried to convince herself of the truth of all that stuff she'd told herself last night, about emotions fading with the passage of time, but she knew now that it was only wishful thinking.

Seated in a corner of the garage with a clear view

out the door and along Gasoline Alley, she'd been working on some drawings of the suspension system and had seen Steve approaching even before Jack had noticed him.

She had caught sight of him, and time had fallen away for her, the seven years evaporating as though they had never been. He was still the most handsome man she had ever seen, the thick, blond hair sun-bleached to the color of wheatfields above the lean, deeply tanned face, the body that still moved with that easy, almost feline grace. There were changes, though, that she could see as she stood in a dim corner of the garage, studying him.

He was broader than he had been, the youthful slimness at twenty-five filled out by maturity at thirty-two, his chest broad and deep, his arms and shoulders powerfully muscled. His face had changed, as well, and here the changes were more subtle and somehow disturbing. The face that had been cheerful and open at twenty-five was no longer easy to read; the eyes were guarded, the smile cynical, with lines carved into the lean cheeks where none had been before. It was still a handsome face, so handsome that beautiful women all over the world pursued him, but it was a disturbing face now, with a sensuality and a hint of cruelty that had not been there seven years ago.

One thing hadn't changed, though. The sight of him had literally caught her breath, as his emotional impact was translated into physical terms. It had taken all her self-control to parry Ms. Sharpe's questions while he stood so near that every nerve in her body was tinglingly aware of him. Even now, as she resumed her seat in the corner, she was acutely conscious of his every movement, of the low rumble of his voice from across the busy garage.

"Kitty?" Her head snapped up as Jack called her name. "Come over here a minute, will you?"

"Sure, Jack," she answered calmly enough, but she laid her clipboard aside with care, for her hands had begun to tremble.

"Could you give Steve an outline of the chassis alterations?" Jack asked as she joined them.

"Sure," she said again, and drew in a slow, deep breath to steady her shaky voice.

"I'll leave you to it, then," Jack said, leaving Kitty to take the seat he had vacated.

"What do you want to know?" She sank onto the bench beside Steve, careful not to touch him, though he seemed totally unaware of her. As she described the alterations she had engineered he listened politely, the way he might listen to a stranger. It seemed almost surreal, for since his first greeting outside he had given no indication that they had ever been more than the most distant of acquaintances. He might have completely forgotten all that had passed between them, and part of her watched him in astonishment, for she was using all the control she possessed to conceal her reactions to him.

It was as if she were aware of him with every cell in her body, as if, even with her eyes closed, she could see him. He leaned closer to see the blueprint she held and his knee brushed hers, sending a tingle of electricity over her skin. His thigh muscles strained the fabric of his trousers as he moved; the hand that pointed something out on the drawing was square and brown and long-fingered, and she couldn't stop herself from remembering the way those hands had caressed her, the feel of his strong body against her, holding her, as they kissed. . . .

"I—I beg your pardon?" She realized that he had asked her a question that she hadn't even heard, and she felt herself flush with embarrassment as she stammered out an apology. "I'm sorry; I didn't hear your question."

"I just asked," he said, with no acknowledgement of her discomfiture beyond a lifted eyebrow, "what you've done with the new rules about the ground-effects devices."

"Well, since the skirts which helped create negative air pressure under the car were banned, we sculpted the underside of the car in a more concave shape to increase the negative pressure, and that, along with some reshaping of the rear wing, should pull the car down onto the track and give you as much ground effect as you had last year. There's only so much we can tell from wind-tunnel tests, but when you drive tomorrow we'll have a better idea." She paused, then looked into his eyes. "I think we've built you a good car."

Steve returned her gaze for a long moment, then nodded. "Let's see if it fits, then."

He stood and peeled off his jacket, tossing it onto the bench as he stepped over to the car. He looked down at it, gleaming scarlet beneath the overhead bulb, and ran his fingertips lightly along the wing. "It's a pretty car," he said, half to himself, and Kitty smiled.

"It is, isn't it?" she agreed as he levered himself into the driving seat. Once in the car he was almost lying on his back, legs extended into the nose. He rested his hands for a moment on the small steering wheel, fingered the tiny gearshift, then raised his arms above his head.

"Buckle me in, will you?" he asked Kitty. "I might as well see if the belt length is okay."

"Oh—uh, OK." She hesitated for a fraction of a second, then stepped forward. It was a reasonable request; within the tight confines of the cockpit the driver was unable to snap the six-point safety harness into the buckle that lay just above his waist and had to be assisted by a crew member while he sat with arms raised out of the way. It was just, she thought as she reached across Steve for the two shoulder belts, that she didn't want to be so close to him. With the shoulder belts snapped into place she reached over for the waist belts, then leaned down into the car, reaching between Steve's thighs for the inner-leg belts.

Her face was deeply flushed and her breathing shallow as she fumbled for the belts; she was intensely, almost painfully, aware of him. The warm, male scent of him surrounded her, a heady mixture of Gauloises cigarettes, spicy aftershave and something that was uniquely Steve, and the closeness required to fasten the harness was playing havoc with her pulses. The brush of her hands against the thin fabric of his shirt as she snapped the shoulder belts in place, the hard muscles of his waist beneath her fingers and now, as she leaned over him, the pressure of his chest against her shoulder, the hard thigh against her arm, were resurrecting feelings she had believed dead and buried.

She tried to fasten the harness quickly, but her hands were suddenly clumsy, fumbling with the buckle, dropping belts, so that when the last one clicked into place and she could straighten and back away she had to brace herself against the wall for a moment, breathing slowly and willing her face to cool. She hadn't known she could feel this way, not after so many years. It was as though she had known the touch of his hand, the strength of his body only yesterday, and she suddenly wanted to know them again. Oh, Lord, how she wanted to know them again.

She felt the attraction so strongly that it seemed

surprising it was not visible in the air around her, yet
Steve seemed completely unaware of her. He thanked
her with a nod and an impersonal glance, then turned
to speak to Jack as the chief rejoined them. Steve then
proceeded to ignore Kitty for the rest of the afternoon.

She couldn't ignore him, however. Last night's
deliberate reliving of that last weekend together, and
seeing Steve again today, had made a mockery of her
belief that she had forgotten anything about him, but
for him things seemed to be different. She couldn't
really believe he had forgotten that dreadful evening;
if she studied his profile she could see the slight bump
that marred the once-perfect straightness of his nose,
but the incident obviously meant nothing to him now.
Probably she lived in his memory as only one in a
series of conquests, she thought cynically, and was
surprised at the stab of pain that thought caused.

And yet, wasn't it better this way? Wasn't it better
that he treat her as a stranger? Wasn't it?

She was unable to relax until he left the garage with
Jack about thirty minutes before Kitty had finished for
the day, and the tension of the afternoon left her with
a throbbing headache that threatened to be with her
for some time. She drove home without really seeing
the streets she passed through and walked up the steps
to her back door massaging the taut muscles at the
nape of her neck with one hand, wincing as her fingers
probed and kneaded. A long, hot shower might help.
She crossed the kitchen and made for the bathroom,
unbuttoning her crew shirt as she went, peeling off her
work clothes while the shower ran hot, and stepped
under the spray with a sigh of relief.

The warm water eased her tight muscles, and she
leaned against the tile while it drummed on her back,
her mind a blank. At length she emerged and dressed

in a mint-green sundress of soft cotton, with wide shoulder straps and an embroidered yoke onto which the body of the dress was gathered. She wasn't really hungry enough to go to the trouble of preparing a meal, so instead she took a can of strawberry soda and went to sit on the front porch to enjoy the slowly cooling evening air.

The porch stretched the width of the house, which was split into two rather long and narrow apartments situated side by side. This duplex arrangement offered some of the advantages of an apartment, each unit being small enough for a single person or a couple, with some of the advantages of a house, such as privacy and front and back yards.

For Kitty there was another plus, the provision of very nice neighbors. Shelley Thomas had been Shelley Emerson when she and Kitty were high-school friends and had met her husband, Jim, in college. Shelley was a children's librarian at one of the north-side branches of the Indianapolis public library, and Jim was a senior medical student. Living next door to them, Kitty never had a chance to feel really lonely, for she knew she had only to knock on the wall if she wanted company.

When Kitty stepped out onto the porch with her soda Shelley was already there, seated on the old-fashioned glider, her cap of curly, ash-blond hair bent over a book.

"Hi, Shel, are you all by yourself this evening?"

"Yeah, unfortunately." Shelley wrinkled her freckled nose. "Now that Jim is doing this surgery rotation, it seems like I never see him. He spends every third night at the hospital, and even on the nights he comes home it's not until eleven or twelve, and he's so tired he just collapses. So much for the glamour of medicine!" She grinned and lifted her shoulders in a philosophical shrug, and Kitty dropped into the glider, laughing.

"At least he'll have a month off after graduation," she reminded Shelley, "and that's only a month away."

"But after that his internship starts, and that's supposed to be even worse!"

"Just think about the vacation!" Kitty laughed at her. "Quit dwelling on what comes after!"

"You're right." Shelley sighed, resigned. "I might as well not worry about it. Now"—she folded her long legs beneath her and grinned at Kitty—"tell me about your day. Did the great Steve Duncan put in an appearance?" Her tone was dry, but her eyes sparkled with an interest she couldn't suppress.

"Yes, he showed up." Kitty sipped her soda, and Shelley leaned forward impatiently.

"Well, what happened? Did he remember you? Did he say anything?" Shelley knew that Kitty had grown up next door to Steve Duncan and had surmised that she'd had a teen-age crush on him. She knew no more than that, but to Kitty's dismay Shelley's romantic heart had immediately begun hoping for some sort of relationship to blossom when Kitty and Steve met again.

"He said hello," Kitty replied dryly. "And he did remember me, I suppose, but he couldn't have been less interested if he'd tried."

"Aw-w-w," Shelley groaned in disappointment. "Didn't he say *any*thing else?"

"Yeah. He asked me how we compensated for the rules changes that reduced the ground-effects levels from last year."

Shelley was clearly crushed. "I won't even ask what that means, because I wouldn't understand it anyway, but is that all?"

"That's all." Kitty shrugged. "We knew each other a long time ago, Shelley. I guess we just don't have anything in common anymore."

"You have the car in common," Shelley offered hopefully.

"He has *that* in common with Jack, Shelley! You might as well stop trying to make some kind of great romance out of it; there's nothing there."

"Well, tell me what went on at the Speedway today. Was the opening of practice exciting?"

"Do you know," Kitty grinned ruefully, "I was so busy with our car and the great man's arrival that I'll have to watch the news to see what went on!"

"What's happening tomorrow?"

"Things will get busy tomorrow. Steve's going to drive at least a few laps, and then we'll really start finding out what's wrong with the car."

"What could be wrong? You've been working on it for months!"

"Oh, there'll be things wrong, all right," Kitty predicted darkly. "Don't you remember Murphy's Law?"

"If anything can go wrong . . . ?"

"It will!" Kitty's laughter trailed off into silence as she looked over Shelley's shoulder at the street.

"Oh, Lord," she said faintly. "Speak of the devil . . ."

"What's the matter?" Shelley twisted around to follow Kitty's gaze, then turned back, puzzled. "Kitty, what's the matter?"

"See that black car, the outrageously expensive-looking one? Well, that's a Lamborghini Countach SS, and unless I'm very mistaken, it's the car Steve bought two years ago after he won the Italian Grand Prix."

"It is?" Shelley breathed and shot Kitty an incredulous glance before turning to watch the low-slung black car purr to a stop in front of the house. "My God," she said weakly, "that's actually Steve Duncan." She glared accusingly at Kitty. "I thought you said he wasn't interested in you!"

"He *wasn't!*" Kitty hissed, and Shelley favored her with another frankly disbelieving glance.

"Then why is he coming up *here?*"

"I can't imagine."

"Well, I can!"

"Shelley!" Kitty bit back any further denials. Shelley wouldn't believe her anyway, not with Steve on his way up the walk. Tall, lean, his handsome, high-cheekboned face faintly smiling, he was elegantly dressed in a dove-gray, summer-weight suit, with a cream silk shirt and a pewter-colored tie. Kitty said nothing, only rose as he stepped lightly onto the porch.

"Good evening, Kitty."

"Hello, Steve." She inclined her head, then turned as he looked over her shoulder at Shelley. "Shelley, I'd like you to meet Steve Duncan. Steve, my neighbor, Shelley Thomas."

He stepped forward to shake her hand, the famous smile turned full on. "A pleasure to meet you, Miss Thomas."

He held her hand a fraction longer than necessary, and Kitty spoke, just a bit dryly, from beside him. "It's Mrs. Thomas," she said, and he released Shelley's hand slowly.

"I'd like to meet Mr. Thomas some time." He smiled and Shelley, normally the most matter-of-fact of women, said something uncharacteristically girlish and giggly.

With a final murmured word to Shelley he turned back to Kitty. "May I come in?"

She regarded him coolly, her instinctive reaction to his nearness warring with a complete inability to understand his presence. "Of course."

She preceded him toward the door, saying, "I'll see you later," to Shelley, who was watching them with eyes alight.

Inside her living room he looked around appreciatively at her comfortable furniture upholstered in a nubby, oatmeal-colored fabric, at the prints and photographs on the off-white walls. The overall impression was of casual yet elegant comfort.

"Very nice." He nodded and repeated, "Very nice."

"Thank you," Kitty said, then paused, watching as he prowled the room. "Why are you here, Steve?"

"To take you to dinner." The well-shaped mouth lifted in a small smile as she stared at him.

"To take me to . . . ? What on earth for?"

"To talk over old times?" He shrugged. "Or have you already eaten?"

"Well, no, but—" A small warning bell had gone off in Kitty's brain. She wasn't at all sure she wanted to talk over "old times"; the discussion could get very sticky. She hedged. "I don't think—"

"You said you haven't eaten." He smiled appealingly. "Come on, Kitty; I'm hungry and I don't want to eat alone."

"Oh . . . all right." She gave in, unable to resist that smile, and he nodded again.

"Right. Then go and get dressed. I have reservations for 8:00."

Bemused, a little surprised at herself, Kitty obediently went to change, unable to understand quite how she had been maneuvered into this. She knew it was probably the height of foolishness to spend time alone with Steve. She wasn't in love with him, of course, but her physical reaction to him was at least as dangerous as love could be. Even greeting him on the porch had affected her, though she'd been able to hide it under a cool demeanor, or hoped she'd been able to hide it.

Cold water splashed on her cheeks cooled the pink flush there, and she made up carefully, emphasizing her large brown eyes with their thick fringe of dark lashes and accenting the softness of her bow-shaped mouth with a sheen of gloss. She hesitated a long moment before her open closet, then nodded to herself as she reached for a hanger.

For someone as petite as she was, finding cocktail or evening dresses that made her look her age without looking as if she were dressing up in her mother's clothes was always a challenge, but the dress she laid across her bed was a triumph of careful shopping. It had been rather expensive, but she had been unable to resist it once she had tried it on and seen what it did for her. Made of a wonderfully fluid copper-colored crepe, it had delicate diamanté shoulder straps above a bodice cut straight across front and back, rested lightly on the soft swell of her breasts and bloused gently above the waist. The skirt was a slim tulip wrap, demure when she stood still but parting with each step to reveal a glimpse of shapely leg.

She slipped it on over nothing more than brief, lacy panties and silky pantyhose, then regarded herself in the mirror with a smile of satisfaction. She looked very different from the starry-eyed sixteen-year-old Steve had known. Perhaps, in a way, this could be a new beginning for them. Steve appeared to have forgotten their last, catastrophic evening together, and his boredom this afternoon had given way to some sort of interest this evening. Perhaps that interest could grow, given some subtle encouragement.

She stepped into strappy, narrow-heeled sandals

that would bring her a bit closer to Steve's height, picked up a matching clutch bag in copper-colored snakeskin and gave herself a last encouraging grin in the mirror as she left the room.

When she paused in the kitchen doorway, Steve was standing by the mantel, looking at a framed photograph of Kitty and John taken on Kitty's six-teenth birthday. She stood, silently watching him, arrested by the expression on his face, for it was harsh, almost grim, the lines cut deeply into cheeks and forehead. She felt a stab of guilt; he must be remembering his friendship with John and regretting its end.

As she moved into the room he turned, and that grim expression might never have been, for it was gone in the blink of an eye. He smiled warmly at her, then complimented her on her dress, and the words she might have said, the apology she would have made, went unuttered. He took a gossamer shawl from her to drape around her shoulders, and she wanted to speak, but somehow the time wasn't right. She couldn't say the things she wanted to say to that charming, sophisticated mask, but later a time would come when she could tell him how she felt.

Gracefully she allowed him to lead her to the low-slung, menacingly powerful black car and assist her into the seat with exquisite care. The car snarled into life and slid away from the curb, and Steve threw her a smiling glance.

"Don't you want to know where we're going?"

"I'll trust your judgement." She matched his light tone, her eyes on the passing traffic. "Just tell me when we've arrived." She was a bit less blasé when they pulled up to the entrance of the newest, tallest, most luxurious hotel in Indianapolis, but she hid it well, watching with polite indifference as Steve sent

an awestruck parking attendant off with his car, then
taking the arm he offered to walk very straight and tall
beside him into the hotel.

The narrow heels of her sandals clicked across the
terrazzo floor of the vast atrium, a breathtaking tour
de force of architecture. Above them the hotel soared
skyward, the rooms on each floor opening onto balconies encircling the atrium, which rose the full height of
the building. Plantings trailed streamers of green from
the balconies, full-sized trees grew in tubs scattered
around the atrium, a fountain splashed and gurgled in
the center and a glass elevator glided upward opposite
them.

Kitty kept her face calm, but her eyes darted about
the huge area, discovering new delights everywhere
she looked. Steve's voice and eyes were amused when
he bent his head to ask her, "Do you like it?"

"It's breathtaking," she replied honestly, and he
laughed, the indulgent laugh of an adult giving a treat
to a child. Kitty stiffened beside him.

She was as adult as he, and she wanted him to know
it, but he said only, "I'm glad you approve," and led
her toward an escalator to the mezzanine. The restaurant they were making for was on an outcrop of the
balcony, looking out over the atrium. Trees in large
tubs were scattered among the tables, lit by twinkling
fairy lights strung through their leaves, while more of
the lights formed a canopy overhead.

The maître d' greeted Steve effusively and led them
to a secluded table overlooking the atrium and partially screened from the rest of the room by one of the
trees. He held Kitty's chair for her, assured Steve that
their waiter and the sommelier would join them
promptly and finally bowed himself off, leaving them
alone.

Kitty laid her bag aside and eased her shawl off her

shoulders, suddenly ill at ease. She didn't know where to look, but when she could do no more "settling" she had to look up at Steve.

"Are you comfortable?" he asked courteously, his face unreadable.

"Yes, thank you."

"Good." He studied her face for a few seconds, his expression grave. "Now we can talk."

Chapter Five

$\mathcal{V}$ery carefully Kitty took a sip of her water and replaced the glass on the table. The suddenness of Steve's last remark surprised her, and now that the issue had been raised she was unable to put the words of her apology together and get them said. She struggled to find a way to express her confused thoughts, but was saved from floundering into a disjointed explanation by the arrival of the waiter to take their drink order. Steve dealt with him quickly, ordering bourbon and branch water for himself and the gin and tonic Kitty requested. The waiter melted away, and Steve turned back to Kitty, who was nervously fidgeting with her napkin.

He watched her face for a moment, waiting, but as she drew a deep breath and parted her lips to speak he raised a hand to forestall her.

"No," he said. "I have to tell you something first." He dropped his eyes to the white linen cloth on the table, seeming to be as ill at ease as Kitty herself, until he looked up again.

"Kitty, I asked you to dinner tonight because we have things to talk about, things that—" He broke off as the waiter appeared with their drinks and waited in silence until the man had served them and departed. "There are things that have to be said," Steve went on, "before we can work together for the next month. We have to talk, and I thought you'd prefer to do that away from Jack and the crew."

Kitty lifted her drink with a hand that trembled slightly and took a deep swallow, welcoming the warmth of the alcohol running through her veins. Her hand was steadier as she set her glass back on the table.

"Steve, I—I've waited a long time, hoping someday I'd have the opportunity to tell you how sorry—how very sorry—I am for what I did." Her voice shook and she drew another deep breath before she could continue. "What I did—was wrong. My reasons for doing it were wrong. I know that I can never undo the damage I did; I regret that more than I can ever tell you." She studied the tablecloth for a moment, then looked up at him, her face grave. "I know it can't change anything, Steve, but I wish it had never happened."

He held her troubled gaze for a long moment, then looked down, watching his own fingers as they toyed with his glass. "Thank you," he said at last. "I know that wasn't easy to say." He seemed about to say something more, but the waiter returned with large, leather-bound menus, and in the flurry of discussion that accompanied their choice of entrees and then the protracted discussion between Steve and the sommelier over a suitable wine, the moment was lost.

They spoke very little as they ate, neither one able to do justice to the beautifully presented food, but when she had finished as much as she could of her lobster Thermidor, Kitty looked up to see Steve watching her, his face somber once again. He glanced away while the waiter removed their plates and poured coffee, then his eyes returned to hers, reading confusion and unease in their dark-brown depths.

"I know it was difficult for you to say what you did," he said again, picking up the conversation where they'd left it almost an hour before, "but I appreciate it. I wondered"—he had lowered his gaze to his cup, studying the inky depths of the coffee as though fascinated—"if you understood, at the time." He looked across the table at her, and this time Kitty was the one to drop her gaze.

"At the time," she said slowly, "nothing. But just afterward, I understood a lot. How my actions affected not just me, but so many others, how irresponsible I'd been, how—wrong—I'd been."

He nodded and sipped his coffee. "There was no way you could have understood everything. You were too young for that, and now, though you understand more of it, you don't understand everything. I doubt if you ever can."

"Steve, I—" She broke off, searching for the words to say, then began again. "Steve, I've waited seven years to say this, and I don't know any fancy way to do it. Steve—I'm sorry for what I did, and for the pain it caused you."

"Thank you," he said, very formally. "I accept your apology. I would like to apologize as well for the wrong I did you."

"There's no need—" she began in protest, but he cut her off smoothly with a change of subject.

"I was very sorry to hear about your father. I know how much you must miss him."

"I do," she said simply, "but it's been over a year now. The hurt lessens. I think he would have chosen to go that way, too—quickly."

"Was it his heart?"

"Mm-hm. They told us it happens like that sometimes, with no warning."

He reached out to cover her hand, and for a moment they sat in silence, remembering Frank Gordon.

"Steve?"

"Mmm?"

"I'm glad I had the chance to talk to you. I've waited a long time for that, and for the chance for us to be friends again." Their eyes met as she spoke, so she saw the brief flash of strong emotion cross his face before he schooled it back to impassivity.

"I don't think so," he said quietly, so quietly that at first Kitty didn't understand. She shook her head briefly, involuntarily, but he went on, his quiet words striking her like stones.

"Too many things have happened for that. I don't know if you understand, even yet, how I felt. I did something that I'm still ashamed of. I took advantage of a girl—not a woman, a girl—and the fact that she was asking for it doesn't excuse me.

"In doing so, I had my nose broken, I lost a friend and I learned something about myself that I still find difficult to accept. I don't enjoy the memories, Kitty; I'd like to forget them, but when I look at you, I remember." He shook his head, his face grim.

"No, Kitty. I understand your feelings, but I don't

think we can be friends. We're going to be co-workers for the next four weeks, but that's all we'll be. Ever."

There was nothing Kitty could say to that; there was nothing anyone could say. She dropped her eyes from the face of the stranger opposite her, the stranger she had foolishly thought she could transform into the Steve she had grown up with. She saw now just how foolish she had been to naïvely expect to be able to roll back the years, to pretend that the past had never happened.

"I don't hate you, Kitty," Steve said, his words striking her like tiny knives. "I just don't feel much of anything for you. We can work together this month, but that's all."

Numb, Kitty nodded weakly, unable to meet his eyes. She felt cold and sick, frozen to the very core of her being, her silly hopes and imaginings shattered beyond repair. "I understand," she whispered. "I understand." There was nothing more to say, and she fell silent.

The silence between them stretched and stretched, taut as a violin string, vibrating with tension, until Kitty opened her mouth to say something, anything, to break it. She was forestalled, though, by a commotion across the room. She turned, startled by the noise, to look for the cause of it and heard Steve swear tiredly under his breath as a group of men, laughing and just a tiny bit drunk, bore down on their table.

She remained seated, watching with growing amusement as Steve rose to greet the group, all race drivers or crew members, she realized when she sorted them out. There were only six of them, not the mob they had seemed at first, two crew members and four drivers from other racing teams. Of the six, she had met five of them at the track, though she wasn't well acquainted with them, and the sixth she recognized from television and news pictures.

He was Marco Rissoli, Italian, and a Formula One driver like Steve, who had come to Indianapolis to drive in his first 500 this year. He was young, like most European drivers, 25 or 26, not tall but strongly built, with the sensuously carved face and curly hair of a Roman statue and the voluble, volatile temperament that was so typically Italian.

The dark, liquid eyes that rested on her with such frank admiration were typically Italian as well, and she found herself smiling easily back at him, enjoying the respite from Steve's wounding indifference. Though he was clearly reluctant, Steve was forced to allow the other men to greet her, but he made certain that their remarks were brief, standing by Kitty's chair like a guard. Marco Rissoli was left until last and might have been ignored altogether, had he not shouldered his way through the group and bent to take her hand.

"Signorina," he murmured and lifted her hand to his lips, "I am at a disadvantage, for I have never had the pleasure of meeting you. My name is Marco Rissoli, and you are . . . ?"

"She's Kitty Gordon and she's on my crew," Steve said curtly before Kitty could speak. She glanced up at him in surprise, noting the belligerent set of his jaw, then looked back at Marco, who was speaking again.

"Kitty?" Marco said slowly, his English heavily accented but fluent. "But this is a small cat, is it not?"

"Yes, it is." Kitty laughed at his comically puzzled expression. "But it's also a nickname for Katharine."

"A very pretty one." He still held her hand, and now he drew her gently toward him. "Will you dance with me, Miss Kitty Gordon?"

The dance floor was filling with couples as a band began to play, but Kitty hesitated, withdrawing her hand from Marco's. She wasn't really in the mood to dance, but suddenly she had to get away from Steve, if only for the length of one dance, or she knew she would burst into humiliating tears. "Thank you," she said. "I'd like that. If you don't mind, Steve?" She turned inquiring eyes on him, but he merely shrugged indifferently, so she took the hand that Marco offered and allowed herself to be led to the dance floor.

Turning into Marco Rissoli's arms as they joined the other dancers, she glanced over his shoulder at Steve, but he was lighting a cigarette, head bent, oblivious to her presence. Cursing her own stupidity, she jerked her eyes away from him, staring blindly at the other dancers, willing herself not to care. Marco led her into the dance, and with perhaps more bravado than prudence she looked up into his gratified eyes and smiled.

"Your Steve is not pleased that you are dancing with me," he murmured in her ear, cleverly executing a quick turn that put her slightly off balance and enabled him to pull her close.

"He's not my Steve!" Kitty said sharply, a little breathless from her sudden contact with his hard chest.

Marco gave a soft, satisfied laugh against her hair. "That is good. You and I, we make a better pair."

"Oh, really?" Kitty pushed against his shoulder, levering herself slightly away from him.

"Yes, really," he mimicked her, easily thwarting her efforts to create a space between them. "Steve is too tall, but you and I are suited to each other; our hair, our eyes, are even the same color. Just think how good we look together!"

Kitty had to laugh aloud at his mock-serious arguments. "You make us sound like a pair of bookends!"

"Ah, but we dance so beautifully together, as well." He spun her around again and then bent her back in a dip that took her completely by surprise and forced her to cling to him for support in what could only look like an ardent embrace. Her face was flushed when he set her on her feet again, and his lips curved in a satisfied smile. "You are beautiful, little one. So beautiful, like the moon in the midnight sky." His murmurings had the sound of a much-used script for seduction, and Kitty began to smile, biting her lip to control the laughter that threatened to break out. "So beautiful," Marco went on, "like a goddess. And I—"

"And you are a naughty boy, Marco!" The laughter won out and Kitty leaned her head on his shoulder, trying to stifle the giggles. When she had them under control again she looked up at him, her eyes sparkling with amusement. "Do girls actually fall for that line?"

He grimaced ruefully. "But of course! Any woman wants to be a goddess! Do you not wish—"

"I'm not a goddess," she chuckled, "and I certainly can't take that sort of thing seriously!"

"But why . . . ?"

"Let's just say I saw through it."

He regarded her shrewdly for a moment. "And you are not particularly . . . ah . . . ripe for such things just now?"

"Not just now," she agreed, and his eyes flicked toward Steve, who was still seated at the table. "But," she added hastily, having intercepted that glance, "things can change, you know."

His eyes met hers for a long moment, and then he nodded, and his mouth widened in a grin. "Then I shall not give up hope," he told her as the song ended and he led her back to Steve. "I will see you again, little one."

He paused beside her chair, kissed her fingers lightly, nodded to Steve and left to rejoin his companions. Kitty had begun to wish she hadn't given Marco quite so much encouragement, and she slid into her chair, avoiding Steve's eyes, and picked up her wineglass to sip the dry white wine they had had with their meal.

Before the glass reached her lips her wrist was seized in a viselike grip. The wine splashed over her fingers as she involuntarily jerked against his grasp, and then he took the glass from her and set it on the table. Quickly, roughly, he wiped the wine from her fingers with his linen napkin, then jerked her to her feet.

"What are you—"

"We're leaving," he growled, scooping up her purse and shawl and pushing them into her hands.

"But I—"

"We're leaving. Now." He dropped some bills onto the table and pushed her before him through the restaurant and into the elevators, his fingers clamped on her upper arm with a force that made her wince. She had to trot to keep up with him as they crossed the atrium, followed by curious eyes as others noted their hurried progress. They had a brief wait for the Lamborghini, and Kitty stood in a frozen silence, her arm held in his punishing grip, utterly unable to understand why Steve was suddenly so angry.

She had no choice but to allow herself to be handed into the car and sat tensely silent as he pulled out onto the street and accelerated with a roar. She stood it for as long as she could, then turned slightly so that she could see his profile in the light of the street lights flicking by. She had no idea why, but he was furiously

angry; the hard lines of his face and rigid set of his jaw
told their own tale, but it didn't make sense.

"Steve?" she said hesitantly. "What is—"

"Shut up!" he barked without looking at her. "Just
shut up!" Astonished, Kitty stared mutely at him for a
moment, then, despite the taut anger in his face, she
tried again.

"What's wrong, Ste—"

"I said *shut up!*" He flicked one daggerlike glance at
her, pinning her to the smooth leather of the deep
bucket seat, then swung the car around a corner with
a jerk of the wheel and a squeal of tires, throwing
Kitty against the restraint of her safety belts. "I'll talk
to you—in private—at your house." It was less a
promise than a threat, and Kitty subsided, her own
anger warring with a sensation somewhere between
nervousness and outright fear. It held her silent until
he braked the car to a stop in front of her house.

"All right, Steve," she began, anger winning out.
"Just what is all this about?"

By the time she finished the sentence she was
talking to an empty seat. Ignoring her, he had
whipped out of the car, slammed his door and strode
around to open hers and jerk her out onto the
sidewalk. She stumbled after him as he dragged her
up the walk, his fingers bruising the soft flesh of her
upper arm, his roughness angering her so that she
hung back, sputtering protests.

"Let *go* of me! Steve, you can't do this! Let me *go!*"
Her words were low-voiced, for she didn't want to
wake Shelley and Jim, but her furious vehemence was
not diminished by a lack of volume. Steve ignored her
completely, hauling her up the steps and depositing
her at the door with no regard for her protests, which
continued in an incensed whisper as he took her bag
from her, rummaged in it for her key, opened her

door and shoved her inside. He followed her in, kicking the door closed behind him, and stood poised, arms folded across his chest, following her with his eyes as she moved to the center of the room and turned, bristling, to face him.

"I don't know what you think you're doing!" she hissed. *"And* I don't have any idea what you're so angry about, so maybe you'll be good enough to explain!"

"I'll be happy to explain." He came farther into the room to confront her. "I don't know, or care, what you've done in the last seven years, but when it reflects on my racing team, then I *do* care!"

"But what did I *do?*" Kitty spread her hands in bewilderment. "I know you don't like me; I understand that, but what are you so angry about?"

"Wouldn't you agree that for a member of one racing team to make a spectacle of herself with a member of another racing team might be open to misinterpretation by the press? Or, if the situation *is* what the press assumes, that it might, at the very least, provide ample fodder for exploitation?"

"I still don't know what you're so angry about! I wasn't making a spectacle of myself—unless you're talking about my dancing with Marco?"

"Unless?" he sneered. "What else? Of all the people you could pick to wrap yourself around on a dance floor, he's got to be the worst! I don't know if you like that oily gigolo type or if you just can't tell the difference, but keep in mind that what you do reflects on the rest of the crew. If you don't care about your own reputation, at least have some consideration for them."

"You . . . ! I . . . !" Kitty sputtered helplessly for a moment, then collected herself. "I did not, repeat *not*, wrap myself around anyone, and even if I had, it would be no concern of yours!" She took two steps toward him and stared up into his hard face, quivering with righteous indignation.

"Now I think it's time for you to go. Thank you for the dinner. I'm glad we had an opportunity to talk. Good night!" Her sentences were clipped, angry and very much to the point, but he refused to move.

"Oh no, Kitty," he said softly, threateningly. "You don't order me out the door." He took a step closer to her and Kitty forced herself to stand her ground despite the thunderous anger that darkened his face.

"I will if I want to!" she snapped, nearly as angry as he was by now. "I made a mistake a long time ago, Steve, but that doesn't give you the right to order me around in my own home. I think you should leave!"

"Well, I don't!" He took one last step and caught her arms in a steely grip before she could back away.

Rather than indulge in an undignified, and probably useless, struggle to free herself, Kitty stood rigid in his grasp, glaring furiously up at him.

"I'll leave when I'm ready, and I'm not ready yet! Anyway, I don't know why you're so anxious for me to leave—unless you made an arrangement with Rissoli while you were hanging all over him?"

"I was not—" Kitty gasped, almost spitting with rage. "But I think I'd prefer *his* company to *yours!*" she added nastily. "He wouldn't manhandle me!"

"You little—" His hands tightened painfully on the soft flesh of her upper arms, shaking her, as if he'd like to do more, as if he'd like to punish her but was holding himself under tight control. "You have a nasty little mouth, don't you? I ought to—" A muscle in his jaw twitched uncontrollably, and he broke off with a muttered curse, jerking her against him and crushing his mouth onto hers in an angry, punishing kiss.

She did struggle then, frantically, fighting the

strength of his arms around her, twisting her head to evade his cruel mouth, but his arms were like steel bands, and one hand came up to twist into her hair, forcing her face up to his. He ground her lips against her teeth until she gave a tiny moan in her throat and went limp, defeated, the resistance drained from her. As he felt her sag weakly against him the character of his kiss changed, and he gently probed her mouth, forcing her lips apart and seeking the sweetness within.

Had she been able to think of anything at all she would have thought his angry kiss would touch no chord within her, that after seven years, after all the hurtful things that had been said and done, there was nothing left between them, but she would have been wrong. Her surrender to his domination had left her with no defenses, no barriers to the response that knifed through her as her lips parted beneath his. She melted against him, the present and past swirling together in her mind as the magic began again, the same magic that had drawn her to him seven years before.

He shifted his feet slightly to take more of her weight against him, and the movement, the feel of him, brought a torrent of memories flooding back. So lost in the past was she that when he lifted his head she clung for a moment, tried to pull him down to her, forcing her heavy lids open only when he set her away from him, pulling her clinging hands from around his neck.

"Just remember," he said, his soft voice heavy with contempt, "whose crew you're on."

A scorching shame flooded through Kitty at the realization of what she had done, and she backed quickly away from him, out of reach.

"Just *you* remember," she told him in a voice that

shook despite her efforts to steady it, "what we talked about tonight."

"Don't worry." He showed his teeth in a wolfish grin. "We're no more friends now than we were before. I won't forget that." He turned to the door, then paused with his hand on the knob and looked back at her. "See that *you* don't." Then he was gone.

For long moments she simply stood and stared at the door, unable to comprehend the reasons for what had just happened, unable, for the first moments, to think at all. It was the cooling of her overheated body, causing her to shiver, that brought her back to reality and a drowning sense of shame.

How, *how*, could she have done that? She turned away from the door, arms crossed protectively over her breasts, goose bumps prickling her arms as a chill ran over her skin. How could she have abandoned herself so utterly to Steve's kiss, a kiss of anger, contempt, punishment?

Maybe he was right about her, she thought despairingly. Maybe she had done as he'd accused her; maybe she had "wrapped herself around Marco Rissoli" on the dance floor. She didn't think so, but then, she'd been dancing, not watching. Maybe, no, probably, she should never have agreed to dance with the man, but after the things Steve had told her she had snatched at the chance to get away from that table, away from him.

She felt like such a fool! She had gone with him in such a hopeful mood this evening, such a naive, stupid, starry-eyed mood, she now saw in the clear light of hindsight. She'd been a silly idiot, trying to see things through rose-colored glasses, pretending she could wipe away all the bitterness and hurt as if that dreadful night had never happened.

She would never accuse Steve of being such a sadist

as to have enjoyed spelling out the facts to her, but after all she'd done to him there had to have been a certain satisfaction in putting her in her place. It must have been the icing on the cake of his evening for her to surrender so completely to his punitive kiss.

At the touch of his lips the present had slipped away, leaving her caught in a web spun from the magic of the past. With one kiss he had taken a twenty-three-year-old woman and transformed her into the starry-eyed teen-ager who had fancied herself in love with him. She smiled a bitter little smile into the darkness of her living room. If he'd wanted to punish her he'd succeeded beyond his wildest dreams; she only hoped he would consider that she'd been punished enough and leave her alone from now on.

Not surprisingly, she slept badly, waking with the same sense of foreboding that had haunted her dreams. By the time she had stood under a steaming shower, though, toweled herself roughly and dragged a brush through her slightly damp hair, her natural strength of spirit was beginning to reassert itself. Steve had got through to her last night, breached the wall around her emotions, but she could see that it didn't happen again. She wasn't sure just how, but she would make sure of it.

She dressed quickly in her work clothes: jeans, the red shirt with the team logo and red-suede running shoes. Her hair was brushed back into a ponytail at her nape and caught with a red scarf, echoing the color of the shirt. She grimaced at herself in the mirror as she left the room. Red was a perfectly nice color, but two solid months of wearing red every day was too much.

In her small, sunny kitchen she lifted the filter off the coffeepot and reached for one of a row of colorful mugs on the shelf above the sink.

"Damn!" The mug slipped from her fingers and shattered on the floor, and the little incident, trivial though it was, caused tears to start to her eyes. Which showed, she thought in disgust, just how steady her nerves were, brave thoughts notwithstanding. Unfortunately, they didn't get any steadier as she drove through the early-morning traffic toward the Speedway.

The garage area was already crowded, and she wove her way on foot through the throng, a small, slight figure in bright-scarlet shirt and jeans, which should have made her look unfeminine but instead clung lightly to the curves of her figure so that she resembled a small, bright bird as she made her way through the crowd of men in Gasoline Alley.

Her steps slowed fractionally as she neared the garage, her inner turmoil reasserting itself, but her entry was an anticlimax, for Steve had yet to arrive. She glanced around the garage as she stepped inside, registering his absence with a relaxation of the tension that gripped her. She was given no chance to enjoy that moment of relaxation, though, for Jack was already barking orders like a drill sergeant, determined to have everything absolutely perfect for Steve's first run in the car. By the time Steve did arrive Kitty was immersed in her own preparations and merely glanced up to register his presence, then bent her head to her work again.

She had no opportunity to worry about him, for they were all caught up in the flurry of preparations. While she was carefully checking the chassis to make certain it had sustained no damage in the last few days as the engine was removed and remounted, Steve was donning his fireproof clothing.

All drivers wore basically the same set of flame-resistant protective clothing when they drove, for fire was the greatest and most deadly danger to a race driver. Steve had stripped off his jeans and team shirt, under which he was wearing the first layer of fire protection, long underwear made of flame-resistant Nomex fiber. His socks were Nomex as well, and over this layer he donned a one-piece coverall-type driving suit made of three layers of Nomex. It was cream colored, with the Amtex logo, his name and assorted other insignia appliquéd on it, and was elasticized at wrists and ankles to prevent flames from entering. Flexible Nomex driving shoes were part of the outfit, as were Nomex gloves and a knitted balaclava hood, which covered his head, neck and face, save for his eyes and nose.

When Steve was nearly ready, Jack glanced around the garage at the others. "OK, everybody who's going to the pits, get your suits on! Come on, step on it! I want this car on the track sometime this month!" Kitty joined the others in a rush for the bright-red Nomex suits that hung ready for them.

One-piece coveralls, similar in design to Steve's driving suit, they were glossy red, elasticized at the waist, wrists and ankles, and liberally bedecked with the same logos and insignia. Kitty pulled hers on over her jeans and shirt, knowing she would be awfully warm wearing all those layers, but not willing to strip down to her underwear as some of the men did after she had pulled on her suit and left the garage.

After they had dressed the others joined Kitty outside, where she was running a finger around the neck of her suit, already warm in the morning sun. She'd be boiled alive inside this thing before long. Which was, of course, infinitely preferable to being burned alive. She sobered suddenly. All this protective clothing seemed like too much of a good thing sometimes, but it was for the best reason of all.

Steve walked out of the garage carrying his gloves, balaclava and helmet, closely followed by the car, as the crew opened the wide doors and pushed it out along Gasoline Alley toward the pits. The pit area was a hive of activity, and the noise as they entered was deafening, so they found themselves shouting to each other while they finished their preparations.

Steve stood calmly amid the din, pulling the balaclava over his head and adjusting the fabric until it was comfortable, the bottom of it tucked inside the neck of his driving suit to prevent flames from reaching his neck or head. His helmet went over it, with the Nomex skirt around the bottom of that tucked into the suit as well. He stepped into the car and raised his arms to be buckled in, and Kitty felt herself flush as she recalled her response to his nearness while performing that task yesterday. This time Rick White fastened the harness, then handed Steve his gloves and fastened the strap that ran from the top of the helmet to Steve's left shoulder to hold his head steady against the centrifugal force generated by 500 miles of left turns.

Steve pulled on his gloves, turning to look up at Jack, who was speaking, and then glancing at the rest of the crew. He looked straight at Kitty, but he was a stranger, his expression masked by the helmet, a space-age model that bore a striking resemblance to those worn by the villain in popular outer-space adventure movies. His eyes held hers for a long moment, but she couldn't read the message there, and then they moved on.

The crew attached the external starter to the car and fired the engine with a shattering roar, and Kitty held her breath as they pulled the starter away and thumped Steve's helmet to signal that he was cleared to go. Two of them ran with the car, pushing it by the rear wing until Steve accelerated away from them and down the pit lane, then out of the pits and onto the track. He kept to the inside, below the white line that separated the racing part of the track from the lane used by slower traffic when accelerating, and disappeared into the first turn. He would be out of their sight until he left the fourth turn and came down the main straightaway, but he was in touch with them via a two-way radio transmitter built into his helmet.

Jack and Kitty both wore headsets and could speak both to each other and to Steve, but in case the electronic system failed they had, as a backup, the traditional trackside signs. A member of the crew stood by the wall dividing the pit area from the track with a set of large signs and a chalkboard. The signs bore standard messages and numbers used to give a driver his times, and the chalkboard could be used for any unusual messages. As the driver entered the main straightaway from the fourth turn the young man with the signs would lean over the low wall, holding a sign at arm's length so the driver could read it as he shot past at something over 200 miles an hour.

Jack was talking to Steve, following his progress around the track, but Kitty pushed the mouthpiece away from her lips and listened with half her attention, watching her stopwatch as Steve made this first circuit. His time was slow, as expected, and he drove past to begin his second lap. The day, begun on such a surge of excitement, became round after round of simple hard work as Steve drove several laps, then pulled into the pits for minor adjustments of one sort or another, then went out for several more laps and repeated the process.

Kitty was kept very busy, for the minor complaints were split about evenly between her, as chassis expert, and Jack, as engine expert. When the long day was finally over for them Steve hadn't even had the car up to speed, but no one was dissatisfied with their efforts.

Speed would come later. After the shakedown period Steve would begin pushing the car to see just how fast it would go. How fast without spinning out or becoming airborne, of course, and that was where Kitty's more subtle refinements would prove their worth. If the aerodynamics of their car were better than those of the other cars, and if their engine was that little bit better, and if Steve's driving excelled as well, then they just might win this race.

An awful lot could happen during the next four weeks, though, and they all trudged back to the garage preoccupied with work to be done. It was late before Kitty left the track, and only as she drove home through the dusk did she realize that Steve had done exactly as he'd promised, treating her as just another crew member. By neither word nor action had he given any indication that he and Kitty were more than co-workers. It was as if the past had ceased to exist for him, leaving her as nothing more than someone he worked with, but didn't like very well.

Chapter Six

Steve continued to treat her like a particularly dull spot on the wall, and Kitty forced herself to be content with that. With increasing frequency and determined firmness she told herself how content she was as the days passed and nothing changed. Sometimes she had the eerie sensation of being invisible when his eyes slid past her without registering her presence in any way, and despite her determination to the contrary, it bothered her, for against her better judgement and despite what he had said to her, she wished they could be friends.

Perhaps, if she could have made herself unconscious of Steve, it wouldn't have mattered, but she was constantly aware of him with that sixth sense that told her when he was near. She couldn't keep her eyes from following him as he moved around the garage,

watching the play of muscles in his back and arms as
he helped lift the engine from the car, the sheen of
sweat on his brown chest when he peeled off the
heavy driving suit, the gleam of the sun on his
wheat-blond hair. Time and again she tore her eyes
away, trying to drown herself in her work, and time
and again she would glance up from her papers or
tools and her wayward gaze would stray back to him.

Somehow his indifference was more wounding than
overt hostility. At least if he were openly hostile she
would know that he was conscious of her presence,
but this way she was nothing.

She no longer loved him, of course; that childish
infatuation had died a merciful death ages ago, but
she still remembered. She remembered the way his
hands had caressed her, creating a need and a delight
such as she had never imagined before that night. She
had tried to forget that, but his kiss, angry and
punishing as it had been, had broken the lock she'd
kept on her mind.

No, she no longer loved him, but he had been her
only lover, and perhaps it was natural that memories
of him should have a particular power over her. She
even considered, in a moment of uncustomary cyni-
cism, the possibility that taking another lover might
erase those memories, but discarded the idea of
cold-bloodedly starting an affair as repellent to her.
She would have to struggle to overcome her own
weakness, without recourse to other men, and ignore
Steve if she possibly could.

That became more difficult when the girls began to
arrive. Invariably beautiful, faultlessly groomed and
expensively dressed, they would wave their visitors'
passes at the guard and brave the crush of Gasoline
Alley to cling to Steve's arm, giggle fatuously up at his
every word and waft clouds of expensive perfume

around the garage. It was maddening to watch, because Steve, though charming to all of them, treated them, Kitty thought, like pet dogs, sending them off with a pat on the head and a kind but condescending word to await his pleasure.

And pleasure it would be, she thought sourly late on one sweltering afternoon. She was seated in a corner of the garage, trying to work out how sharply the rear wing could be angled before the increased wind resistance negated the desired downward pressure, but she was finding it difficult to concentrate.

"Oooh, Steve! Do you really go *two hundred* miles an *hour?*" Ginger, the very buxom brunette who was speaking clung to his arm, leaning forward to display her nearly indecent décolletage to better advantage.

"Not in the corners." Indulgently amused, Steve's eyes moved appreciatively over Ginger's ripe curves. "But in the straightaway much faster."

"Oooh!" The piercing squeal drew all the eyes in the garage, the men's frankly appreciative of the woman's tight slacks and brief top, Kitty's frankly annoyed. How Steve could put up with Ginger and those like her Kitty had no idea. If asked for the sum of two plus two, Ginger would probably be stumped, and she would certainly never be considered a clever conversationalist. Of course, it wasn't her conversation that Steve was interested in.

The girl took a tottering step in her impossibly high heels, stumbling, whether accidentally or by design, into Steve's apparently willing arms. She giggled again, pouting full, red lips up at him as he responded with a heavy-lidded bedroom smile, and young Jimmy Miller, blushing furiously beneath his flaming hair, hurried forward with a battered folding chair.

"Why, thank you, honey. You're very kind." Syrupy-sweet, Ginger's voice now held a faint trace of a Southern drawl, and Kitty could bear it no longer. Gathering a sheaf of plans and diagrams, she escaped to the hurly-burly outside, preferring the crowded Alley to the cloying atmosphere inside the garage. A discarded rear tire, wide and treadless, lay on its side by the door, a comfortable perch.

She unfolded her papers on her knee and glanced around appreciatively, enjoying the din outside after Ginger's giggles, then bent over her calculations.

"Kitty!" She recognized the heavy accent even before she looked up from her papers and smiled warmly, watching Marco come across from his garage, which was almost directly across the way.

"Hello, Marco. Have you been out today?" He was wearing his driving suit, and he nodded, but with a little grimace.

"I was out, but there is a problem in the steering, so . . ." He shrugged. "They take it apart and I wait, and maybe I can go out again before the day is over. And why are you out here?"

"Same reason—problems, problems." She glanced at the thick sheaf of papers on her clipboard and mimicked his shrug. "There's always work to do, isn't there?"

"It appears so." He slid onto the tire beside her, an arm around her waist, pulling her close. "You should let me help you. These figures and plans are not for someone as lovely as you—"

"Ah-ah-ah!" She moved the clipboard out of his reach, tapping his wrist like a reproving schoolmarm. "You're still a naughty boy, Marco, trying to steal our secrets like that!"

"I? Steal secrets?" His look of wounded innocence was beautifully done, but the gleam of amusement deep in his dark eyes gave him away.

"Yes, you—steal secrets." The wounded look deepened and she could no longer contain her laughter, resting her hand weakly on his shoulder as she gasped, "Honestly, Marco, do people actually believe the things you say?"

"Certainly they do." He drew himself up, wrapped in an air of offended dignity, and she giggled again. "Why do you not believe me?"

"Because you're as transparent as glass, that's why!"

"And because you're not in love with me?"

"Right." She shook her head regretfully. "But I think I could be your friend."

"Very well—but if you want a lover . . . ?"

"Stop it!" She poked him in the ribs with her elbow. "And behave yourself!" They were laughing together when Ginger emerged from the garage, closely followed by Steve.

Marco cocked an amused eyebrow at the girl as she twined her arms around Steve's neck and gave him a long, intense kiss before he pulled her hands away and sent her off with a slap on the bottom. She squealed in playful excitement, and Kitty wondered again how he could put up with her. He hadn't chosen her, though, for her sparkling wit, she reminded herself.

The girl walked away, and Steve turned back to fix Kitty with a look of disgust equal to her own. "Do you think," he said with icy contempt, "you could carry on your affairs somewhere less in the public eye? There are reporters all over this place."

Kitty rose unhurriedly, her face calm. "Yes, there are a lot of reporters, aren't there? Just think," she smiled sweetly at him as she sauntered back toward the door, "we might even see you and Ginger," she waved a hand in the direction the other girl had gone, "on TV tonight. Bye, Marco!" She waved, he waved back and she paused in the doorway. "In case you haven't heard, Steve, the reporters don't bother me anymore. I don't give them a good interview." She favored him with another saccharine smile and vanished.

She had handled that rather well, she thought, none of her inner agitation showing on the surface. She did that with the reporters, too; she was becoming very good at hiding her feelings. She had discussed her work briefly with a few reporters in her first days at the Speedway, but when the questions became more personal—how did she get her job? how did she get along with Steve?—she stopped cooperating. Not that she was unpleasant, she simply looked at them with wide, guileless eyes and gave brief, boring, uninformative answers, deliberately misunderstanding the double-edged questions. Word had spread among the press fraternity with gratifying speed, and now she was rarely approached. It was more peaceful that way.

Her relationship with Steve was not so peaceful after those barbed remarks. For the rest of the day he found fault with everything in the car that she was responsible for, and it was only with the greatest effort that she kept a fingertip hold on her fraying temper. It was more than a little unfair of him, she fumed, to exchange that exhibitionist kiss with Ginger smack in the middle of Gasoline Alley and then act like Simon Legree because Kitty was sitting laughing with a friend.

The next day began little better, for Steve picked at her unrelentingly as they prepared to put the car on the track. The others watched in wary surprise, unable to understand his sudden change of demeanor. She judged herself vindicated, though, when she stood in the pits, clipboard and electronic stopwatch in hand, and recorded the times he turned.

He had held back until now, carefully pacing himself, shaking the car down and uncovering the small problems without trying for real speed. His speed had increased a little each day, but this afternoon was cool and cloudy, perfect racing weather, with no great heat to damage the engine and no distracting shadows on the track; it was late in the day and there were few others on the track, so he was able to push the car, testing its limits.

Lap after lap Steve flashed past, moving so fast that the eye could not keep up, seeing only a scarlet blur as the car passed in front of them. Lap after lap Kitty clocked his speed, recording his times in a column that grew more impressive with each new entry.

She had been listening with half an ear to the terse conversation between Steve and Jack on her headset, but after the twenty-eighth lap she let out a whoop of joy, her anger at Steve forgotten in the elation of the moment.

"One ninety-six point two eight eight!" she cried. "We did it! Steve, we did it! We broke one ninety-five!" She seized Jack's arm, bouncing on her toes in excitement. "Look, Jack! Isn't it great?"

Jack was grinning happily back at her as he told Steve to bring the car in on the next lap, and the rest of the crew were laughing and back slapping. If Steve could turn such a quick lap now, with two days yet to go before the first weekend of time trials, he stood a very good chance of breaking the magical barrier of a 200-mile-per-hour average for one two-and-a-half-mile lap and an even better chance of capturing the coveted "pole" position for the start of the race.

They were waving and cheering when the scarlet car rolled into the pits, and Steve's gloved fist was raised in a victory salute. The general elation accompanied them back to the garage, where they were waylaid by a flock of reporters. While Steve and Jack dealt with them the crew "put the car to bed" for the night and drifted away, pausing to say a few words to the press on their way out.

Kitty was left alone in the garage at last, but she waited, continuing her work. She had some questions for Jack, and anyway, she preferred to avoid the reporters if she could.

"You're still here?" Her head, bent over some figures, snapped up as the door swung open and Steve walked in.

"Yes, I want to see Jack before he leaves."

"You're too late, then. He went off with Bill Martindale about fifteen minutes ago."

"Oh, rats! Did he say where he was going?"

"Out for a beer somewhere and then home, I guess." Steve shrugged and unzipped his driving suit to peel it off his shoulders. Suddenly embarrassed, Kitty turned away as he stripped off the protective layers and pulled on street clothes. "What are you working so hard on, anyway?" he asked, and Kitty looked up again to see that he was nearly dressed, pulling on a blue, button-down shirt as he spoke.

"Oh, just . . . just the wing angle." She indicated a complicated diagram on the page in her hand. "I'm going to reset it tomorrow."

"What for?"

She ignored him and stood, collecting her papers, anxious to leave since there was no reason to stay. Anxious as well to avoid being alone with Steve.

"Where are you running off to?" He put out a hand to hinder her in her clearing away.

"Home." She shrugged. "Where else?"

"Without congratulating me on my times today?"

"Of course not." Kitty smiled with genuine pleasure. "That last lap was terrific! We should get a two-hundred-plus time out of that car yet!"

"We'll get a two-hundred lap all right," he said with absolute confidence. "If I can turn one-ninety-six, I can turn two hundred. Which brings to mind the question of why you're changing the wing angle. How come?"

"Because." Irritated by both his questioning of her decision and his demanding tone of voice, Kitty gave a deliberately provocative answer and was rewarded by a narrowing of Steve's eyes and a tightening of his jaw.

"Very funny, Kitty. Not too mature, but mildly amusing. Can you just answer the question?"

"I think you already know the answer. I'm going to sharpen that angle every time you drive until the times are as good as we can get. There's nothing new about that."

"There's no need for it, either. Just leave it as it is and I'll *drive* it quicker."

"Maybe you will, but I'll reset the wing anyway." Kitty slid the last of the papers into her briefcase and snapped it shut, straightening with it in her hand and taking two steps toward the door before coming to an abrupt halt as Steve stepped in front of her to block her way.

"I said, leave it alone," he repeated, and Kitty froze, staring at him with a rising anger.

"I heard what you said," she told him carefully, "but as *I* said, the wing will be reset."

"No." The one soft-spoken syllable was a lit match to the fuse of Kitty's fury.

"Who do you think you are?" she gasped. "*I'm* the chassis engineer, remember? There's no reason for me to do things any differently than any other chassis specialist, and there's no need for coaching from the driver!"

"Look, I just said you don't have to keep playing around with the wing. Leave it the way it is!"

"And I just said I'm going to reset it, and you don't have any say in the matter!" She stalked past him, but never reached the door, for she was caught by the arm and spun roughly around. "Stop it!" she snapped, and jerked free of his grasp. "You don't tell me how to do my job and I won't tell you how to do yours. You wouldn't be saying any of this to a man, to a *real* chassis specialist, would you? Well, let me tell you, Steven Duncan, I *am* a real chassis specialist, and it's *my* responsibility to see that the car you drive has the best chassis possible! I did the calculations and engineered the modifications and drew the designs for that car! All *you* did was get in and steer!" Her voice dropped lower, husky with anger, as she went relentlessly on, beyond heeding the warning flash of fury in his eyes.

"You're a good driver, Steve, no one can deny that, but without a good car you're not even an also-ran. Without a good car you're nothing!" She turned on her heel and would have stormed out of the garage but for the large hand that seized her arm and jerked her around to face him again.

"I'm nothing, am I?" he asked very softly, twisting Kitty's arm behind her back, forcing her close against him, her head falling back as she glared up into his face. "We'll see . . ."

She had gone one step too far, Kitty could see that in the glittering gray of his eyes as his face came down to hers. In a surge of panic she began to struggle uselessly against his greater strength. She would have turned away, but he wound his fingers into her hair and forced her face up to his to take her mouth in a kiss of angry punishment.

It was less a caress than an attack, a deliberate assertion of superior strength. His mouth oppressed her, taking for his own pleasure, uncaring of hers as he punished her for her impertinence. One of his arms was around her, crushing her against the rock-hard bulk of him so tightly that she couldn't move, couldn't breathe. . . .

She struggled furiously, fruitlessly, against that hateful, contemptuous kiss, wriggling and squirming helplessly. She was furious at her own feminine weakness, hating her inability to fight him effectively, hating him for using his superior strength to force her to submit.

Her efforts were humiliatingly ineffective, and tears of rage filled her eyes as he effortlessly thwarted her attempts to free herself. Not until her struggles had weakened and finally ceased in surrender did he release her, pushing her slightly away from him so that she staggered and had to catch herself against the wall. He made no move to help her, but stood with arms folded, watching her. His face was impassive, but his lips were compressed in a tight line as he took in her shattered appearance.

"What happened to the tough engineer?" he jeered softly. "Could it be you're not as omnipotent as you think?"

"You—you're disgusting!" she spat at him, and he smiled.

"You disappoint me, Kitty. I expected something much more original from you. Unless, of course, your energies are all being wasted on that Italian gigolo friend of yours."

Kitty sucked in a furious breath, fighting for some

kind of self-control. "It's too bad," she said with taut sarcasm, "that you're disappointed, you—you *creep!*" She grabbed up her purse and brushed past him out the door and along Gasoline Alley, painfully aware of soft, mocking laughter following her.

It was a relief to escape the garage while the men donned their fire suits. Kitty slumped onto the tire beside the door and leaned her head on hands that shook slightly with tension. She couldn't bring herself to speak to Steve; she had barely looked at him after one venomous glare when he had walked into the garage that morning, a glare to which he had responded with a taunting half smile that brought hot color to her face.

Being near him was almost more than she could bear, forcing her to remember that humiliating kiss. Her face flamed again; she could feel the warmth in her cheeks and fanned herself with her clipboard.

"Good morning, Kitty!" Recognizing Marco's cheerful voice, she looked up and returned his wave and greeting.

He dropped onto the tire beside her and kissed her cheek lightly. "You are so pink." He brushed a fingertip down her cheek. "Is something wrong?"

"What? Oh, no." She laughed lightly. "I'm just warm." She smiled into his laughing brown eyes, genuinely glad to see him. That he was a womanizer of some repute she had learned through the grapevine since meeting him, but she knew her chances of falling for his practiced charm were nil. She had seen straight through him at their first meeting, and he had made no effort to push their relationship beyond a casual friendship.

"I'm just warm," she said again, indicating her fire

suit, and he nodded, smiling but not really convinced. One skeptical eyebrow rose just a bit, then lifted higher when Steve appeared in the doorway and Kitty quickly averted her face.

"You are angry with my friend Steve?" he murmured with a smile in his voice. "Then perhaps you will turn to me?"

"It's not like that!" she whispered, painfully aware of Steve only a few feet away.

"Oh, no? I do not believe you but . . ." His words trailed off, then he said something in violent Italian under his breath. Kitty didn't understand Italian, but she knew swearing when she heard it, and she followed Marco's eyes back toward the main gate of Gasoline Alley.

A stunningly beautiful woman was walking in their direction, and Kitty wasn't really surprised when Steve strode past them to greet her. Very tall, very slim, very blond, she was elegantly dressed and exquisitely made up and walked into Steve's arms with the sort of studied grace Kitty associated with dancers and models. She was watching Steve and the woman with the same disdain she'd felt for all his empty-headed girlfriends when she felt Marco stiffen beside her as the two kissed.

Surprised, she slanted a glance at him, then turned her head to look more closely, for his face was set in rigidly angry lines and the hand that rested on his thigh was clenched into a fist. She touched it lightly with her fingertips and he started, as though he had forgotten her presence.

"*Si?*" He glanced at her briefly, then his eyes flicked back to the others, as though he hated to look but could not look away.

"Who is she, Marco?" Kitty murmured.

"Irina van Damm. She's Dutch, a model."

"She's very beautiful," she said gently.

The hand beneath her fingers tightened into a fist again. "Yes. She is beautiful," he agreed tersely.

"Are you in love with her?"

Marco looked down at her with a frown, which changed to bleak regret when he saw no mockery in her face, only gentle compassion. "Yes," he said heavily. "I am in love with her."

"Then why don't you—" Kitty began, but he cut her off with a quick flare of anger.

"There are reasons," he said harshly, "why I have no right to—to speak to Irina."

"No right to speak to her? That's ridiculous! You have every—"

"Basta!" His hand chopped sharply downward in a silencing gesture. "That is enough! There are things that you don't know, that no one can understand except myself and Irina." Shocked into silence by his furious outburst, Kitty stared at Marco with wide, startled eyes. "This," he said in a taut voice, "is one of those things."

"Marco, I—I apologize," Kitty stammered. "I didn't mean to pry."

The rigid anger began to leave Marco's face, and he managed a thin smile. "I know that, and I understand that you meant only to help. There are some things, though, that no one can help with." Kitty nodded silently, and Marco's eyes returned to Steve and Irina. "Anyway," he went on bitterly, "the two of them, they even look as if they belong together, do they not?"

Watching them, Kitty was forced to admit that they did indeed make a striking couple. Both were tall; Irina van Damm must be about five feet ten inches, for with high heels she was as tall as Steve, and they were both blond, both strikingly handsome. Irina's hair was cut in a fashionably short, sleek cap, and her eyes were a blue so vivid that it could be seen even from a distance. They looked like a matched set, made to order.

Well, they were welcome to each other. Steve had made it more than clear that the threads that had bound them together in the past had all been sundered beyond repair by Kitty's ill-advised actions. He was certainly free to conduct his love life how he chose, and she didn't care what he did. It was too bad, though, that he should be seeing a woman Marco loved; it obviously hurt Marco badly. It was too bad; everything was too bad.

"Kitty, will you help me?" Marco whispered in her ear. She looked at him in surprise and then began to shake her head as understanding dawned.

"Oh, no, Marco. I'm sorry, but, no."

"What can it hurt?" He took her hand in both of his and gave her a little-boy smile. "It is only a little playacting."

"I shouldn't . . ." she began.

"It is wrong of me to ask, I know, but I don't want their pity!" There was bitter pride in that, male pride, the pride of a man stung by the sight of "his" woman with another man, but Kitty understood. Her pride had taken a beating in the past few days, and suddenly she wanted to help.

"OK," she whispered. "I'll help." His face brightened and she hastened to add, "But only so far, Marco. Don't get carried away."

"Of course not," he murmured indignantly as he rose, pulling her to her feet, but she didn't quite like the gleam in his eye.

"*Buon giorno,* Irina. It is wonderful to see you again."

"Hello, Marco." She bent slightly to allow him to kiss first one cheek, then the other, then straightened and smiled expectantly at Kitty, a smile that did not reach her sky-blue eyes. Kitty didn't really care what Steve or Marco thought, but on the simple level of feminine pride she was acutely aware of the contrast between herself and the Dutch girl.

Not only was Irina tall, beautifully dressed and perfectly groomed, but not a wayward strand of golden hair nor a bead of perspiration marred her perfection, and the mauve linen pantsuit she wore showed her graceful figure to stunning advantage. Kitty, by contrast, was dressed in a bulky fire suit, wisps of her hair were beginning to escape the scarf that caught it back at the nape of her neck and her face was flushed and shining from the heat. Self-consciously she brushed a damp ebony tendril off her forehead and returned Irina's gracious smile with a wan effort at one of her own as Marco began the introductions.

"Irina van Damm, may I introduce Kitty Gordon?" Marco slipped a proprietorial arm around her waist and pulled her close against him. "She is—"

"She is a member of my crew," Steve interrupted rudely, with a glance of distaste at Marco's hand resting on Kitty's waist, "and she undoubtedly has work to do."

Kitty's color rose angrily, but she answered calmly enough. "I don't have anything at all to do right this minute, Steve. I'm just waiting for the guys to bring the car out. And talking to Marco, of course." She smiled up at Marco, who returned her smile with one that had no doubt melted feminine hearts all over his native Bologna. Only his eyes gave him away, sparkling with a private message, and Kitty, looking into them, was hard pressed not to giggle.

She was saved by the opening of the main garage door as the car was pushed out. She would have turned away to gather up her things, but Marco, to her astonishment, pulled her close and kissed her firmly on the lips before striding off toward his own garage, leaving her staring after him in disbelief.

When she turned back she met Steve's eyes, watching her with cold contempt. She held his gaze defiantly for a moment, then looked away, her own eyes bleak. She already knew what he thought of her, he'd made that more than plain, and it didn't matter, she told herself. After all, she had no right to care.

Her response to his kiss that first night had been purely physical, her awareness of him since then only a natural reaction to the presence of a man who had once been her lover. Her only responses to his cruel kiss of the day before had been shock and anger. It didn't matter *what* he thought of her!

And Irina . . . Kitty had almost forgotten her, but she picked up her things and straightened to find the Dutch girl watching her with a strange, speculative expression. Kitty blinked, and suddenly Irina's eyes held nothing, only cool disinterest.

"I'm happy to make your acquaintance, Miss Gordon." She extended one slim, cool hand and Kitty suppressed an urge to wipe her own rather grubby one on her pants before shaking hands. Defiantly she stuck out her hand, grime and all, and returned Irina's brief, well-bred handshake before excusing herself to follow the car into the pits. It was all so confused; Marco loved Irina who, for some reason, did not love him, and Irina was one of Steve's girls, and Steve didn't want Kitty to see Marco. It was all a horrible tangled-up mess!

She shook her head. It wasn't important; the race was important. She followed the car into the pits, emptying her mind of anything but last-minute preparations for the next day's qualifications.

Chapter Seven

". . . expecting a crowd of over 300,000 fans for the opening day of qualifications. Already cars are lining up on West 16th Street, waiting for the gates to open, and . . ." Kitty only half heard the tinny voice of the radio announcer as she wove her way through the pandemonium of Gasoline Alley. This was Saturday, the first of four days of qualifications, of "time trials." The two weekends before the weekend of the race itself were qualification days, and Kitty was very aware that the race was only fourteen days away. The countdown had begun.

The rules governing qualifications were horribly convoluted and complicated, but basically each driver, over those two weekends, was attempting to earn a place in the field of thirty-three cars that would actually compete in the race. Beyond earning a place in the field, however, they were earning a place as near the front of the starting "grid" as they could. When the field of thirty-three cars was lined up on the track in eleven rows of three they would be arranged in order according to which cars had qualified fastest on each of the four days, and the fastest qualifier on this first day would occupy the coveted "pole" position on the inside of the first row.

Said to be the most advantageous position from which to start the race, the pole also carried with it prestige and a substantial cash prize, and it was the goal sought by Steve and his team.

For them, and for several of the other entrants, experienced drivers with good cars and good crews, a place in the field was almost a foregone conclusion, but for many it would be an achievement to be in the race at all. For the unfortunate who was sitting in the number thirty-three slot at any time during the four days, each competitor's run was a harrowing experience, for he was the "man on the bubble." Each time a driver made a qualifying run faster than his, the man currently on the bubble, the slowest driver, was "bumped," or dropped from the field.

Each car was allowed only one complete qualifying run of four laps, not counting two warm-up laps; if the driver detected a problem with his car or was dissatisfied with his time before the four laps were completed, he could abort that run and wait his turn to try again. Once a run had been completed and the time entered into the record, though, that car was officially committed to the time recorded. If the car were then bumped it was out of the race, though the driver was free to seek another car in which to qualify.

Not that Steve's team expected him to have to face the nail-biting tension of the man on the bubble; their worries concerned his chances of securing the pole.

The car was now ready, fueled with the alcohol fuel used in championship racing, despite the fact that Gasoline Alley retained its traditional, if anachronistic, name. The crew dressed for the pits and Steve for driving, and they proceeded to the pit area where the sound of the huge crowd, which had been a steady background accompaniment at the garage, was now a solid wall of noise against which their puny shouts were a poor weapon.

With the headsets they were able to communicate, but instructions were not really needed by the well-rehearsed members of the team. They took their places quickly: the five-man pit crew, who would refuel the car and change the tires during the race; the sign man, out by the track; Jack; Kitty; and the others behind the pit wall.

Steve's concentration had been narrowing since he awoke that morning, all his attention focusing on the few short laps he would drive that day. It was always like this before he drove, the progressive tuning-out of all extraneous stimuli. He stood in the pits at the last minute, adjusting the balaclava comfortably over his head and neck, already beginning to sweat beneath all the layers of protective clothing.

Jack stood at his elbow, releasing his particular brand of tension by barking a rapid stream of last-minute instructions at Steve, who let his eyes slide absently over his crew and heard not a word of Jack's harangue. He pulled the back of the balaclava down and tucked it smoothly inside his driving suit, then pulled the fabric up to cover his chin and mouth.

His fingers stilled suddenly as his eyes touched Kitty, passed on and then jerked back, almost against his will. He was moving toward her, pulling the balaclava down below his mouth again, striding

through the people crowded around him even before
the sudden impulse was translated into thought. The
idea made no sense, of course, but he knew exactly
what he was going to do and wasted no mental energy
searching for reasons.

He reached Kitty in three long strides, grinning
down into her surprised brown eyes as he reached out
to pull her close. He had a brief glimpse of her eyes
widening even more as he bent to kiss her, then his
own eyes closed as he took her lips. He kissed her
slowly, the contact searching and sweet, and felt the
quick rush of response that softened her body in his
arms before he lifted his head to smile down into her
bewildered eyes.

"That's for luck, Kitten," he told her, then pulled
the balaclava back into place and stepped over the low
pit wall. She wasn't consciously in his thoughts as he
levered himself into the car and raised his arms for the
harness to be fastened, but somewhere deep within
him one vibrating thread of tension had been stilled.

He was cool, ice-cold, as he waited while the engine
was fired, his total being concentrated on the task
ahead of him. He saw one of the track stewards give
them the signal to go for their qualification run, felt a
crewman give him an "all-clear" thump on the helmet
and let out the clutch as the car began to roll, pushed
by two crewman who ran with it until Steve accelerated away from them.

Into the first turn and down the short straightaway
beyond it he stayed low on the track, in the acceleration lane, gathering speed so that as he left the second
turn for the backstretch he could move up onto the
racing surface. He was not yet at racing speed, but he
had two laps to reach it before he either left the track
to await another turn or took his qualifying attempt.
Through the third and fourth turns he was feeling out

the car and the track surface, which was cool, as he preferred it. He entered the main straightaway again, satisfied with the conditions for his run.

He accelerated down the straightaway, his concentration now on speed, on driving four laps, ten miles, as quickly as he possibly could. Driving was automatic: shifting gears; pressing pedals; turning the steering wheel, all slight movements of controls specifically designed for economy of movement. Steve had no need to think about what he was doing, but could focus his attention on the track ahead, which unwound in a series of endless left turns. The huge crowd wasn't even a backdrop to his driving, for the field of his vision was bounded by the track walls streaming past, and not even the roar of 300,000 shouting fans could overwhelm the roar of the engine behind his head.

He knew before he entered the fourth turn that this would be his qualifying run, and when he passed 200 miles per hour on the main straight he raised one gloved fist, signaling to the stewards that he would take this attempt. Above him green flags twirled from the starter's tower as he crossed the yard-wide strip of the original brick paving that marked the start/finish line, and his attempt had begun.

Each qualifying attempt was four laps of the track, with the speed for those four laps averaged. Steve knew he was running quickly; he could feel it with some sort of driver's sixth sense as he finished lap three and flashed beneath the white flag which signaled one lap to go, and then, with that last lap done, took the checkered flags.

Easing off his speed as the run ended, Steve relaxed and lifted his attention from the track ahead of him to the crowd all around him, on their feet now, cheering and waving while he acknowledged their accolade

with a raised hand as he passed. His crew were as wild
with glee as the crowd had been, laughing and shouting and clapping him on the back before a larger
crowd of well-wishers, press and track officials swirled
around him, carrying him out of the pits and back to
the garage.

Kitty watched him go at the center of that crowd,
which had cut her off from him as neatly as a closed
gate, and felt strangely forlorn. Steve's time had been
outstanding, just over 199 miles per hour, but even
the exhilaration she had felt when his official time was
announced had faded when he vanished so quickly,
without even a glance for her. And yet, what did she
expect? she asked herself angrily.

What did she expect? A thank-you kiss to make a
pair with his good-luck kiss? She was an idiot to even
think about it. The man didn't like her; he had made
that more than clear. The good-luck kiss had obviously been nothing more than a joke; he'd only kissed *her*
because it would have looked funny if he'd kissed
Jack!

Around her the crew was gathering up equipment,
preparing to take the car back to the garage, but
Kitty's work for the next few hours was out here, in
the grandstand that rose behind the pit area. Acting as
a sort of combination football scout and industrial
spy, she would time their competitors, noting any
idiosyncrasies of cars or drivers that might affect their
racing. She watched the crew and the car leave the
pits, trailed by a flock of reporters, then she climbed
into the grandstand and settled her baseball-style
cap—provided by Amtex and emblazoned with the
team's logo—more firmly on her head and clicked her
stopwatch as another car shot past under the green
flag.

She remained absorbed in her task, for though it was painstaking and repetitive, it never became monotonous. There was simply too much that might—and often did—happen. There were a few accidents; one car lost a wheel for no apparent reason almost directly opposite Kitty. She watched, horrified, as the car slid along the outer wall, trailing sparks and smoke until it came to a stop. As the fire crews sprinted toward him the driver climbed out, turned to give the tireless axle hub an enraged kick, then calmly walked away.

He was lucky. It was a chilling fact, and one which Kitty had to force to the back of her mind, but the truth was that despite all the recent improvements in safety equipment and regulations, auto racing remained a very dangerous sport. She had trained herself to be matter-of-fact about the risks, as had everyone in racing, for the risks were always there. Sometimes drivers were hurt, and occasionally they died, but many, no *most*, of them simply retired when they felt the time had come.

She watched a group of officials walking the track to make sure no small bits of debris remained to cause other accidents; then the OK was given, another car rolled out and the time trials were under way again. Sometime around noon redheaded Jimmy Miller brought her a can of soda and some sandwiches, which she nibbled between qualifying runs. By four P.M. no one had topped Steve's speed, though several of the veteran drivers had come dangerously close.

Jack came out to check her notes and stood scratching his head and muttering under his breath. "Well, hell!" he growled in disgust. "I was hoping to get this over with early today, but these three," he indicated drivers whose times had been very close to Steve's before they cut their runs short, "are going to try it again, and they just might catch us." He handed the clipboard back to Kitty. "I guess we can't relax yet. Just keep your fingers crossed that nobody gets lucky." He touched the bill of his cap in a little salute and left her.

A blue-and-white car rolled away as Kitty made her way back down to the pits to wait with Jack. She watched Marco, who had drawn one of the last spots in the qualifying order, begin his attempt. He came around fast on the first preparatory lap, but Kitty heard an ominous sputter under the whine of his engine, and when he reappeared in the fourth turn, instead of an upraised fist she saw a plume of smoke from his engine.

His car wasn't on fire, fortunately, but it was obvious that something was seriously wrong with his engine, and he was almost as angry and frustrated at losing this first-day qualifying opportunity as the driver who had lost his tire had been. She watched with a pang of sympathy as he told his crew chief in rapid-fire and highly emotional Italian, punctuated by a great many short, sharp gestures, what had apparently gone wrong. To have a mechanical failure after so much preparation was hideously frustrating, and she reached out to touch his arm as he stalked past her toward Gasoline Alley. He stopped short and turned a black scowl on her.

"I'm sorry something went wrong, Marco," she said gently. "I know what a disappointment it is."

His scowl lightened and he sighed heavily, then his lips curved in a wry grin. "Thank you, little one. I am sorry I glowered at you."

"That's okay. You're allowed a glower or two."

He laughed aloud at that and wrapped her in his arms for a bear hug. "Thank you for your kindness," he said again, kissing her cheek lightly as he released her, then turning to follow his crippled car back to the garage.

Kitty watched him for a moment, then turned to look back at the track, stopping halfway as her eyes met Steve's, gray and chilly and contemptuous.

Kitty could only stare at him in surprise for a moment and then try to return his icy regard with a defiant glare of her own, but it was too late. He turned away to say something to Jack, and she stood glaring impotently at the back of his head. She had done nothing wrong, after all, and it was infuriating that she should allow Steve's snap judgments of her behavior to bother her. She went back to her task of timing and charting, but now it was difficult to concentrate. She was tired, and the beginnings of a headache had begun to nag at her when the day finally ended at six.

The rest of the crew members were noisily rejoicing, for Steve's time had stood up to all the challenges and he would be this year's "pole-sitter," but Kitty found it difficult to join in the jubilation. Steve had crushed her enthusiasm with that one cold glance.

"You're coming, aren't you, Kitty?" Rick White, who was an engine mechanic and the fuel man on the pit crew, was walking beside her as they returned to the garage. She heard the question, but had been lost in thought and had missed whatever came before.

"I'm sorry, Rick, I didn't catch all that," she apologized with a rueful smile. "Am I coming where?"

"To dinner with the rest of us. To celebrate. We'll go have a steak and a couple of drinks somewhere."

"I don't think . . ." she began, shaking her head, but then, over Rick's shoulder, she saw Steve watching her with mocking amusement. He expected her to say no; he thought she was afraid to go. Her chin came up and she smiled brightly up at Rick, her decision made for her.

"Sure, I'll come. I don't have my car today, though; will you give me a lift?"

Rick's reply of "Sure thing!" was prompt and gratified, and Kitty felt a twinge of guilt at using him this way. Lanky, dark-haired Rick was a pleasant young man, and she didn't want to hurt him. He had made it clear that he was interested in her when she joined the crew, and it had required patience and tact for her to discourage his overtures while maintaining a casual friendship. It was obvious that he was reading more into her words than a simple request for transportation, and she knew that it was her fault for asking him, rather than Jack or someone else, for a ride.

Still, she'd seen a flash of anger on Steve's face when she asked for that ride. It almost made it worth the trouble she knew she'd have with Rick.

She had agreed to go with them, but she had no intention of staying more than a short time at whatever steakhouse they frequented. She could always call a taxi to take her home if no one else was leaving. She was surprised, and a bit embarrassed as well, when they arrived at one of Indianapolis's nicer restaurants, for like the rest of them she still wore her work clothes.

She wasn't at all sure they'd even be allowed in; it was the type of restaurant that looked like it would have a dress code of some sort, but they were welcomed, and she understood why when they entered the bar. The crowd there was about evenly divided between well-dressed couples out for the evening and members of the racing fraternity, dressed pretty much as Kitty and the others were.

It was a gathering place for many of the crews and drivers during the month of May, and the management, who might in other circumstances have insisted on ties and jackets for their customers, knew good business when they saw it; it gave the place a certain cachet to be an in-spot for the racing crowd.

Kitty looked around at the other bar patrons and slipped away to the powder room to make some quick repairs. Racing in-spot or not, her appearance was a little too far below par. After a light application of makeup and with her hair loose about her shoulders, she looked more feminine, she thought, regarding herself in the mirror. Still out of place in her shirt and jeans, but at least a little more like a girl. She shrugged at her image and made her way back to the bar to take the chair Rick had held for her at their large, noisy table. A cocktail waitress was taking their orders, and Steve, who had mysteriously ended up seated on Kitty's other side, ordered his usual bourbon and branch water before turning to Kitty.

"The lady will have . . . ?" He raised a querying eyebrow at Kitty. "The usual?" She nodded shortly, furious at his proprietorial air, but unable to do anything about it without creating a scene. "Gin and tonic," he told the waitress with a smile that had her fluttering her eyelashes at him in a scarcely veiled invitation.

Clenching her teeth, Kitty half turned away from him to smile at Rick, who was watching her through narrowed eyes after witnessing Steve's casual assumption of familiarity. He returned her smile guardedly after a moment, but she thought tiredly that if he was going to begin acting possessive simply because she had asked him for a lift she would have to make it very clear, very soon, that their relationship was not, and would not be, more than friendly. In the meantime

. . . She took her eyes from Rick's and smiled across the table at Jack, who she was absolutely certain would read nothing more than she intended into a smile.

The drinks arrived quickly, and Jack proposed a toast to Steve, then one to the crew, then a toast was drunk to the car, and one to Jack, and one to winning the pole position, and then the bartender brought them a round of drinks on the house. . . . Kitty tried to refuse the new rounds of drinks bought by race fans, tried to sip hers slowly, but by the time they went into the dining room she was feeling distinctly tipsy. She thought food would help, but a robust red wine and more toasts accompanied their chateaubriand, and by the end of the meal she no longer minded the muzziness and had completely forgotten her plans to leave early.

They moved back to the lounge, where a band was playing beside a small dance floor, and the lights were romantically low.

"Uh, Kitty?" Jimmy Miller stood before her, his freckled face as red as his hair. "Would you like to—uh—dance? To—uh—celebrate, you know?"

She smiled up at him and rose, resting a hand on her chair back as she did so, for her legs felt just a touch unsteady. They were fine by the time she and Jimmy reached the floor, however, and she danced uninhibitedly to the fast tune the band was playing. She was laughing as she walked back to the table with Jimmy, and before she could sit down another of the crew had risen to lead her back to the floor.

Once the dancing had begun it couldn't end until she had danced with each of them, even Jack, who steered her through a sedate fox trot and then startled them all by dipping her as the song crescendoed to its end.

"Jack, you sly devil," she laughed breathlessly at him as they left the floor for the table where the rest of the crew was applauding Jack's dancing talents. "You're full of surprises, aren't you?"

He smiled complacently. "Joy says I have hidden depths."

She laughed again at his expression. "Well, Joy should know, shouldn't she?" Jack blushed beet-red, and Kitty reached up to kiss his weathered cheek as they reached the table and the moment she had been dreading.

Steve had watched her dance marathon with cynical amusement, but now he rose from his chair and extended his hand.

"Oh, thank you, Steve, but I'm really tired after all that . . ." She tried to excuse herself, but the crew wouldn't hear of it.

"You can't quit now, Kitty," they chorused. "Only one more. It's a slow one; it won't be tiring." Steve said nothing, only took her hand and propelled her before him to join the other dancers as the lights dimmed and the band slid into a slow, dreamy number.

He turned her into his arms, pulling her close and holding her hand against his chest. Somewhere in the befogged recesses of her mind was a little voice telling her she should resist, that she didn't want to dance with him at all, and definitely not so closely. She should resist, but the spicy scent of his aftershave and the warm scent of his skin surrounded her; they moved easily together to the gently seductive strains of the music, and fire began to run along her veins, born of the wine, or the music, or his nearness. Her protests were never uttered, and the hand that might have pushed him away slid up instead to rest lightly against his neck. At her small movement of capitula-

tion his arm tightened around her, and he released her
right hand to bring his other arm around her as well.

They swayed as one to the music, barely moving,
and the desire she had fought so hard to deny washed
through Kitty, making nonsense of the antipathy
between them, for neither could deny this mutual
need. Steve's hands moved restlessly over her back
and she twined hers around his neck, clinging to the
warm, hard strength of him, trembling as his knee
nudged between hers and his lips explored her throat.

The music swelled, and she moved her head the
tiniest bit; then his seeking mouth found hers, clung
and lifted reluctantly as the last note died away.
Dazed, disoriented, she let him lead her back to the
table.

The men were watching them, oddly subdued, and
through the mists that seemed to hold her mind
entrapped Kitty dimly realized what she and Steve
must have looked like on the dance floor, wrapped in
an all-too-obviously passionate embrace. Though she
realized that she couldn't worry about it, for the spell
Steve had woven still surrounded her.

Passive, unprotesting, she waited while he bid the
others good night and announced that he was taking
her home. Rick turned reproachful eyes on her, but
she only stared blankly at him for a moment, then
turned back to Steve. There was no room in her
awareness for anything but him, her eyes following his
movements as he picked up her purse and his jacket.
Later she might care that the rest of the crew undoubtedly thought Steve was taking her back to her
apartment to make love to her, but right now it didn't
matter; it was what she thought herself.

She moved in a dream, unaware of the drive home,
or the walk to her door, or anything at all until he
took her into his arms in her living room and she came

alive again. His arms slid around her, tightening slowly until she was lifted onto her toes, clinging to his shoulders, her head thrown back, her body arched against his, reveling in his strength as she watched him, watched his head bend near, nearer, saw the glitter in the gray eyes, the sensual curve of his mouth. . . . Her eyes fluttered closed, and his lips touched hers, lightly at first, exploring, and then captured hers in a passionate demand.

Her lips softened, parting willingly beneath his, welcoming the searching exploration of his tongue, meeting his kiss with her own. Their mouths met, lifted, slanted across each other, twisted as they kissed with a starving hunger which was not appeased by kissing, but which demanded more and more. Desire shot through Kitty like a flame, melting her against Steve, her slim body pliant beneath his hands as they stroked her back, slipping up to curve around her throat, slipping down to shape the soft curves of her hips, pulling her hard against him so that she could feel his need for her. Her hands were moving restlessly over his chest and shoulders as she returned his kisses with an urgency that matched his, and he lifted her into his arms to carry her to the sofa, where he sat with her across his lap.

Kitty's hands moved to shakily unbutton his shirt and slip inside as she pressed against him. She needed to touch him, to run her palms over the mat of curly hair, to stroke the hard planes of muscle and bone, discover the smooth heat of his skin. His hands had dispensed with her buttons, and he pushed the red team shirt off her shoulders, the hard, slightly rough touch of his palms following it as he slid it off her arms.

A quick tug and the shirt slid to the floor as Steve traced a fingertip along the edge of one lace bra cup, sending a shiver of pure sensation over Kitty's heated skin. The fingertip followed the line of the lace to the closure in the cleft between her breasts, deftly freed it and pushed the wisp of lace off her shoulders to join the red shirt on the floor. Kitty made a little purring sound in her throat, arching against him as he cupped her breasts in his hands, his thumbs teasing the nipples to taut peaks.

Her own hands were busy on errands of their own, memorizing the contours of him, then twisting in his hair as his mouth moved down her throat, teasing her until she moaned softly, urgently, and he took what he had sought. Their bodies moved together, twisting to slip down until they were lying on the sofa, Kitty clinging to Steve, reveling in his weight on her, which was no weight at all, really, but what she wanted more than anything else.

She had needed this, waited for this, for *him*, for so long, and it felt so right; it was all she'd ever lived for. . . . Her surrender was willing, complete; she waited only for his possession.

When he left her abruptly, pushing her away and rising to stand with his back to her, she didn't understand. She lay weakly against the cushions, staring up at him with blank, uncomprehending eyes. Something about the rigid set of his broad shoulders, silhouetted against the pale light from the window, filled her with dread.

"Steve?" Her voice was a husky whisper, and she rose from the sofa, snatching up her shirt from the floor and slipping her arms into it. "Steve?" she said again.

"Don't touch me!" She had reached out to him, but flinched sharply back as he snarled the warning. She stared at him for a moment, then must have made some slight sound or movement, for he whirled around, freezing her where she stood. "No!" he barked. "No!"

"What—"

"No! It won't happen again!" She stepped back from him, retreating in the face of his anger, suddenly totally sober, and cold, as cold as ice, all the way through to her bones.

"What are you talking about?" she asked in desperation, pulling her shirt closed and clutching it together in front of her.

"It won't happen again, the way it did before. I won't do that. I *can't* do that."

"Can't do *what?*" Kitty finally shouted back, and he faced her across the width of the small room, his arms held stiffly at his sides, his face grim in the dim light that filtered in from the streetlight outside.

"I can't let what happened between us happen again. I can't," he said very distinctly, the words striking Kitty like tiny knives, leaving a thousand bleeding wounds behind them, "allow myself to be seduced again into doing something I will regret so deeply. I will not allow you to seduce me again."

"But I wasn't," Kitty breathed, horrified at the conclusion he'd drawn. "I wasn't trying to seduce you!"

"You don't *have* to try!" he said bitterly. "It just seems to come naturally." He jerked his shirt back onto his shoulders, letting it hang loose while he refastened his belt buckle, which Kitty realized, to her horror, she must have undone. "You don't have to try at all."

He showed his teeth in a smile that was not a smile at all, and Kitty moved toward him pleadingly, one hand out in a gesture of supplication. "Steve, no. That's not what I was doing."

"Maybe not." He was clearly unconvinced. "But

whatever it was you *were* doing, I won't let that
happen again. Too much damage was caused last
time. What I told you before still stands—you can't
pretend the past never happened. I forgot that for a
little while, but I won't forget it again, I promise
you."

Her lips parted to say something, to try somehow to
make him understand that her actions were not what
they seemed, but he was gone even as she drew breath
to speak. What use would it have been even if she *had*
spoken? she wondered; the weight of evidence against
her was overwhelming. A wave of humiliated shame
washed over her; she had given Steve all the reason in
the world to assume the things he had—her behavior
had been an open invitation to seduction.

Moving stiffly, she crossed the few feet to the sofa
and crumpled onto it, bowing her head into her hands
as if to hide from herself. She would have liked to
blame her behavior on all the alcohol she'd drunk, on
fatigue or extenuating circumstances or *something*,
but she knew she'd be lying to herself. She couldn't
blame her actions on anything but the fact that, even
after all this time, after all the hurt and bitterness, she
wanted Steve to make love to her, wanted it more
than she wanted anything else in the world.

She moaned low in her throat, a sound of pure
anguish. Why should she want him to make love to
her, a man who had told her clearly that he wanted no
relationship with her at all? She had persuaded
him—no, she corrected herself angrily, she had seduced him—once before, and it had caused them both
irreparable damage, and others as well. She thought
of John and Steve and the friendship they had shared
until she, with her unthinking greed, had taken something she wanted and in doing so had torn the friends
apart. She groaned again.

Steve was a bitter, cynical man now, not the man he'd been when she'd lured him into bed; she was responsible, at least in part, for the changes in him. And Kitty herself had not escaped unscathed. Her relationship with her brother had been irrevocably altered, the man she'd thought she loved lost to her, her own emotions locked in a deepfreeze for seven years. Yes, she'd done more damage on that stormy night than she'd ever have imagined possible. So why, *why*, had she allowed herself to come so close to repeating that mistake? Why did she still, knowing all she knew, ache for his kiss, his touch?

Because she loved him.

The thought leaped, unbidden and unwanted, to her brain, and in the same instant that she was frantically denying it to herself she knew the truth of it.

Oh, dear God, she loved him. As the tears came she wrapped her arms protectively around herself and sat rocking to and fro, huddled into a ball of misery. The tears fell for a long time.

Chapter Eight

"Hey, Kitty, what's wrong with you? You look terrible!" Jack frowned at her pale face and the shadows under her eyes. "If you drank too much last night there's some aspirin in the garage and beer in the refrigerator. You know—hair of the dog."

"No thanks, Jack." Kitty shuddered at the thought of beer at eight A.M. "I don't have a hangover."

"Then what's the matter with you? You act like you didn't sleep at—" Jack realized what he was saying and broke off in mid-sentence, his weathered cheeks flushing brick red.

Kitty looked away for an embarrassed moment, then forced herself to meet his eyes. "I'm *OK*, Jack." She stressed the second word. "There's nothing to worry about." Her gaze was clear and candid, and after a moment Jack cleared his throat and nodded.

"Well . . . that's OK then, I guess," he said uncertainly, and Kitty nodded.

"There's nothing, Jack," she repeated. "I'll see you later." She walked away, looking back and waving at him once as she strode off toward the grandstand behind the pit area. She was back at her scouting; Jack, Rick and a couple of the others were going to take the engine apart. Everyone else had the day off since Steve, having qualified, wouldn't be driving again that day.

It helped Kitty to have something to do, something to think about to take her mind off the night before. She could only feel agonizing shame at the way she'd reacted to Steve and something akin to despair at the discovery that she loved him still, after all the heartbreak and all the years. She shook her head to clear away the unwelcome thoughts and stuck her sunglasses on her nose, concentrating fiercely on the bright blue car that was just leaving the pits.

Sitting in the middle of the happy crowd, warmed by the bright May sunshine, Kitty was able to push those tormenting thoughts to the back of her mind and involve herself in the task at hand, so that the morning passed quickly, and even enjoyably. By noon it was warm sitting full in the sun, Kitty was thirsty and the first faint rumblings from within were signaling the approach of lunchtime. She knew that Jack would have someone bring lunch up to her, and she was scanning the crowd while yet another car warmed up for a run when she saw him.

Like her, Steve was wearing one of the Amtex baseball caps, and that was what she glimpsed first, moving up through the grandstand. It was pushed to the back of his head and a lock of straw-colored hair had fallen across his forehead, gleaming in the noon sunlight as he looked around, searching for Kitty in the throng. She knew she should wave, or stand up, do something to catch his attention and guide him to her, but it was hard, after what had so recently passed between them, to deliberately call his attention to her.

That was a disgustingly cowardly attitude, she knew, and giving herself a sharp mental kick in the pants she forced herself to stand, raising one arm above her head and waving when Steve looked in her direction. He acknowledged her with a nod in her direction as she caught his eye, and then he climbed more quickly toward her, his hands full of their lunch.

Somehow he had made it all the way into the bleachers with two-foot-long coney-dogs, chips, big dill pickles and two large paper cups of beer, all balanced precariously on a flimsy cardboard tray from the concession stand. Kitty had been dreading the moment when she would be face to face with Steve again, and now that it had arrived she could not quite look him in the eye.

He was juggling their lunch as he stepped carefully over the feet of the people crowded onto the bleachers between Kitty and the aisle, and she looked at his shirt front rather than his face as she reached up to help him with the food. Ordinarily one of the mechanics brought her lunch to her, and today of all days she wished that there had been no change in the routine. She was filled with a burning, scalding sense of shame every time her thoughts returned to her behavior last night, and facing Steve in the hard, bright light of day was so embarrassing as to be almost painful.

He had made it humiliatingly clear what he thought of her, and she was forced to admit that he had reason for that assessment, so she hoped fervently that he would simply leave her the food and go on his way. It seemed that he had other ideas, though, for he waited politely while the lady next to Kitty moved down the wooden bench, then took the seat she had freed.

"Ooops!" he was muttering under his breath. "Grab that pickle, will you, and I'll . . . just . . . Ah, no you don't, you—!" He muttered an imprecation and caught a hot dog that was threatening to slide off the tray, while Kitty retrieved the wayward pickle and caught a bag of potato chips as it fell.

"Thanks." She took the coney he handed her along with her pickle and potato chips and set the paper cup of beer between her feet after taking a thirsty swallow.

"Mustard, relish and onions OK?" he asked. "I just got what I usually have on both of them."

"Uh . . . that . . . that's fine," Kitty stammered, her attention carefully focused on her hot dog. "I like them this way." She took a bite and nodded approval. "I . . . uh . . . didn't expect to see you here today." She glanced up briefly and found him watching her, frowning. "You don't have to . . . to stay, if you don't want to."

His frown deepened. "I'm not here to give you a hard time, Kitty; I didn't plan this. I just happened to be in the garage with nothing to do when Jack needed someone to bring your lunch up."

"Oh." Kitty felt her face redden again at the realization that she'd committed another faux pas. "Well . . . thank you."

"Look, Kitty"—Steve took her chin in his fingers and turned her face up to his, noting the flush in her cheeks and the distress in her eyes—"like I said, I didn't come up here to give you a hard time. I think we've said all there is to say. I just want to check out the opposition for a little while, OK?"

"OK." Kitty managed a feeble response to his

rather tight smile, then fumbled for her stopwatch as a car came around into the straightaway. Struggling to activate the watch and balance her hot dog at the same time, she couldn't prevent the clipboard from sliding off her knees.

"You time, I'll write." Steve retrieved the clipboard and set it on his own knee. "That way you'll have one hand free to eat with."

"Thanks." Kitty's reply was distracted as she retreated into her work, and as the car came into the straight, she followed it with her eyes until it crossed directly in front of her. She hit the lap button. "I appreciate it." She showed the watch to Steve, who noted the time on her chart. "He's not doing too badly, is he?"

"Hm-mm. Not bad at all. Anything unusual about his car?"

"Not really. His wing shape is a little different from ours, but I think ours is more effective."

"You *would* think so, since you designed it," Steve teased with a grin. "I just hope you're right."

"I'm right," Kitty asserted firmly, and hit the button on the stopwatch again. "One eighty-nine point two-oh-six for the second lap."

"Got it." Steve wrote the figure on the chart, took another bite of his hot dog and squinted up the track toward the head of the straightaway.

Kitty slanted a furtive glance at his profile, hard and tanned and handsome, and felt her eyes suddenly fill with tears. This was what it could have been like if she and Steve had remained friends. They could have had this all along, this easy camaraderie, this sharing of simple things, of work and ideas and even hot dogs. They could have had this if only she hadn't been thoughtless and greedy and snatched at what she wanted when she had no right to do so.

"Hey, wake up!" Steve nudged her with his elbow. "Here he comes!" Kitty blinked fiercely at the tears, refusing to allow them to spill over, and pulled her mind back to the job at hand.

She was in a pensive mood as she drove home that evening, automatically threading her way through the heavy traffic leaving the track, her mind filled with images of Steve. He had spent the afternoon in the grandstand with her, helping with timing and charting, punctuating their businesslike discussion of racing with occasional pungent comments on the other drivers that sent Kitty into gales of laughter. The images of him laughing, carefree, tore at her heart, for now she knew just what she had lost.

When Kitty stepped up onto the front porch on her way inside, Shelley was seated cross-legged in the glider, eating a sandwich and reading a magazine balanced on her lap.

"Hi, Kitty! Did you work today?"

"Um-hm. It's seven-day weeks from now on."

"That sounds like Jim's schedule!" Shelley grimaced.

"Where is your phantom husband, by the way?"

"The hospital, same as always. Whatever you hear, the glamorous life of a medical student's wife is grossly overrated!"

Kitty joined Shelley's laughter. "If you'd like some company, give me a minute to change and I'll join you."

She peeled off her work clothes, had a quick wash and slipped on pink shorts and a matching cap-sleeved T-shirt, then made herself a peanut-butter sandwich and carried it and a glass of milk out to the porch.

"It feels so good," she told Shelley between bites, "to wear a color other than red! A month of red shirts and red fire suits and I may never wear that color again!"

"It would be a shame if you didn't; it's such a good color for you, with your black hair. I know what you mean, though. Just imagine if you were a nurse and had to wear the same white uniforms all the time. Ugh!"

They girl-talked for an hour before Shelley excused herself to work on a story-hour presentation for the next day, and Kitty took her plate and glass into the kitchen to wash them. She was running hot water into the dishpan when she heard the doorbell chime. Shelley must need to borrow a cup of sugar, or something, she thought. Though Shelley was an inspired cook, she was a scatterbrained shopper and frequently found herself without some vital ingredient for a dish that was already half prepared. Kitty walked quickly to the door, wiping her hands on a dish towel.

"Do you need to borrow something, Shel—" she began as she pulled the door open, then stopped in surprise, staring at the man who stood on the porch. "Marco! Why are you . . . ? I mean—I'm sorry, won't you come in?"

He was smiling indulgently at her confusion. "*I* am sorry. You were not expecting company. I will go." He bent his head in a small bow and took a step back, but Kitty touched his arm lightly.

"No, please come in, Marco. I'm sorry I was so rude."

"If you are certain . . . ?"

"Of course. Please come in." She stepped back, holding the door open, and he followed her inside.

"This is for you." He held up a bottle of white wine with a little shrug. "It is a small thing, but . . ."

"It's very thoughtful of you. Thank you." She let

him put it in her hands, then handed it back. "Will you open it? I'll get some glasses."

He drew the cork while she took wineglasses down and put some cheese and crackers on a tray. Seated on the sofa, glass in hand, she looked at him in inquiry.

"Why are you here?"

"A social visit." His shoulders lifted again in that small shrug. "Nothing more." He raised his glass, and she touched hers to it, then sipped the light, golden wine, enjoying its cool fruity tang.

"Mmm. This is delicious wine, Marco. Thank you for bringing it." She leaned her head against the back of the sofa and closed her eyes, allowing herself to relax. Her eyes opened wide when a hand closed on her shoulder and she found herself staring blankly at Marco's dark face, only inches from her own.

"Marco, what are you—" Her question was abruptly stifled by his lips as he pulled her toward him to kiss her on the mouth.

For a moment she was too surprised to do anything at all but let him kiss her, then she began to struggle. She wedged her arms against his shoulders and pushed with all her strength, but he held her easily, his arms and shoulders, like those of any race driver, immensely strong. Truly angry now, she shifted her tactics, reaching up to twist her fingers into his thick, black curls and pulling hard.

It worked. He jerked his head up, drawing his breath in a hiss of pain and scowling down at Kitty's furious face. "Why did you do that?" he demanded with an expression of outraged hurt that would have been comical if Kitty hadn't been so angry.

"Because I don't want you to kiss me!" she snapped, pushing ineffectually at his shoulders.

"But why not? I told you before, we are a good match."

"You're in love with Irina!" she reminded him furiously, and again he shrugged.

"*Si*. But she doesn't love me, and you and I could have a good time, could we not?"

"No, we could not! And let me *go!*" At last he released her, and she quickly rose and moved away from the sofa. "We could not have a 'good time,' Marco," she repeated, and indicated the door. "I think you should go now."

He rose slowly from the sofa. "I have made a mistake. I am sorry." He took a step toward the door, then paused and looked back at her. "Kitty?"

"Yes?" Her voice was distinctly chilly, and he lifted his shoulders in another little shrug.

"Could we not . . . be friends?"

His face was a comical mixture of little-boy chagrin and wounded male pride, and Kitty answered with more exasperation than anger. "I'd like to be friends, Marco, but not if you mean the kind of friends that—"

"No, no, no. I mean only friends, no more."

"Then why . . . ?"

He stared at the carpet beneath his feet, for all the world like a naughty boy being chastised, and she had to smile as he muttered, "I am a man, you are a woman. . . ."

"Well, I would like to be your friend, Marco," she said more kindly, "but that's all. You love someone else, and I—" She caught herself in time and rephrased it. "As attractive a man as you are, Marco, I'm not in love with you."

"Then we shall be friends," he said lightly, but his eyes on her were shrewd, as though he guessed what she had so nearly said. She allowed him to seat her on the sofa again and refill her glass, feeling rather strongly that she had perhaps been too quick to forgive. He had accepted her decision so readily, though, that she felt as if the pass had been more an expression of the Mediterranean male's sexual identity than a serious attempt to make love to her. And it was impossible to stay angry with him when he turned on the little-boy charm, for there was no real malice in him at all.

He refilled his own glass, then ostentatiously chose a deep armchair instead of his former place beside her. She grinned in recognition of the gesture and leaned back comfortably against the sofa cushions. For several seconds she studied his face.

"What happened between you and Irina?" she asked softly, and Marco's head snapped up. "What happened?" Kitty repeated, and smiled gently. "You may as well tell me. I seem to be involved in some sort of triangle, or quadrangle, or something, through no fault of my own, so I'd like to know just why Irina looks at me the way she does and why Steve keeps warning me against you."

He shrugged, dropping his eyes to his glass, uncharacteristically ill at ease. "It is a very old story," he muttered. "You would not be interested."

"Try me." He looked up again, and Kitty nodded. "I'm in a very awkward position here, Marco, because I don't know whatever it is that everyone else knows. Anyway, it might help you to talk about it."

He regarded her steadily for a long moment, his dark eyes somber and a little bit angry; then he nodded, one short nod.

"We knew each other," he said softly, "some time ago, two years ago to be exact. We were . . . together. She followed the Grand Prix circuit when she had time off from her modeling, and we were together. For a year we were. Irina loved me, she told me she did, and I cared for her. I suppose she felt we would be married someday." Kitty had been looking at the wine in her glass, but her head came up with a jerk at that.

"Oh, yes," he said, with a small, bitter smile. "That is the way things were with us, but I was not ready to accept it. I was young, a racer, and there are always women. . . ." He shrugged. "You know what I mean."

Kitty nodded; she knew very well about the women, the groupies they were sometimes called, who followed racing and the drivers.

"Yes, you know about the women. Well, I was used to these women—I am a man, after all." He spread his hands. "And I was not . . . faithful . . . to Irina."

Kitty sucked in a little disapproving breath, and Marco shot her a quick, defensive glance, then dropped his eyes to the carpet beneath his feet.

"I know. It was wrong. But the fact remains that I was not faithful to Irina." He grimaced in self-condemnation. "I was a fool; I thought I could—what is it you Americans say? That I could eat my cake?"

"Have your cake and eat it, too," Kitty supplied, and he nodded.

"Yes, that is it. I thought I could have Irina and still, if another girl were there and Irina was not . . . It meant nothing to me. I know," he added as he saw the disapproval in Kitty's face, "that I was wrong. I know that now, but *then* I was afraid. I was afraid to admit that I needed Irina, afraid to commit myself to something so permanent as marriage. And, anyway, things have always been different for a man than for a woman.

"I know now that this is not right, I understand this, but when I was growing up, in *Italia,* things were different." He looked to Kitty, appealing for under-standing, and she nodded slowly. Her woman's sym-pathies were all with Irina, of course, but she could, in a way, understand Marco's point of view, considering his background.

"Did Irina ever . . . ?" she asked hesitantly, and he shook his head emphatically.

"No! And, of course, that makes what I did all the more wrong. But I did these things, and one of the girls talked about it. She talked," he said bitterly, "and it got into the papers in France and Italy and other places as well, perhaps, and that was the end. *Pffft!*"

"Did Irina talk to you?" Kitty asked softly, and he laughed, a brief laugh that held no humor at all.

"I suppose you could call it that, what she did. She came to my hotel room, I was in France at the time, in Nice, and she had one of the papers. It was one of the sort of papers which—which take the truth, and—"

"I know what you mean," Kitty said quietly. "Was it very bad?"

"As bad as it could be. What I had done, that was bad enough, but this paper had taken the things that girl said and made them into something . . ." He faltered, then finished in a torrent of incomprehensible, but obviously angry, Italian.

"She said nothing. She just came to my room and tossed that paper on the table. I—fool that I was—I tried to explain, to give some sort of explanation, but she had no ears for my stupid words. She waited until I was silent, and then she took off the pendant I had given her." He lifted a thin gold chain he wore around his neck so that Kitty could see the pendant on it. A small oval medallion of gold, it was engraved with a flowing initial "I," and a sparkling diamond was set into the design.

"It's lovely," Kitty said gently.

"She took it off and dropped it to the floor, and then she said goodbye. And she was gone."

Kitty sat silently for a long moment while Marco lifted his wineglass and drained it. She sipped her own wine, scarcely tasting it, her mind on what she had just learned. "I think I'm beginning to understand. Since then, Marco, how have you lived?"

"How have I lived?" He was confused.

"The girls," she prompted, and he shrugged.

"It has not been the same since then. I have gone out with women, yes," he said as Kitty raised her eyebrows in disbelief, "but not like before. I no longer wish to live that way."

"Then why, with me, have you acted the way you did?"

He shrugged again, ill at ease. "I am a man, you are a woman . . ."

"That's a rotten reason, Marco! And if that's the way you think, it's no wonder your reputation isn't very good! How do you expect Irina to know you've changed if it looks as though you're still doing the same things?"

"What difference would it make?" He rose abruptly from his chair and took a couple of jerky strides to the middle of the room, then turned angrily to Kitty. "What difference would it make now? She said goodbye to me; it is all over. It was all over two years ago."

"But she still thinks, and Steve does too, I guess, that you're seeing that kind of woman, living that kind of life. Don't they?" Kitty came to her feet, her own anger growing. "Don't they?"

"*I* don't know what they think." Marco shrugged again, but his guilty face gave him away.

"Really, Marco, did you have to make it look as if I were another of your groupies?" Kitty's anger was fading to exasperation nearly as rapidly as it had flared, but she didn't feel like letting Marco off the hook just yet. "Didn't you think that it might make things a little difficult for me at the track?"

It was clear that Marco hadn't considered this possibility, for his face fell with an almost comic suddenness. "Have I done that?" he cried. "I am sorry, Kitty! I must come to your garage and explain. I will—"

"No, no, no. You don't need to do that, Marco. No one has been giving me a hard time—yet—but I wanted you to think about what might happen."

"This is not happening to you?" Relief warred with anger in his face, but relief won out.

"Not yet," Kitty admitted. "But you know how that kind of gossip gets spread, and I don't want it spreading about me."

"You are right, of course." Marco studied his hands, his face serious. "You are right, as well, when you say that I have involved you in that situation without your knowledge. It was wrong of me and I apologize."

"That's OK, Marco. You don't—"

"I also wish to apologize," he continued as though she hadn't spoken, "for my behavior this evening. To act this way toward a lady such as yourself is unforgivable. I very much regret doing such a thing."

"I know you do," Kitty said gently. "I accept your apology." He had been standing half turned away from her, but now he faced her, extending one hand. When she placed hers in it he lifted it and bent his dark head to lightly kiss her fingers in a gesture that was very Continental, very graceful and almost unbearably sweet.

"Mille grazie," he murmured, releasing her hand slowly. "Thank you." His smile widened back into his habitual expression of teasing lechery, but his eyes

slipped past her for a moment to the mantel clock and widened in disbelief. "I had no idea of the time!" he exclaimed, and Kitty glanced over her shoulder to see that it was nearly eleven.

"I must go," Marco said. "I should not have stayed so late, boring you with my problems."

"Don't be silly; you know I wasn't bored." She walked beside him to the door.

"I hope you were not." He opened the door, then paused. "Thank you for being so generous as to forgive me for my behavior. I am most sorry—"

"Shhh." She touched her fingers lightly to his lips. "It's forgotten."

"You are very kind," he said quietly and inclined his head in a gesture that was almost a bow. "Good night, Kitty." He leaped down the steps and crossed the grass to his car, waving once more as he got in and then pulling away with a roar.

Kitty smiled as his taillights disappeared. Race drivers were all the same; it wasn't enough for them to drive the most powerful cars in the world on racecourses, but they had to own powerful cars—Marco's was a Ferrari—and drive fast on the streets as well.

With their highly developed reflexes and superb driving skills race drivers were statistically safer than the average driver, but that was hard to keep in mind the next morning when the scarlet Ferrari roared into the parking lot, screeching to a halt a few feet from a badly startled Kitty.

"You scared me to death!" she gasped as he climbed out of the car. "Do you always drive like that?"

"But of course! Anyway, that is nothing. You should see the way my mother drives! She is a maniac in her Fiat!"

"Your mother? I don't believe it!" They walked toward Gasoline Alley, laughing together.

"On my honor as your friend!" Marco raised one hand in affirmation. "I swear it is true. All of Bologna is frightened of her!" His happy face sobered. "Am I still your friend, Kitty? In spite of my very bad behavior?"

"Of course. Just so we both understand—"

"I understand," he interrupted her. "And I wish to apologize for—"

"You already apologized. It's forgotten. Friends?"

"Friends!" He draped an arm around her shoulders, and Kitty smiled up at him as they passed through the gate and into Gasoline Alley. She was glad that Marco had confided in her; it was a relief to have at least some idea why Irina had taken an instant dislike to her and why Steve disapproved so strongly of Marco. It was too bad Irina did not know how Marco felt about her and too bad that Marco's Italian *macho* pride would not let him go to her and apologize. Perhaps she could persuade him to abandon that pride and talk to Irina.

"Marco—" she began, but he spoke across her, his voice low and urgent.

"Steve is watching you, and he is angry. Do you wish me to speak to him, to explain?"

Kitty glanced quickly at the Amtex garage where Steve, already dressed for driving, was indeed leaning against the doorframe watching them, his face hard and his eyes very cold.

"No." She looked up at Marco's worried face and smiled reassuringly. "Don't try to talk to him; it's not that big a problem."

"But if it becomes so, you will tell me?"

"I'll tell you. Don't worry about it now, just go to work." She gave him a little push toward his own

garage and another bright smile, then walked on
toward Steve with the smile still in place.

"Good morning, Steve." She greeted him with the
pleasant courtesy of co-workers who don't know each
other very well and brushed past him to enter the
garage. Damn Steve Duncan, anyway! She yanked
her fire suit off its peg with uncustomary force. Where
did he get off giving her dirty looks because she talked
to Marco? With the parade of—of *females* he had
marching in and out of the garage, he should be the
last person to pass judgment on anyone else's social
life!

And if he said one word to her about Marco, she'd
tell him so, in language he would understand! She
looked over her shoulder, aiming a glare at the spot
where his back had been, only to find him watching
her, his face bleak. The anger in her eyes died after a
moment, and she turned away to finish zipping her fire
suit, aware of nothing but a huge empty ache of regret
for what might have been and could no longer be.

Chapter Nine

Steve watched for a moment as Kitty zipped herself into her fire suit, then thrust himself angrily away from the doorframe and stalked outside. Why the hell he should care one way or the other he didn't know, but it galled him to see her batting her eyelashes at that damned Italian. Couldn't she see what he was—or didn't she care? His hand tightened into a fist, crumpling his heavy driving gloves, until he realized what he was doing and deliberately relaxed.

He didn't understand any of it, not the way she acted nor the way he felt, and it was driving him insane! As he'd told her that first evening, whatever had been between them seven years before was over; they couldn't be friends, or anything else, after all that had happened.

And yet there was still something there. He shook

his head irritably as if to shake off the unwelcome
thought. It was the last thing he'd wanted to discover
about himself, but he'd been forced to face the fact
that something of the spell still existed. That was the
way it felt, the way it had felt at the time, as if she had
woven a spell to ensnare him. There had to be some
explanation for the obsession she became for him
when she was sixteen.

She had haunted his dreams, driven him nearly
insane without even trying, and when she *had* tried
she had pushed him over the thin line dividing responsibility from madness. He still remembered, far more
vividly than he wanted to, the taste of her mouth, the
feel of her body, her eager response to his lovemaking.

Angrily he clamped a lid on the thoughts, hating
them, hating their power to stir him, even at this
distance in time, painfully aware that the small
woman in that garage could still arouse the same
response in him. Why? Why couldn't he get her out of
his mind?

He knew exactly what kind of woman she'd become; her "relationship" with Rissoli, whose amorous
exploits were common knowledge, was evidence
enough of that, and still . . . No, he was just confus-
ing his memories of her with the reality, idealizing
her, even though he knew what she was. It might take
a little more time, but he'd stamp those foolish,
rose-colored memories out until he could see her as
no more than his chassis engineer.

Beside him the garage door squeaked open and the
car's nose appeared as it was pushed out. Steve
straightened to walk beside it toward the pits, deliberately emptying his mind of extraneous details, narrowing his concentration to the task at hand. It was a

useful talent, this tunnel vision of thought, for it enabled him to keep his full attention on his driving.

As he strode through the throng he was dimly aware of the people around him, some of them reporters, but he passed by, deaf and blind to their presence, allowing nothing to break his concentration. He knew that the press were used to him ignoring them and that they had come to regard Haskell as an ally, but even Haskell knew better than to speak to Steve before he drove.

He felt good about the car this morning, confident, ready to push for as much speed as the machine was capable of, and his mood was infectious. It was still early; only a couple of other cars were on the track to get in his way. It was slightly overcast, so there would be no glare or distracting shadows on the track, and the air was cool, though the day would probably turn sultry later.

He watched the others drive past as he donned the rest of his protective clothing and climbed into the car, sliding down into the semireclining driving position. Jack bent over him to fasten his safety harness, shouting one last-minute comment before they switched to the headsets.

"They're bringing more cars out, Steve. Try to get some speed before it's too crowded out there!"

Steve nodded, then returned his eyes to the pavement in front of him. He felt the thump when the starter was attached to the car and lightly pressed the accelerator as they fired the engine. The engine vibration masked the removal of the starter, but when someone tapped the top of his helmet in the "all clear" he let out the clutch and began to roll forward, aided by two crewmen pushing the car.

Steadily accelerating, he slid to the right to leave

the pits, then almost immediately began to swing left
into the first turn. He was low on the track, to the left
of the white line that marked the acceleration lane,
and as he picked up speed he wove slightly from side
to side, "scuffing" his tires to bring the rubber up to
racing temperature.

The other two cars passed above him as he left the
second turn and he spoke into the microphone built
into his helmet.

"Anybody else out yet, Jack?"

"Nope," the reply crackled through the speaker.
"There's just the three of you."

"I'm moving, then."

"Gotcha!"

As Jack spoke Steve increased his speed and let the
car slide across the line and onto the racing surface in
the middle of the backstretch. The motions of steering, braking, shifting gears and then accelerating
again were automatic, almost instinctive, freeing his
mind to concentrate on the track ahead and behind,
the way the car handled, the sound of the engine. It
was all good, and he knew with a sort of sixth sense
that he could run very quickly today, quicker than he
had yet this year.

Out of the fourth turn and down the main straight
he flicked his eyes off the track for an instant to see the
sign man holding out a board that read, "Steve: GO."
He went. The grandstands outside the low white wall
were invisible to him, a blur as he passed, his concentration on the track. One of the other early birds was
slowing, going in; Steve passed him in the fourth turn,
even as he saw another car emerge from the pits at the
far end of the straight.

His speeds for the first several laps were good and
steadily increasing, reported to him by Kitty in a voice

that grew more excited with each lap until, as he completed the ninth, he heard her shouting into her headset, "Jack, look! Steve! You did it! That was two hundred point zero one six!"

Steve's face broke into a broad grin as he steered into the turn, and he gave a whoop of glee that he knew must have almost deafened the others. Two hundred plus! He'd broken the magic barrier for the first time this year, and now felt that he might really win this thing after all.

On the tenth lap Jack spoke again, his voice sharpened by irritation or anxiety. "They're bringing Watson's car from the garage, Steve. I'll tell you when he's coming out, so watch for him. He takes up more of the track than he's entitled to."

Steve murmured his assent, well aware of what Jack meant. Mike Watson was a rookie; he had never driven in the 500 before and, as far as Steve was concerned, it showed. A drag racer, Watson was not yet accustomed to the oval track, and though he got quick times, Steve felt he got them at the expense of safe driving.

After another three laps Steve saw Watson's blue-and-white car emerging from the pits as he shot past and into the first turn. By the time Steve saw the car again Watson was up to speed and perhaps a quarter of a lap ahead. He followed Watson around the track once, closing the gap between them, and then as they left the fourth turn Watson moved toward the outside, providing Steve with room to pass on the inside as they swept down the main straight.

He took advantage of it, moving up on Watson's left. His right front tire was even with Watson's left rear when, for some inexplicable reason, the blue-and-white car bobbled toward him. Steve saw it

coming and without being aware of it swore softly
under his breath in the instant before Watson's tire
brushed his and both cars went out of control.

As the more experienced driver, Steve recovered
first, but he was still behind Watson, trying to avoid a
real collision as Watson slid across the track, brushing
the outside wall, and then caromed back toward
the inside again. Still swearing in that steady undertone, Steve braked hard, allowing his car to scrape
along the pit wall before swerving to the outside to
avoid Watson as he hit the wall with a crunch and slid
along it.

Steve came to rest against the outside wall, almost
on top of the start/finish line, with the starter waving
the yellow caution flag overhead. There was a moment of silence as the engine died and the scrape of
metal on concrete ended, a moment in which, incon-
gruously, Steve heard a clear, sweet trill of birdsong.

Why the bloody hell, he thought in frustrated fury
as he released his harness and climbed out of the car,
why the hell Watson hadn't bothered to learn how to
drive on an oval track before entering this race was
something Steve didn't begin to understand. As he
came to his feet on the asphalt surface of the track the
fire crew reached him, prepared to spray fire-
extinguishing foam on the car, or on Steve himself, if
either of them happened to be on fire.

They weren't, and Steve stood slightly back from
the car, mentally assessing the damage as the fire crew
completed their check. Watson had certainly done a
dandy job. Steve scowled at the crumpled fiberglass of
the car's body, knowing that there was undoubtedly
some structural damage as well. It would be two days,
at least, before he drove again, even if the crew
worked twenty-hour days to locate and repair all the
damage.

He swore once, very quietly, but very vehemently, and swung around to walk back to the pits. He could see his crew waiting tensely by the wall and waved reassurance to them while he waited for two cars to drive past him at the sedate eighty-mile-per-hour speed limit mandated by the yellow flag.

"It's OK," he shouted when he was near enough to be heard. "I'm fine. It was only a bump." A hell of a damned nuisance of a bump, but still only a bump.

Only a bump. Kitty could not, under any circumstances, regard what she had just witnessed as "only a bump." She'd stood, frozen in shock, watching the accident happen, knowing there was nothing she could do to prevent it, to stop the horror from happening. It almost seemed that her heart stopped as well, while one thought ran through her mind again and again, like a broken record. I love him. I love him. I love him.

When he got out of the car on his own she drew a long shuddering breath, feeling her muscles begin to tremble after being held rigid for so long. She felt as though she had died a small death in those endless moments when the unthinkable might have happened, for she had glimpsed what the world would be like without him in it, cold and dark and empty.

"I didn't hit hard," Steve was saying, and Kitty forcibly jerked her mind back to the business at hand, "but Kitty," he looked around for her, "will have to go over the left side. There may be some structural damage, and the steering felt a little bit loose after I hit."

Kitty couldn't have spoken at that moment without bursting into tears, so she nodded, fighting to achieve a measure of his matter-of-fact calm. She had thought that her professional cool was better established than it had proven to be as she had watched with freezing horror the two cars sliding across the track. She would, she knew, relive that moment in slow-motion nightmares for weeks to come, but Steve's cool acceptance was helping her to regain control. He was describing the steering problem, and she had to concentrate on what he was saying, had to pull her mind away from the accident itself and back to the work at hand.

"You just leave that to us," Jack cut across Steve's explanations. "You have to go over to the hospital and get yourself checked out."

"I know, I know." Steve nodded, with a grimace of annoyance. The Speedway required that any driver involved in any accident, however minor, must immediately be examined by the doctors at the track hospital in the infield, even if he appeared unhurt. "It just seems silly to go to a hospital. If I'm in good enough shape—"

"Don't seem silly to me," Jack growled. "Go! Kitty, you go with him."

"But . . . I . . . ." Kitty began to stammer a protest, remembering those cold eyes on her that morning. "We have to check the car," she protested.

"The guys'll get the car back to the garage, and by the time you're done at the hospital we'll be ready for you. Anyway," he grinned at Steve, "somebody has to go with Steve in case he faints or something." Steve grinned at the gibe, and Kitty had to smile herself, albeit weakly, at the thought of Steve fainting. "Now, go on!" Jack gave her a push, and reluctantly she went, looking back over her shoulder at the car as it was pushed off the track.

"Don't worry," Steve said derisively. "This won't take long, and then you can get back to your car."

"Good." Kitty mimicked his tone. "I'd hate to waste too much time on you."

"You don't have to. And I won't faint, either. I'd hate to be left lying in the middle of the road while you went for a stretcher."

"What stretcher? I'd just throw you over my shoulder in a fireman's lift."

"You mean you wouldn't leave me there?" Steve raised his eyebrows in mock surprise. "I'd have thought you'd be only too glad to see me come off that track in pieces."

Kitty froze as the color left her face, staring at him in shocked horror, the image created by his careless words suddenly more than she could bear. "That's a lousy thing to say," she said in a low, shaking voice.

He stared at her in surprise for a moment and might have said something else, but an ambulance rolled up beside them.

"Want a lift?" the driver called to them, and Steve grinned and nodded.

"You bet! Anything to escape those vultures!" He jerked his thumb at the crowd of reporters waiting at the gate for news of the accident. The few in the pits when the accident had occurred had been brushed off with a curt "Later," but this group would follow them to the hospital and into the exam room if given the chance.

The ambulance attendant swung the back doors open and they climbed in, Kitty averting her face from Steve's questioning eyes, too shaken to face him. She stared at the floor as they rode through the crowd, almost physically sick with the horror of what might have happened.

She had kept it out of her mind all month, adopting the racing fraternity's matter-of-fact attitude, but the

accident and that one casually cruel remark had
shattered her defenses. He was someone she worked
with, the driver of her team's car, but he was also the
man she loved, and he might have been injured or
killed in that blink of an eye.

She looked at her hands and saw that they were
shaking; *she* was shaking, and she gripped the edge of
the hard seat until her knuckles whitened as the
ambulance lurched along the service road to the
hospital. They climbed out in front of the white
clapboard building and were led quickly through the
reception area.

Kitty hung back and would have stayed in the
reception room, but Steve seized her arm and pulled
her along with a brusque "Come on" as he followed a
white-coated doctor to one of the curtained treatment
cubicles. She was recovering her composure, pushing
her emotions back behind that professional barrier,
and though she didn't know why he wanted her there,
she followed him calmly enough as he entered the
treatment room.

He sat on the high table and Kitty stood in a corner,
as far out of the doctor's way as she could place
herself. He was a genial man in his fifties, with
thinning hair and a cheerful manner, and he joined
them after collecting Steve's chart from a rack by the
nurses' station.

"Well, Steve, what did you do to yourself this
time?" he asked, flipping through the chart to note
something on a blank page.

"To tell you the truth, Gil, I don't think I did
anything at all. I brushed the wall with the left-side
tires, but the impact was light. The only thing I even
bumped was my arm."

"Let's see it, then." Gil laid the chart aside and

glanced at Kitty, "If you'd just wait outside, Miss . . . ?"

"No." Steve shook his head. "She's my watchdog this time." Gil looked at Kitty, then back at Steve, and gave a snort of laughter.

"Well, if Steve doesn't mind, I don't mind, but you don't have to stand in that corner. Have a seat over here, miss; you'll be more comfortable."

She smiled her thanks and took the chair he indicated. "Thank you, but what do you mean by watchdog?"

Gil chuckled again. "Jack always has someone ride herd on Steve when he's over here, and tell him exactly what was said, because he doesn't trust this one," he jerked his head at Steve, "to report any bad news."

"But he knows I will, huh? OK, Doctor, I won't leave anything out."

"That's the way to deal with this guy," the doctor agreed. "Don't let him get away with anything." As they talked Steve had been stripping off his driving suit and protective clothing, resuming his position on the table clad only in small, tight briefs. Kitty wanted to look away but was mesmerized by the sight of him, more beautiful even than she had remembered.

His body had filled out since he was twenty-five, and the physical exertion of driving race cars had left him with heavily muscled arms and shoulders and a broad, powerful chest. He was deeply tanned, the thick, curling hair on his chest and arms bleached golden by the sun. His legs were long and tanned and powerful, his hips and stomach lean and hard. A sheen of sweat gleamed beneath the bright overhead light as he moved, and Kitty's mouth was dry, her palms damp, as she watched him with hungry eyes.

His left arm had indeed been hit; there was an angry red mark, which would become a bruise, just above the elbow, but the doctor pronounced it trivial. More important was the check for any head injury, which was done even when none was suspected. Kitty waited until it was completed and the doctor had departed, pronouncing Steve perfectly all right, then she stood.

"I—" Her voice was a husky whisper and she cleared her throat. "I'll wait for you outside."

"Why?" He slid off the table, frankly amused, watching the pink in her cheeks. "It's a little silly to suddenly be shy now, isn't it?"

Her chin came up at the taunt, and she dropped onto the chair again, folding her arms across her chest. "All right. Go ahead."

One dark gold eyebrow went up, but he only reached over to lift his driving suit from the table, the muscles bunching and sliding beneath the brown skin of his back. Kitty dropped her eyes, staring at the floor, listening to the rustle of fabric and the rasp of the long zipper. She rose again and turned to go, but a large hand on her shoulder held her back.

"Wait a minute." She slowly raised her eyes to his. "What was the matter with you—back in the pits?"

"What?" She stared at him for a moment, then shook her head dismissively. "Oh, nothing. It was nothing."

"It wasn't nothing. You were white as a ghost. I thought for a minute you were going to faint."

"Well, I wasn't!" she snapped defensively. "And it was no big deal. It was just—" She sought frantically for some way to explain her reaction to his remark. "It was just that, even if we're not . . . friends, you don't need to think I'd wish you harm."

"That's all? You looked more upset than that." He wasn't convinced, and she shook her head angrily.

"Look, I was a little shook up. I'd never seen an accident that close, and it bothered me. That's *all!*"

"OK, OK," he agreed, but he watched her with a curious expression as she preceded him from the room.

They heard the voices before they reached the reception room, one raised angrily, the other placating.

". . . drove right into me!" someone was saying. "There ought to be rules about that kind of thing!"

"The TV people will have it on tape, Mike," said the placating voice, and Kitty looked up at Steve in surprised comprehension. It was Mike Watson talking so angrily about the accident and blaming Steve! Steve nodded, his mouth tightening, but said nothing as he walked toward the doorway. "The stewards will review the tape," the placating voice continued. "You don't have to do anything."

"I still say they shouldn't allow people on the track unless they know what they're doing!"

"I couldn't agree with you more, Watson," Steve said as he stepped through the open door, a note of hard amusement underlying the courteous words. Watson spun around, his face a deep red.

"Yeah—uh—sure," he muttered, his bravado evaporating and his face flushing even darker.

Steve nodded politely at Watson's companion and left the building with Kitty, caught between indignation and laughter, following him. The ambulance had waited to drive them back to the garage, and she held her tongue until the doors banged closed.

Indignation bubbled over first. "Of all the nerve!" she sputtered. "How can he say things like that? But what *you* said! Oh, Steve, that was marvelous. And he certainly deserved it!"

"Don't be too hard on him," Steve cautioned, and she frowned in surprise. "I know I embarrassed him, but maybe that'll teach him to keep his mouth shut. This place is always crawling with reporters, and they'll print anything you say, however trivial, and make a mountain out of a molehill like that remark of his. He has to learn to keep quiet, even when he's scared and shook up because he caused what could have been a bad accident."

"Then it *was* his fault," she said with satisfaction.

"Oh, yes." Steve briefly sketched in what had happened. "But with any luck it's put a good scare into him and he'll drive more carefully after this." He paused, then changed the subject.

"By the way, when you tear the car down, check the steering system and the axles carefully. He didn't really hit me hard, and I didn't really hit the wall hard, either, but something didn't feel right, and there's no telling what kind of damage was done."

"OK." She was as coolly businesslike as he was. "How did the wing work out, anyway?"

"It's good. I think it helped get the two hundred."

"Congratulations on that, in case I didn't tell you already. I'll make sure the wing's reset at the same angle."

She was talking so calmly that she surprised herself. It was amazing that she could hide the love she felt; it seemed to blaze through her whenever she looked at him or heard his voice. It was even more amazing that she could talk about the steering system with half her attention while her eyes followed his every move. The hard line of his cheek as he turned to look out the window, the muscles of his thigh outlined by the shiny

Nomex when he braced himself as the ambulance swung around a turn, the long, brown fingers that curled around her arm as he helped her out of the ambulance, all were etched into her memory, keepsakes for the time when he would be gone again.

She accepted the fact that when the month of May was over he would go back to Europe and the Grand Prix and she would go on to another job in racing, and while their paths might cross again, it was unlikely. The memories of these few minutes of empathy would be saved for those empty days in the future.

The empty days could be in the present, she realized as they walked around the ambulance, for Irina van Damm was standing outside the garage, looking expectantly toward them.

"Irina!" Steve shouted her name in welcome and ran the last yards to the garage, leaving Kitty to approach more slowly, an unwilling audience as he wrapped his arms around the tall Dutch girl and swung her in a circle. "Where did you come from?" he asked when he'd set her, laughing, on her feet again. "I thought you were shooting in New York this week?"

"So did I, but at the last minute they canceled it. Some sort of problem with the ad campaign, so they will reschedule it for next month." She shrugged her tanned shoulders and smiled prettily at him. "I am glad it was postponed. It is more exciting to be here with the racing."

"You're my best fan." Steve kissed her lightly, an arm around her slender waist pulling her close. Kitty averted her eyes and lowered her head as she brushed past to enter the garage, unnoticed by either of them. She felt cold and numb and unutterably weary, but she had a job to do. After collecting the tools she needed she turned dull eyes to the scarlet car being carefully dismantled and began her search for subtle signs of damage.

Work was the only thing that got her through the rest of that endless week. She immersed herself in it, arriving at the Speedway at dawn, staying until dark, absorbing herself in each tiny detail, blocking everything else from her mind. She tried to exhaust herself, but still she lay awake long into the night, aching with love, burning with jealousy as she imagined Steve and Irina together, talking, laughing, making love.

Always she was painfully aware that her month of working with Steve was slipping away. There was the second weekend of qualifications to come, and then a week during which cars were allowed on the track only on Thursday, Carburetion Day. In addition to checking the carburetion of the engines, the teams would practice their pit stops on Thursday, and then they would all return to their garages to make their final preparations for Sunday's race.

By Friday the strain was beginning to show in her shadowed, haunted eyes, in the pallor of her face that careful makeup could not quite conceal and a weight loss that showed quickly on someone so petite. Always slim, she was now almost thin, the bones of her face pressing against the skin, her ribs visible below the swell of her breasts.

She didn't think anyone had noticed, but on that Friday Marco stopped her on her way to lunch, and his greeting was not reassuring.

"You look terrible!" He scowled. "What have you done to yourself?"

"I haven't done anything," she muttered defensively, staring at the pavement beneath her feet. "I've been working, that's all."

"Then working is not good for you. Come. I will buy you lunch." He took her hand to pull her along, but she resisted.

"Marco, no! You don't have to buy me lunch; I have something to eat."

He paused to look quizzically at her. "What?"

"A—an apple," she admitted after a moment's hesitation, and he snorted in disgust.

"That is nothing! I am buying lunch for you, and you will eat it." It wasn't a request, and she resignedly allowed herself to be led to the track cafeteria, which catered exclusively to the racing fraternity. The food was far from *cordon bleu,* but it was filling, and Marco watched with hawklike vigilance as she forced down the meal he had chosen for her.

When she pushed her plate away and picked up her coffee cup he leaned back and folded his arms, smiling at her in satisfaction. "That is better. You need to eat, a little girl like you are."

"I'll bet that's what your mother told you," she teased, and he grinned in amused agreement.

"Every day, when I would not eat my pasta. And she was right."

"Mothers always are, I guess." In spite of herself she sounded a little wistful.

"Your mother is . . . ?"

"She died when I was young; I don't remember her, but I always wanted a mother. When I was little I used to imagine that Steve's mother was mine as well."

"You knew Steve then?"

"They were our neighbors," she said, her tone closing the subject, and Marco did not pursue it.

"What are you doing next week while the track is closed?" he asked her, and she grinned.

"We're doing what everyone else is doing," she told him. "Taking the car apart and putting it back together again."

"Ah, yes," he laughed. "You mechanics are so busy, while we poor drivers have nothing to do. Is Steve going to help take the car apart?"

"No," she answered casually. "I heard him tell Jack that after he drives this afternoon he's leaving for Florida to visit his parents. He'll be back for the carburetion runs."

Marco nodded. "I had forgotten that he cannot drive this weekend either, while the rest of us qualify. It will make a nice holiday for him."

Kitty drank the rest of her coffee without replying to that, and they rose to move toward the door. "Kitty?" She looked around at Marco. "Will you come with me to a party this evening?"

"What party?" she asked suspiciously and was ashamed of herself when he frowned ruefully.

"It is a real party," he reassured her. "I am not going to make myself so disagreeable again. It is the reception that is being given for the drivers this evening. You must have heard about it?"

Kitty nodded.

"Well, I would not ask you, for I know you do not wish to be where Steve is, but if he is leaving to visit his parents, then will you come with me?"

"Oh, Marco, I don't know. I don't really feel like a party."

"It is only for a little while, but—I do not want to go alone to this."

"You don't have to go at all," she offered, and he shook his head.

"That is the problem. My sponsor insists that I attend—for 'public relations.'" He said the words with distaste, and Kitty had to grin in sympathy. "So, will you come with me?"

"Oh . . . all right." She gave in, unable to resist the appeal, and he caught her in his arms, there in the middle of the crowded cafeteria, to give her an ebullient hug.

Chapter Ten

She wished she felt some of that ebullience as she dressed for the reception. She looked good; the black crepe cocktail dress was so simple as to be almost plain, with a halter-necked bodice which left her shoulders bare and a softly flared skirt that swirled around her knees as she walked. It was a warm evening, and the lacy black shawl she draped around her shoulders was more for show than warmth. Black, narrow-heeled sandals and a black satin bag completed the ensemble, and she wound her hair into an ebony chignon low on her neck, ornamented with a glittery rhinestone comb.

Marco's appreciative reaction was confirmation of her own assessment, but beneath the carefully applied makeup she felt only weary and vaguely depressed, and she wished the evening were over before it had even begun.

The reception was what she had expected, large, noisy and lavish, with a buffet arranged on one side of the enormous hotel ballroom and a bar doing a brisk business, as well as waiters circulating with champagne and a band playing at one end of the room.

She felt curiously detached from it all, an observer rather than a participant, as she let Marco lead her into the crowd, press a drink into her hand and begin circulating among the elegantly dressed guests. She spoke when spoken to, laughed brittlely at innumerable bad jokes, pretended an interest in the shallow conversation and felt the beginnings of a headache nagging at the back of her skull.

After endless minutes of dutiful sociability Marco steered her toward the dancers, swearing under his breath in Italian.

"They are not paying me enough," he murmured in her ear as he took her in his arms and moved into the dance, "for them to expect me to deal with this!" He changed to a girlish simper. " 'Do you enjoy racing, Mr. Rissoli? Oh, it is so exciting, Mr. Rissoli.' *Eccetera, eccetera.* Without you here, Kitty, I would go mad!"

Kitty giggled at his wickedly accurate portrayal of the people they had spoken to. "I'm not doing anything to keep you from going mad," she protested, "but if you seem about to strike, I'll hold you back."

"Promise me that you will. It would look very bad in the papers: 'Race driver attacks wealthy woman wearing vulgar jewelry.' "

"Marco!" She tapped his cheek with a reproving finger. "You mustn't be unkind!"

"*Si.*" He hung his head, shamefaced but teasing underneath. "You are good for me, just as I said. You have a kind heart." His arm tightened around her as he murmured the words and they danced in silence for several minutes.

"*Dio!*" Marco's harsh whisper jerked Kitty from a near trance, and she looked up at his face. He kept her close, so that she could see only the taut angle of his jaw and the suddenly deep lines carved beside his mouth.

"Marco, what is it?"

"Shhh." He pressed her face into his shoulder, but she resisted.

"Marco, what is going on?" She jerked her head back and frowned up at him. "Tell me!"

"Someone came in," he replied vaguely, and she pounced on the remark, disturbed without knowing why.

"Who?" And then, over his shoulder, she saw them.

Steve took Irina into his arms as they reached the dance floor, and together they moved so smoothly that it looked as if their steps had been choreographed. Jealousy stabbed through Kitty with a pain that was almost physical, and she jerked her eyes away, focusing her gaze on Marco's collar.

"*Si.*" He had felt her stiffen. "I guessed the way things are for you. It hurts you to watch them, just as it does me." He turned her away from the other two in a quick step, then turned again, and Kitty saw the two gleaming golden heads, so close together. Suddenly her headache was a throbbing pain.

"Marco, I—will you excuse me for a few minutes?"

"Of course, but is something wrong?"

"No. No, of course not. I'd just like to—to freshen up."

"Certainly." He led her off the floor, turning

toward the bar as Kitty made her way along the side of the crowded room.

She had to escape the heat, the noise, the smoke-laden air for a few minutes. She was alone momentarily, having stepped out of the swirling crowd and into the lee of an enormous potted palm. There were French doors behind her, opening onto a balcony, and she looked longingly at the cool night outside. Marco was across the room at the bar; he wouldn't notice if she stepped out for a moment. She pressed the latch and slipped through the door.

The night had gone cool, and she pulled her shawl more closely around her shoulders, breathing deeply of the clean air, relishing the quiet after the din inside. She walked to the end of the balcony, out of the light, and leaned against the waist-high balustrade, looking out over a small park without really seeing it.

"Not enjoying the party?"

The voice coming from behind startled her, and she spun around to stare in surprise at the man who stood watching her.

"Steve! You scared me!"

He closed the door and walked across to brace himself against the balustrade beside her. "Sorry, I didn't mean to. Weren't you enjoying the party?"

"Mmm. It just got to be too hot and noisy," she said noncommittally and turned away from him to look out at the park again. She didn't know what he was doing here with Irina when he was supposed to be on a plane to Florida, and she didn't want to know. She just wanted him to go away and leave her alone. Her silence didn't seem to bother him, though. She heard the rustle of fabric and the crunch of cellophane as he took out a cigarette, then the *snick* of a lighter and the scent of tobacco smoke. He let the stream of smoke drift away on the breeze and half turned to look at her.

"When did you decide to come to this bash?"

"Today." Her brief answer did not invite further comment, but Steve ignored her coolness.

"The Italian Romeo asked you, did he?"

She clenched her teeth at the taunt, fighting down a sharp retort, and said only, "Marco asked me, yes."

"Is he still waiting, or has he already gotten what he wants?"

Her eyes blazed at that, and she looked down to hide the fury in them. "I think," she said lightly, "that Marco and I are both getting what we want from our . . . friendship." In the silence after her words she heard his suddenly indrawn breath.

"Are you really?" His voice was very soft as he dropped his cigarette and crushed it out beneath his heel. "And just what *do* you want, I wonder?"

With a swiftness that caught her completely by surprise he seized her arm and jerked her around, crushing her against him with one steel-hard arm around her waist. Her head was flung back as she stared up at him with wide, startled eyes, alarm growing at the dark anger in his face.

"What do you want?" he repeated softly, almost to himself. "Do you want this?" He captured her mouth in an angry kiss, forcing her lips apart, one hand clamping the back of her neck, thwarting her efforts to twist her head away. His lips lifted fractionally from hers and he whispered, "Or do you want this?" He claimed her mouth again, but this time there was no punishment in the kiss, only a sweet, seductive persuasion that was more powerful than any force.

He savored her mouth, teasing her with tiny kisses, tracing the contours of her lips with his tongue, then parting them to possess her mouth again. All thought of resistance dissolved as the magic took over and she clung to him, her hands sliding up of their own volition to link behind his head, her fingers slipping into the thick blond hair; her body arched against his as she went up on her toes, pulling him down to her.

Her response was complete and almost instinctive, something she could not control. She was only half aware of his hands moving over her shoulders, of the clasp at the neck of her dress parting, and when his lips left hers and found the soft swell of her breast as the black crepe was pushed away she could only welcome his touch.

The cool night air contrasting with the heat of Steve's mouth as it moved over her breast was almost painfully erotic, sending desire shooting through her. Her nipples tightened to hard peaks beneath his lips, and she arched against him, her hands moving over his back beneath his jacket, caressing the hard muscles through the thin silk of his shirt. She gasped against his neck when his hands slid down over her hips and then tightened to lift her almost off her feet into a thrillingly intimate embrace.

That intimacy, and the impossibility of acting on it in such a public place, lent a sense of frustrated urgency to their kisses and caresses as they molded their bodies together, pressing back into the deep shadow at the end of the balcony.

The shaft of light slanting out across the balcony from the ballroom froze them both into immobility for an instant, then Steve straightened slowly, pulling the straps of Kitty's dress up, his bulk shielding her from the view of the couple who stood beside the doors, chatting idly about the race. She was grateful for the consideration he showed in that protective gesture, but her wits were returning, bringing with them shame and a deep anger at both him and at herself.

He bent to pick up her shawl, which had fallen to the ground, and as he did so the other couple turned and reentered the ballroom. Apparently they hadn't even noticed that they weren't alone on the balcony, which wasn't really so surprising, Kitty realized. She and Steve were both dressed in dark colors, and they stood in shadows deep enough to have concealed them, thank heaven, for her own self-contempt was difficult enough to bear.

Steve held the shawl out to her and would have placed it on her shoulders, but she stepped away, snatching it from his hand and wrapping it around her shoulders as if to shield herself from his eyes. He noted the gesture and paused without coming any closer.

"What's the matter?"

"What do you think is the matter?" She laughed bitterly. "You're the matter! Now, will you please let me go back inside? It's getting cold out here." She took two quick steps, but instead of allowing her to pass he caught her wrist and jerked her around to face him.

"You're not going anywhere just yet," he growled, his face dark with anger. "Not until you explain that remark!"

"I don't have to explain anything!"

"Oh, I think you do." His soft voice was heavy with menace. "And you will."

Kitty just glared mutely up at him, her simmering anger apparent in her face. "Can you tell me *why* I should explain anything to you? What possible reason you can have for wanting any explanation at all from me?"

"I've known you for a long time. That's reason enough. I want to know what you meant by that little remark, *and* I want to know what you're doing here with Rissoli."

"What's it to do with you?" Kitty asked nastily. "Anyway, the fact that you and I have known each other for a long time doesn't mean anything anymore! You told me that very plainly. You and I aren't friends anymore; we're not *any*thing anymore! Who I go out with is none of your business. Now let me *go!*" She jerked her arm, but he only tightened his grip until she thought he would break her wrist.

"Then what about that other smart remark? Why am *I* what's the matter?"

"Don't you *know?*" She shook her head in amazement. "Can't you figure it out for yourself? You told me—you *told* me you didn't want anything to do with me, so why are you giving me lectures about my personal life and why are you out here and *why* did you kiss me?" She finished on a near shout and glared up at him, her breast heaving with her rapid, angry breathing.

For a long moment he just glared back at her; then he growled a muffled curse and jerked her against him again. "Why did I kiss you? Why not? You weren't fighting too hard, were you?" As the last cruel, insulting word left his lips and as Kitty gasped in shocked fury, he crushed his lips onto hers again.

This time she fought him, twisting and struggling to free herself, but it was useless. Steve held her too tightly, one arm around her waist almost crushing the breath out of her, a hand twisted in her hair to force her face up to his. His kiss was in no way a caress; he crushed his mouth onto hers, forcing her lips apart, grinding them against her teeth. She pushed at his shoulders, but it was like pushing a brick wall, and even when she pulled at his hair he only said some-

thing short and angry against her mouth and pulled
her arm down to pin it at her side.

She could feel the anger in him like a tangible force,
frightening her, overwhelming her puny resistance so
that her own anger faded, to be replaced by a simple
desire to escape before she was destroyed by this
elemental fury. Her resistance crushed, she sagged
against him, weak tears slipping from beneath her
lowered lids as she waited for his fury to spend itself.

When he finally released her he pushed her slightly
away and she staggered back a pace before she caught
her balance. With trembling fingers she clutched her
shawl around her and reached up to scrub the tears
from her cheeks before looking into Steve's face.

"Why?" she asked him in a low, shaky voice. "Why
are you doing this? Are you trying to punish me? Is
that it? *Is that it?*"

"I don't know!" Steve moved a step away from her
and flung one hand out angrily. "I don't know. Maybe
I am trying to punish you! Do you blame me? Maybe
I've been waiting for seven years to punish you; I had
reason enough, don't you think?"

"No, I *don't* think! I did something wrong, but that
was *seven years ago,* Steve. However you feel about
me, after all this time it's hardly fair to set yourself up
as judge and jury!"

"Not fair?" Steve growled. "They say all's fair—"

"—in love and war?" Kitty mocked. "You've got
your metaphors mixed, haven't you? This can't be
war, not between members of the same team." She
drew a deep, shaky breath. "And it certainly isn't
love!" she snapped, feeling a small surge of satisfaction at the darkening anger in his face. She looked
around for her bag, which she had dropped, but Steve
saw it first and stooped to pick it up. She snatched

it from his outstretched hand and held it in front of her like a shield.

"I wanted to be friends with you again, Steve," she said, her voice low and shaking with emotion. "But not anymore! When this month is over I hope I never have to see you again!"

She brushed past him and into the ballroom, pausing halfway along the room to scan the crowd for Marco. He was dancing with Irina, and Kitty stared in astonishment. They made an unusual couple, Irina so much taller than Marco, and yet there was something very right about the way they looked together. Marco held her tenderly in his arms, her head bent to rest beside his, his eyes closed as they swayed to a slow, dreamy number. He turned, and she saw Irina's face and was astonished anew.

It didn't make sense, didn't fit with anything else that had happened these last weeks, but Irina's face was peaceful, content in the way Kitty associated with love. It could be a trick of the light, or something else, but in that moment Irina looked like a woman in love. Kitty pulled her shawl more tightly around her shoulders and walked quickly from the room, hoping, for Marco's sake, that he had taken her advice and told Irina that he still loved her.

The clerk at the main desk of the hotel called a taxi for her and agreed impassively to deliver a message to Marco.

"Please tell him that I'm not feeling well and that I've taken a taxi home. My name is Gordon. Katharine Gordon."

In the cab she leaned wearily back against the worn upholstery, massaging her throbbing temples and trying vainly not to think. What was happening? What was happening between Irina and Marco; what was happening to Steve, and God in heaven, what was happening to her?

How could she have done that, responded so abandonedly to Steve's lovemaking when he only wanted to punish her for what she had done so long ago? Thank heaven he was going to Florida. She wouldn't have to see him for five days; perhaps by then she'd have her defenses strengthened.

Perhaps, but she knew she was lying to herself. She had no defenses against him; she could only hope that she would be able to avoid being alone with him until the race was over.

"Kitty! There's someone at the gate to see you!"

She looked up at Jimmy and nodded, balancing precariously on one foot as she peeled off her fire suit.

"Okay, Jimmy. Do you know who it is?"

"Nope. Just some guy. You got a boyfriend you haven't told us about?"

"Huh-uh." She shook her head. "I don't know who'd want to see me. Was he going to wait?"

"I guess so."

"Well, I'm about ready to go, anyway." She put her fire suit away and picked up her purse. "See you guys tomorrow." The men who remained in the garage returned her good-bye wave, then bent over the engine again.

The six days since last Friday had passed quickly; it was Thursday evening, the race was on Saturday, and the carburetion tests were over, in a day that had been a surprising anticlimax.

Steve was back from his trip to Florida, and she had dreaded having to face him again, but he had breezed into the garage that morning, said a cheerful "Hello" to them all, blandly given Kitty a message from his mother, who invited her to visit them in Florida if she wished, and got down to the business of the day.

She felt as though she'd missed a scene in a play. When she'd left him on that balcony last week they'd both been angry, furiously angry, and yet today he'd been almost friendly, with no disturbing undercurrents flowing between them at all from the time he arrived until he'd left almost an hour ago. And she had no idea why. Maybe seeing his parents had mellowed his attitude. Whatever the reason, she found this sort of Jekyll-and-Hyde personality transformation unnerving.

"Kitty! *Kitty!*" Her head snapped up and she stared in disbelief at the tall, black-haired man at the gate.

"Johnny?" She began to run. *"Johnny!"* He held his arms wide, and she ran into them, wrapping hers around his neck and giving him a smacking kiss on the cheek. "Oh, Johnny, it's wonderful to see you! But what are you doing here? Why didn't you tell me you were coming? When did you get here? Is Pam with you?"

"Whoa! Give me a chance to answer!" He took her arm, and they walked together toward the parking lot. "Now, let's see—I'm here to see the race, and yes, Pam's here, too, and the boys. We wanted to surprise you; we got here about noon today. Was that everything?" he teased.

"I think so—and don't make fun of me!" She grinned back. "Where are you staying?"

"With Pam's parents. She's there now, with the boys, and her parents are going to baby-sit tonight while Pam and I take you out to dinner."

"Lovely! When are we going?"

"Just as soon as we can get you cleaned up. Did you bring your car today?" She hadn't, so they headed for the parking lot, where he seated her in his car and began maneuvering toward the exit.

"What made you decide to come to the race this year?" Kitty asked as they pulled out into the heavy traffic on 16th Street. "You always said you'd rather stay in New York and listen to the radio than deal with the traffic and the crowds."

"Oh, I don't know," John drawled, looking out the windshield and avoiding her eyes. "Maybe I just wanted to watch my little sister in the pits." His lips curved into a teasing smile. "And maybe I just got a week's vacation at the right time."

"Where are your seats?"

"In the tower terrace, right across from the pits."

"*Really?* Those are about the best seats in the place! How on earth did you get tickets there? I thought they were usually sold out a year in advance!"

"I guess they usually are, but a fellow I know had two tickets he didn't need, so he let me have them."

"He *gave* them to you?" She stared at him. "Johnny, those are almost a hundred dollars a seat!"

"Uh, yeah, I guess they are," he said a little hesitantly.

"You sure have some generous friends," Kitty commented lightly, noticing, but not understanding, John's unease. "Send this friend my way the next time he's giving things away, all right?"

John grinned in amusement, his face lightening again. "I'll do that," he said cheerfully. "The next time he's feeling generous I'll be sure to mention your name."

Kitty returned his grin, but wondered at the uncharacteristic evasiveness of his answers. Not, of course, that it was any business of hers in the first place, but it was unusual for John to be in any way secretive about his life.

Her curious thoughts were pushed to the back of her mind, though, by more important concerns, such as changing rapidly for dinner and renewing her acquaintance with her nephews, Jason, five, and Matt, three and a half, who were ecstatically happy to see Aunt Kitty again.

The restaurant John and Pam took her to was well known for its excellent food and quietly luxurious atmosphere, and the three of them enjoyed their duck à l'orange and caramel mousse immensely. They were sitting back in their chairs with coffee and liqueurs when John asked the question Kitty had subconsciously been dreading.

"Kitty?" He looked across the table at her during a lull in the conversation.

"Hmm?"

"How is it going—you and Steve working together?" Kitty's eyes opened wide, and she darted a nervous glance at Pam. "It's OK," John said. "Pam's always known what happened."

Kitty glanced between the two of them again, then dropped her eyes to the tablecloth, flushing. It was bad enough that John knew what she had done all those years ago, but somehow it was much worse that Pam should know, too. She must despise Kitty for it.

"Kitty," Pam said gently, covering Kitty's hand with her own, "please don't be angry with John for telling me, and please don't be embarrassed. You were very young, and it's not hard to understand."

Kitty slanted her an uncertain look. "Yes, but it's not an easy thing to live with." They smiled with her, and some of the tension eased. She wasn't quite sure, however, how to answer John's question. She fell silent, studying the pattern on the tablecloth for a few moments.

"To what you asked, Johnny, about working with

Steve, there's no real answer. We work together well enough, on the surface, but he doesn't like me, and I don't really expect him to.

"Johnny," she looked across at him, entreaty in her eyes, "I know how angry you were with Steve then, but it was my doing—what happened. I never meant it to be the ruin of your friendship, and"—she searched for the words—"I wish there could be a way for me to put things right."

A strange expression crossed his face, and he met Pam's eyes again, the look they shared holding a message that Kitty didn't comprehend. John sipped his coffee, then met Kitty's worried eyes gravely.

"I appreciate the thought, Kitty," he said slowly, "but a lot of time has passed, and it's not always possible to turn back the clock."

His words stayed in her mind. She had wanted to do that, to turn back the clock and wipe out that dreadful night as if it had never happened, but now she admitted the futility of such wishes. Nothing could wipe it out, for any of them, and she must simply accept responsibility for the damage she had done.

This acceptance seemed to give her an inner calm, a serenity that had been lacking for her. Her work went so well that Jack sent her away at noon on Saturday, her job complete, so that she could watch the 500 Festival parade with Pam and the boys.

The boys were bursting with excitement as they waited for the parade to begin that afternoon. They had an excellent vantage point, for John's company had a branch office overlooking the Meridian Street parade route, and company employees were invited to watch from the windows. Below them one city block of Meridian Street was covered in black-and-white-checkered carpet, symbolic of the checkered flag that signaled the finish of the race. The grandstands erected for dignitaries were below them as well, and all the bands and drill teams would perform there for the television cameras.

Kitty lifted Matt up to sit on the windowsill as they heard the distant rhythms of a marching band, and then they were all plunged into the magic of the parade. There were bands and floats and drill teams, television and movie stars riding in open cars, politicians and local notables, a Festival queen and her court of princesses, all local college co-eds, and the thirty-three drivers, riding in open cars.

Kitty said nothing as Steve came into view, smiling and waving to the crowd, his hair ruffled by the breeze, but her throat tightened when his car drew level with them. Tomorrow was the day everyone had spent so long preparing for, the culmination of all their hopes and efforts, and when it was over they would go their separate ways, all the people who had worked so hard together, and many would not see each other again. Certainly she and Steve would never meet again.

He looked up, and it seemed that he looked directly at her, but she couldn't move. Little Matt waved frantically, but Kitty only stood, eyes wide in an effort to halt the tears that pricked at her eyelids, and watched as he was driven around the corner and out of sight.

It took some time to work their way back to Pam's car through the post-parade crush, and longer still to escape the heavy downtown traffic.

"Are you sure you won't come back and have supper with us, Kitty?" Pam was frowning with concern as she pulled up in front of Kitty's apartment.

"No, Pam, but thanks anyway. It's already six and I'm just going to have supper and loaf around for a

couple of hours and go to bed really early. I have to be
at the track at four A.M. tomorrow, you know!"

"Well, if you're sure . . ."

"Really, it's OK. I'm kind of nervous about tomorrow, and I think I'll be better off by myself. I'll be
sociable again after the race is over."

"I'll hold you to that," Pam told her, the words half
threat, half promise, and they both laughed. "Are you
going to eat a good supper? You need more than just a
can of soup or—"

"Steak and salad OK?" Kitty asked with a teasing
grin. "I bought lots more than I'll ever be able to eat,
but I promise to try, all right?"

"All right," Pam relented, laughing, and Kitty
stepped out of the car. "Sleep well, and good luck
tomorrow!"

"Thanks!" Kitty waved to the boys as Pam drove
away, then went inside to shower and change.
Dressed in a T-shirt and shorts, for the evening was
sultry, she began preparations for her dinner.

She had bought not one, but two enormous steaks,
and had no idea what had possessed her to do such an
extravagant thing. She shrugged; she'd just eat one of
them tonight and the other tomorrow, and then live
on hamburger and tuna fish the rest of the month. She
laid one on the counter and replaced the other in the
refrigerator, straightening as someone knocked on the
front door.

It was probably Shelley, checking to see if she
wanted company, and Kitty was smiling in anticipation as she pulled the door open.

"How are you Shel—" She broke off, staring in
blank surprise, then asked rudely, "What are *you*
doing here?"

Chapter Eleven

Steve lifted one shoulder in a slight shrug. "Is that any way to greet somebody who just stopped by to see you?" he said gently, smiling.

Kitty's eyes narrowed suspiciously. "Probably not," she said coldly, "but why did *you* come by?"

"To see you," he replied, ignoring her hostility.

"You've seen me. Goodbye." She stepped back to close the door, but he blocked it with his body.

"Invite me in, Kitty." It was almost a plea, and so unexpected that she stopped and looked up at him in surprise.

"Why?" she asked bluntly.

"Because I'd like some company. Because I don't want to go back to my hotel room yet."

"Go find Irina; she'll keep you company!" Kitty regretted that unmistakably jealous remark the moment it was uttered, but his eyes held no spark of mocking triumph.

"Kitty, the race is tomorrow," he said wearily. "I need to relax, talk a little, away from crowds and parties. I'll buy dinner for you, if you haven't eaten."

He looked tired, tense; he looked as though he needed to relax. Perhaps there was no more to this request than met the eye, no more than a simple need for company while he prepared himself for the next day's race. After a long moment of studying his grave face, she relented.

"Come in." She stepped back and he followed her inside, closing the screen door with a soft click. In the middle of the living room he halted her with a light hand on her arm.

"Thank you for this, Kitty." He smiled, and she looked gravely back at him for a long moment before replying with a slight twist of her lips, not yet convinced of the wisdom of spending time alone with him. "I'll buy us something for dinner," he offered. "Carry-out, if you don't mind eating here."

"I don't mind eating here."

"What would you like? Chinese? Pizza?"

"Steak and salad?" she suggested, and he raised quizzical eyebrows.

"Where can you get carry-out steak and salad?"

"Here. I was about to fix mine, and I have enough for two," she said indifferently.

"That's terrific, if you don't mind cooking."

"I was going to cook anyway." She shrugged. "One more doesn't make any difference."

"Can I help?"

She didn't know if he meant that, but she would certainly take him up on the offer. He'd invited himself in, so he could help, all right. She led him to the kitchen and seated him at the table while she got out potatoes and a knife.

"There isn't really time to bake potatoes, so you can make French fries out of these while the steaks are marinating."

He groaned and rolled his eyes. "You must have been talking to my mother!" Kitty looked around at him in inquiry, and he laughed.

"I'm not much of a cook, and I never was, but she felt that everyone should know how to peel potatoes. I think I spent half my childhood with a potato and a knife!" He laughed again, and Kitty couldn't stop the giggles that rose inside her.

"Good," she said unfeelingly and grinned at him. "You ought to be good at it."

He groaned again and began peeling.

While he worked, she poured red wine over the steaks, added black pepper and herbs and then made a salad, pausing now and then to turn the steaks in their marinade. When she was done Steve was just finishing the potatoes, and he laid the table for two while she pan-broiled the steaks and fried the potatoes. She added the marinade to the steak pan for the last moments and then poured the savory liquid over the steaks on their serving platter.

When it was set on the table in front of him Steve inhaled deeply and then looked at Kitty with something approaching awe. "This smells marvelous! Do you cook like this all the time?"

"Should I tell you that I do, or should I be honest about all the nights when I have a sandwich and an apple?" She grinned and served him a steak and some potatoes.

"Don't disillusion me." He looked at the ruby-colored wine she poured. "Are we drinking the same thing the steaks had?"

"We could, but this is better stuff, if not in the Lafite-Rothschild class."

"Not bad at all," he announced after a judicious sip. "Quite good, as a matter of fact. Thank you, Kitty," he said, and there was no hint of teasing in his voice or eyes.

"You're welcome, Steve," she replied softly, then bent over her plate as her cheeks warmed under his eyes.

After they had eaten every scrap of the meal he insisted on helping her with the dishes, finishing them in record time, and then led her to the living room and seated her on the sofa while he made coffee. He brought the rest of the wine, as well, a rich burgundy that was sending velvety warmth along her limbs. He handed her a glass and then turned away to flip through her records, select one and place it on the turntable. The haunting strains of "Scheherazade" drifted into the room, and Kitty relaxed against the cushions, head back and eyes closed.

This all seemed so right, as though they had shared many meals, as though they would share many more, comfortable and easy with each other. She wasn't asleep, but floating in a sort of waking dream. Gently he drew her to him, turning her so that she lay across his lap, cradled in his arms. One hand stroked her hair, letting it flow through his fingers like black silk, his touch intimate, sensual, yet without aggression.

She lifted heavy lids and looked up at his face, loving him, loving the hard angle of his cheek and chin, the straight, sun-bleached brows above eyes that could change from the cool, gray glitter of ice to the deep, smoky gray they were now, loving the firm, clean line of his upper lip, the sensual curve of the lower.

She raised a hand to lightly touch his cheek as

though she were afraid he might not be real, and he caught it in his and pressed a kiss into her palm. His lips lingered, then lifted slowly and he gazed down at her, his eyes dark, so dark they were almost black.

"You're so beautiful, Kitten," he murmured. "So beautiful . . ."

He took her face between his hands and bent his head to kiss her gently, touching her eyes, cheeks and finally lips, his kisses butterfly-light, undemanding, giving pleasure while asking nothing in return.

But she wanted to return it, she wanted to please him, and she reached up to hold him to her. Her heart was fluttering against her ribs like a captive bird, and his breathing was no longer steady and unhurried. With a wordless murmur she shifted in his arms, nestling closer, her hand sliding down the strong column of his neck to slip inside his half-opened shirt.

She could feel the heavy beat of his heart as she caressed him, her hands exploring, delighting in the warm, hard muscle, the thick mat of hair that trailed down onto his flat belly. Somehow she freed the rest of his buttons, and he breathed her name into her hair as her arms slid around him.

He captured her willing mouth again, his hands large and warm, circling her throat to lift her face to his. His fingers moved, caressing the length of her neck, then following the V-neck of her T-shirt to trace a tormenting pattern down to the shadowy valley between her breasts. Kitty gasped and arched against him as his fingers pushed the neckline of her shirt aside and slipped inside. Her breasts swelled at his touch, the nipples hardening to taut peaks beneath his thumbs, her own hands busy on his chest and shoulders.

When he caught the hem of her T-shirt and peeled it over her head she pressed against him, rubbing her breasts against his chest and thrilling to the rasp of his chest hair against her skin. The dim glow of the street light outside sent a faint shimmer over her skin, and when Steve raised his head to look at her Kitty followed the path of his gaze without shyness, for she knew he found her beautiful. Her breasts gleamed white against the tan she'd acquired on a few warm afternoons, and as his mouth followed the path his eyes had taken Kitty gave a soundless sigh of pleasure, delighting in the touch and taste and warmth of him, waiting for the consummation of their lovemaking.

His lips were a sweet torture, teasing, rousing; she whimpered softly and moved against him, kissing his neck, his shoulder, her hands moving over his skin, close but needing more closeness. His lips left her breast, sliding up to her neck as his arms tightened, molding her pliant form against him. When he lifted his head again she took his face in her hands, trying to pull him closer, to kiss him, but he resisted, turning to press his lips to her palm.

He released her hand and then, to her surprise, reached over to pick up her T-shirt. Still holding her within the circle of his arms, he slipped it over her head and gently tugged it down, stroking the warm skin of her waist as he let go of the hem. She watched his face uncomprehendingly as he kissed each of her palms in turn, then eased her off his lap and rose to his feet, pulling her with him.

He shrugged his own shirt back on his shoulders and buttoned a couple of buttons, then bent to brush his lips lightly over hers.

"Good night, Kitten," he said softly. "Thank you for dinner."

Then he was gone, moving across the room and out the door as soundlessly as a ghost. She could only stand there while the fire he had lit within faded away to leave her cold and numb, the bewilderment in her eyes replaced by pain. He had gone. But why? Why?

She had wanted him so badly, and she knew that he had wanted her. Why had he gone? Was he still punishing her for what she had done so long ago? If so, it was an effective punishment, for she hurt. She hurt so badly that she didn't think she'd ever get over it, but there could be no other explanation for his actions. He was still so angry with her that he was punishing her, deliberately rousing her desire for him until she was mindless and abandoned, practically begging him to make love to her, and then leaving her aching and empty with need.

She should hate him for that, she *wanted* to hate him, and yet . . . There was no other explanation for his actions but a desire to punish her, but why had he helped her gently on with her shirt, why had he kissed her, that feather-light, fleeting kiss? The tenderness in those gestures was so at odds with his avowed desire to avenge himself on her that she could not reconcile the two.

One was real, and one was not, but how was she to know which was which? The Steve who had tormented her, playing on her susceptibility to his potent attraction, taunting her with her weakness, that Steve wanted revenge, wanted to punish her. The other Steve, the Steve she remembered from her childhood and adolescence, was the tender Steve. He might kiss her, or charm her for a dinner, that tender Steve, but he didn't exist anymore. She'd killed that Steve when she persuaded him to violate his principles, when she shattered his faith in her and in himself, when she shattered his friendship with John.

That Steve was gone, and it was the other one, the hardened, cynical one, who had kissed her and caressed her and then left her this evening. He was

exacting the revenge he had promised, bringing her to
the point of surrender and then leaving her empty,
unfulfilled. She should hate him for that. It would be
easier, so much easier than loving him. When the
tears came, slow and scalding, they lasted a long time.

". . . and it's 3:22 this race-day morning, for all you
early birds already waiting in line. Our traffic 'copter
reports traffic lined up at this hour on West 16th from
Georgetown Road west to . . ."

Her clock radio whirred, clicked, and the announcer's too-cheerful voice jerked Kitty violently awake.
She pushed herself slowly to a sitting position as her
heart rate settled back to normal and was surprised to
find that she felt well rested and alert. Her eyes were
slightly puffy from the tears she had shed, but she
knew that would soon disappear, just as the anguish
of the night before had disappeared. Oh, nothing had
changed in the way Steve felt about her or the way she
felt about him, but somehow it didn't seem so all-
important now; there were other, more important
things to be dealt with.

In the dim predawn light everything seemed clear-
er; clearest of all was the fact that her future lay with
her work. Filled with a sense of calm acceptance, she
showered and dressed and was waiting on the porch
for the taxi Jack had sent to pick her up, which
delivered her to the gates of Gasoline Alley after
threading its way past the long lines of traffic waiting
for the five A.M. opening cannon.

". . . clear skies this morning and a high temperature of ninety-two degrees, with thunder showers
moving into the Indianapolis area later this
afternoon . . ." A concessionaire setting up his stand
had a portable radio beside him, and Kitty absently
noted the weather forecast as she passed. If the rain

held off until one-thirty or two P.M. the race would be completed before it fell. The weather was a constant worry on race day, for these cars, with their treadless tires, ran only on a dry track, and Indiana's notoriously unpredictable weather was not always cooperative.

Inside the Speedway the vast grandstands and acres of grounds were oddly hushed, though already peopled by several thousand race-day workers. Security and medical personnel, concessionaires, fire and rescue crews, ticket takers and parking attendants, all were preparing for the influx of nearly 400,000 race fans who would fill the empty vastness. Gasoline Alley, though, was a teeming hive of activity, the easy camaraderie of earlier days gone as an almost tangible tension enveloped them all.

Last-minute adjustments were made to the cars, questions and orders muttered or shouted. Some ate breakfast in the cafeteria as the sun rose; others attended a Mass said by a priest standing in the bed of a pickup truck parked in Gasoline Alley. A few climbed atop the garage roofs just before five o'clock to watch the first vehicles enter the infield as the cannon boomed and the gates were flung open.

The tension in the air all around them was part of the spiral of excitement and anticipation that would wind slowly to an almost unbearable peak as eleven A.M. approached and then burst in an explosion of noise and speed and color as the green flags were waved and the race began. Kitty could feel it all around her, hear it in the distant noise of the growing crowd as the sun rose in the sky and the cool freshness of early morning gave way to the promise of sultry heat.

She concealed her own nervous excitement better than most of the crew as she went deliberately through her last-minute checklist, but she was perspiring, her palms and forehead damp, whether from nerves or the heaviness of the air she didn't know. Jack's face was red and shining, and he chomped fiercely on his cigar, taking it out and waving it to add emphasis to the staccato flow of his voice as he hurled comments and directives at them all.

The mechanics worked quickly and efficiently, their experience as a team evident in the smoothness with which preparations were completed, though their tension broke through in an occasional sharp oath or muttered imprecation. Steve lounged on a work-bench, back against the wall and legs stretched out before him, a baseball cap tipped over his eyes, his only movement the raising of a coffee mug to his lips.

Had it not been for the hand that held the mug, Kitty thought, he could have been asleep. She smiled to herself; with all his racing experience this must be just another day's work for him. She wished she felt as calm as he looked; it would be wonderful to be so accustomed to it all.

And then she saw his eyes.

Jack had turned his flow of oratory to Steve, who pushed back the baseball cap to reply to a question, and Kitty paused in her work to stare at his eyes. Glittering and intense, they totally belied the indolence of his pose. No one seeing them, hard and clear and bright as diamonds, with a singleness and intensity of purpose that was almost frightening, would ever believe that this man was relaxed.

His face was a mask, betraying no emotion beyond a casual appreciation of Jack's bad jokes. His hands were relaxed, his body still; only his eyes gave him away. And even they revealed nothing when he looked at Kitty. No inner spark of intimacy or malice lit them today; today his concentration was on the race he would be driving, and there was room for nothing else.

And in a way she was emulating him. The love, the hate, the anger she had felt toward him, all were of secondary importance today. Later she would love again, hurt again, but today there was only the race.

"... 500 Festival parade is now circling the two-and-one-half-mile oval. More than 380,000 fans are expected to pass through the gates of the Indianapolis Motor Speedway. . . ." Kitty could hear the distant rattle of drums from an abbreviated version of yesterday's parade circling the track, and the radio announcer was in full cry as their car was rolled out of the garage. They made their way slowly to the pits, assisted by security men who cleared a path through the throng for them.

Their pit was identified now, with Steve's name and number painted on both the pit wall and their fuel tank, installed for the race and emblazoned with the team's name and logo. Around them the other teams were bringing their cars out, completing the same tasks, feeling the same tension.

The minutes were ticking past more quickly now, the excitement building toward that almost unbearable peak as the countdown to the start began in earnest. The steady rumble of the vast crowd made conversation nearly impossible, but those wearing headsets were able to communicate through them as they tested their transmitters and receivers.

With less than an hour to go the track stewards gave the signal, and Steve's car was pushed onto the track and into his inside front-row position in the starting grid. A great shout of approval went up, first from the fans seated on the main straightaway as the scarlet car appeared and then from others around the track as the P.A. announcer reported it. The other thirty-two cars followed quickly, lining up in eleven rows of three. Some drivers were already seated in their cars; others, like Steve, were completing their preparations in the pits before walking onto the track.

He had pulled his balaclava on and was adjusting the fabric over his mouth, his head tipped to one side, listening as Jack fired a volley of last-minute instructions at him, when he glanced up briefly and met Kitty's eyes. His eyes flicked away, but then returned, holding her gaze over Jack's shoulder as they widened and darkened to a smoky gray.

With a curt gesture he cut off Jack's words and moved around him, pushing past a crewman to get to Kitty, who stood watching him in blank surprise. He took her arm, pulling her with him a few steps away from the mechanic she had been advising. Still holding her arm, though lightly, he looked down into her cocoa-colored eyes. He was a stranger, masked in white; only his eyes were recognizable, holding her own with a searching intensity as he spoke.

"Wish me luck, Kitty?" he asked so quietly that she could barely hear him above the din around them.

"Of course." She nodded, puzzled. "Good luck, Steve, and be careful." She smiled and could see his mouth move beneath the fabric of the balaclava in acknowledgment. He released her arm and moved away, but paused after a few steps and turned back, jerking the balaclava down below his mouth as he retraced the distance between them in long strides.

She hadn't seen him turn to her again; she was already moving back toward the crewman when she was seized by the arm and pulled roughly around.

"What in the—" she gasped in astonishment, but further words were smothered by his mouth on hers. This was nothing like the first good-luck kiss they had shared. Uncaring of the thousands of watching eyes he wrapped his arms around her slim form, lifting her onto her toes and bending her backward as he pressed her against him, kissing her with a hot, demanding insistence she was powerless to resist.

Powerless even if she had wanted to resist, for as the passion in the kiss reached her she shivered and melted against him, her hands slipping up to cling to his shoulders as she returned his kiss with ardent intensity. The kiss was long and deep and unashamed, a lovers' kiss, and it left her physically and mentally shaken to the core.

She could only gaze up into his face when he set her on her feet, his hands sliding away from her. She felt the warmth of him slipping away, leaving her chilled in the sultry morning air, and she felt, like a brand, the touch of his fingers as he brushed them lightly across her lips before he turned and left her, and strode onto the track.

The chill was swamped by a hot rush of blood to her cheeks as she came all the way down to earth again, suddenly aware of the avidly curious eyes around her and all too conscious of the speculation Steve's kiss and her obviously enthusiastic response to it would generate. And yet she no more understood his reasons for doing such a thing than the onlookers did. His actions the night before, and now this kiss, made no sense at all unless they were part of some punitive plot so baroque and convoluted that the ultimate resolution of it could not be understood.

There was another explanation, but it was one she was afraid even to consider, for it would be too wonderful if it were true and too horribly painful if it were not and she allowed herself to hope.

"Kitty!" She spun around to see Jack waving her over and was given no more time to consider such absurdly unlikely possibilities, for the final flurry of prerace festivities was leading them to the start of the race.

The events and their sequence were traditional and almost archetypically American. The Purdue University marching band played the national anthem as the university choirmaster sang, an invocation was said in recognition of the Memorial Day holiday and a brass quartet played taps, the haunting notes drifting out over the eerily quiet crowds.

A television celebrity sang "Back Home Again in Indiana," and as he held the last long note some 15,000 multicolored balloons were released to drift into the brilliant blue sky, sent on their way by another thunderous cheer from the crowd.

"It's 10:50 A.M. and the balloons have been released. They're floating overhead now into a beautifully clear race-day sky. The chief steward has given the order for the crews to leave the track. . . ."

Kitty strained to see over the shoulders of the men around her as the crews ran off the track, leaving only one man standing by each car, waiting to start its engine.

". . . and here, to give the traditional command, is the president of the Indianapolis Motor Speedway. . . ."

Hundreds of thousands strained to hear, leaning forward, barely breathing. Kitty felt a shiver of almost unbearable excitement slide over her skin as she held her breath with everyone else. There was a taut pause, and then . . .

"Gentlemen, start your engines!"

The shattering wall of sound created by thirty-three powerful engines overwhelmed even the roar of the huge crowd, and Kitty jumped up and down frantically, looking for the raised hand that would signal to the stewards that Steve's car had been successfully started. It was not unheard of for a car to fail to start, and it was only when she saw Rick straighten, gloved fist in the air, that she breathed a sigh of relief. Rick and the others ran off the track, carrying the heavy external starters; the pace car moved off, and the first row followed.

The field pulled away, the rows a bit irregular, cars weaving from side to side, scuffing the tires to bring them up to racing temperature as they circled the track in the traditional parade lap. Leading the field out of the fourth turn and into the main straightaway, the pace car increased its speed for the pace lap, followed by the racers, who now began attempting to line up in their proper places for the start.

They streamed out of sight around the first turn and Kitty glanced up at the starter's tower, where he held two green flags ready, then turned to watch the head of the main straightaway where the cars would reappear.

". . . the last row is leaving the first turn as the pace car enters the second turn, and I'll pass you over to Bill Carlson on the backstretch."

"Bill Carlson here. The field is entering the backstretch. They're picking up speed—passing us now—the drivers attempting to line up for the start. The pace car is entering turn three, and I'll turn you over to Fred Knight in the short chute."

"Fred Knight here, for the Indianapolis 500 radio network. The field is moving through the chute between turns three and four in good order. The pace car is entering the fourth turn, and I'm turning you over to Paul Payne for the start of the race."

The voices of the radio announcers stationed around the track were becoming higher and more excited in counterpoint to the roar of the crowd and the howl of the engines. Kitty leaned over the pit wall, straining to see as the announcer's voice rose to a crescendo of feverish excitement. Coming through the fourth turn the pace car was traveling at about 130 miles per hour, essentially what a commercially produced automobile was capable of, with the field champing at the bit behind it. Out of that turn the pace car would slip off the inside of the track and into the pits while the field swept down the straightaway to the yard-wide strip of brick that marked the start/ finish line.

"This is Paul Payne, the voice of the 500, to give you the start of the greatest spectacle in racing! The pace car is coming out of the fourth turn as the official starter readies his flags below me. The pace car is entering the pits as the first rows leave the fourth turn—they're moving into the main straight—accelerating—

"The green flag is out! The green flag is out, ladies and gentlemen! The first row has crossed the start/ finish line and the Indianapolis 500 is under way! Ladies and gentlemen, the Indianapolis 500 is under way!"

His words were drowned out by the shriek of engines as the field streamed past down the straightaway. Kitty couldn't be certain, but it looked as though Steve's car led the pack into the turn.

It had begun.

Chapter Twelve

Steve knew he was in the lead when he slid down low on the track to enter the first turn. One good burst of speed as he crossed that strip of brick and he'd left good ol' Joe Taylor in his dust. Beneath his helmet and balaclava his lips curved into a smile as he streaked through the turn, up to the right in the short chute and then back down to the inside and through the second turn, following the "groove," the most efficient path around the oval.

Smooth as silk, he thought, coming up into the backstretch and accelerating past 200 miles per hour. Smooth as silk, but no piece of cake. Joe Taylor had shot out of the turn hot on his heels and was now on his right, doing his best to pass. Steve's grin thinned a little as his peripheral vision picked up the nose of Taylor's white car, and he increased his speed just a bit, enough for him to slip into the groove first, forcing Taylor to follow him into the turn.

He kept his lead and entered the main straight first, leading the pack past the shouting, waving throng and into the first turn again. While Steve completed another lap in first position, others were not so fortunate. At the far end of the backstretch one car was off the track on the grass by the infield fence, apparently with mechanical problems, and as Steve came out of the fourth turn he saw another enter the pits trailing a plume of smoke.

Steve felt sorry for the unfortunates, but not *that* sorry. Attrition due to mechanical problems was a natural part of this race; he only hoped it wouldn't happen to him. Mentally crossing his fingers, he slid into the groove to enter the first turn again.

He managed to keep the lead for the first nine laps, knowing all the while that it couldn't last. In reality, he didn't want to lead throughout the entire race, for though there was a cash prize for each lap a driver led, to maintain that pace would waste fuel, and Steve had no intention of losing the race because he'd exhausted the supply of fuel he was allotted.

Midway through the tenth lap he was challenged again, this time by seasoned veteran Ron Finch, and though Steve tried to prevent it, Finch caught him with a burst of speed and slipped ahead of him into turn three. Steve grinned a bit dryly at the rear of Finch's car. Ron was one hell of a driver, no doubt about it; if the race came down to a duel between the two of them Steve would enjoy every minute of it.

By the time his fuel was running low and his first pit stop was approaching, he had traded first, second and third positions with Finch and a couple of others, and had seen several more cars drop out with mechanical problems. Jack was keeping him posted via the headset on the standing of the cars farther back in the pack, and Steve had a good idea of where everyone was running when he dropped down to the inside of the fourth turn and into the pit lane.

The five-man pit crew was waiting as he rolled up, catching the car and bringing it to a halt while Steve braked and steered into his pit. They worked with a speed and fluidity that were almost balletic, filling the fuel tank, changing the right-side tires—which wore out much more rapidly than the left-side pair—and sending him out again with an "all-clear" thump on the helmet and a push-off—in no more than fifteen seconds.

The pit stops were so brief that Steve barely took his eyes off the pavement ahead of him, just glanced over at Jack, whose mouthed "How's it running?" was drowned out by the noise all around them. Steve gave him a thumbs-up, then looked for Kitty, a few paces to Jack's right. With his helmet on Steve didn't know if she could tell that he was looking at her as he jerked his thumb upward again, but apparently she could, for she smiled and brought the tips of thumb and index finger together in an OK sign.

That was all he could do, for in the next instant someone thumped his helmet. He let out the clutch as they pushed the car and it began to roll forward, and he was back in the race again, less than half a minute after he'd left the track. Moving smoothly up from the acceleration lane into the traffic, he mentally thanked Kitty again for the adjustments she'd made in his steering this year. Last year it had been a bit "loose"; it had oversteered, and he had been unwilling to risk trying to pass in tight spots.

He slipped around one car and tucked himself in behind the next one, "drafting" it, saving his fuel by letting himself be sucked along in its wake, until an opportunity arose to pass again. Thank you, Kitten, from the bottom of my heart, he thought as he swung out and shot past the car he'd drafted, a smile lifting his lips beneath the balaclava. Thank you, Kitten. He'd have to tell her, when the race was over, that her modifications had made the difference.

He'd have to tell her that, and a lot of other things, as well, things that should have been said, talked out, long ago. He left the fourth turn, passed another, slower car and streaked down the main straight past two more before he had to brake for the first turn. Yes, he had a great deal to say to Kitty when this race was over and they were both free of their commitments to Amtex, or the team, or anything else.

He only hoped she'd listen to him and not spit and scratch like the angry kitten she sometimes resembled. He smiled, passing Ron Finch as the other man entered the pits. She'd listen, all right; she'd listen if he had to tie her to a chair first. When he'd said what he had to say they might part and never see each other again, but at least there would be no more confusion and misunderstanding.

With his peripheral vision he caught sight of Mike Watson's blue-and-white car pulling up on his right, and he swore under his breath. Even that fool Watson ought to know better than to pass so near the turn. Steve added just enough speed to edge in front of Watson, but he was forced to enter the turn faster than he liked and came perilously close to the outside wall in the short chute.

As if a switch had been thrown somewhere in his brain all his attention snapped back to the race, thoughts of Kitty shelved for another time. When the race was over he'd think about her, but for now racing was all that mattered.

He was driving well, as well, perhaps, as he had ever driven, and as he pulled into the pits much later for his seventh and, he hoped, final pit stop, he knew intuitively that the race was within his grasp. Something could happen, of course; there was always some unforeseen catastrophe lurking around the corner, waiting to snatch victory away, but barring that Steve knew he had as good a chance as anyone there to take the checkered flag.

The crew knew it, too. It showed in their faces and in the speed and enthusiasm with which they fueled the car and changed the tires. For Steve the fifteen seconds were a respite, his last respite, from the physical strain of the race, which was now making itself felt with a vengeance.

At around the midpoint of the race, lap 100, he had begun to feel the strain his body was under, a strain that would leave him sore and exhausted when the race was over. In some ways this race was more tiring than even Grand Prix, for the centrifugal force generated by all those left turns constantly pulled his body to the right, and the effort required to hold himself steady against it would leave him aching for days. The pit stops were a welcome relief from this strain, a few moments in which to flex neck and shoulders and hands that had grown stiff and cramped.

The stop was a mixed blessing, though, for without the movement of air around him he felt the full impact of the heat. Generated by the huge engine behind him, striking up from the shimmering, melting surface of the track, from tires that would burn an ungloved hand, from the heavy air all around him, heat was his worst enemy. Dressed as he was in multiple layers of closely woven fabric, Steve would have been comfortable in freezing weather; with the temperature of the humid Indiana air hovering around ninety degrees he felt as if he could barely breathe.

Heatstroke wasn't out of the question, and since there wasn't time for him to remove his helmet to drink during the course of the race he did the next best thing, leaning forward as the car was fueled so someone could pour a cupful of cold water down his neck. It almost made up for the loss of air movement, which had given him the sensation, as he slowed to a stop, of driving into an oven. He sighed as the water trickled its coolness down inside his driving suit, then the pneumatic jacks were released and the car thumped back down onto the pavement, someone tapped his helmet and he rolled out to begin lap 176.

He wouldn't stop again, not voluntarily at any rate, until he'd completed 200 laps, all 500 miles of this race. Ron Finch was in the lead again, having gained that position while Steve was in the pits, but he still had one pit stop to make, and when he did, Steve took the lead once again. He was driving hard now, flat out, knowing he had only to maintain his position and the race was his. Ron Finch was now half a lap behind him, and the third-place runner a full lap farther behind. Beneath the sweat-soaked balaclava his lips stretched into a thin smile of competitive pleasure and hard triumph as he drove toward that 500-mile goal.

". . . and this has been a classic duel, ladies and gentlemen! Steve Duncan is less than ten laps away from the checkered flag and driving a magnificent race! Running second is car number 43, driven by Ron Finch, and one lap back in third is . . ."

The crew was nearly hysterical, counting down the laps as Steve streaked past toward the 200-lap completion of the race. Their work was finished; he would not make another pit stop, and his victory was almost assured. Only a catastrophe of unexpected and monumental proportions could prevent it now.

He appeared in the fourth turn and shot down the main straight again, and Kitty jumped up and down with the rest of them, shrieking, "One ninety-five!" as he passed. They watched him disappear into the first turn, and Kitty was stepping back, turning to pick up the clipboard she had dropped, when beside her a crewman, Jimmy Miller, gasped, "My God!"

Startled, she followed his gaze to the starter's tower where the yellow caution flags were being vigorously twirled. She glanced to the left, down the track, and saw that the caution lights, set at intervals around the track, had come on. There had been an accident; somewhere on the track there had been an accident, and she hoped, prayed, that it wasn't . . .

Steve saw it happening in front of him with that queer, slow-motion sort of vision the brain clicks into as disaster strikes. He had followed a pack of cars, five or six of them, into the first turn, and ahead of him he saw Watson's blue-and-white car trying to pass on the inside. It was an insanely risky thing to do, and Watson couldn't pull it off.

Just out of the turn Watson's wheel tapped Joe Taylor, and like marbles in a children's game the two cars veered sharply away from each other, Watson losing control and spinning down onto the infield grass as Taylor slid up to meet the outside wall with sickening force. Somehow he kept his car from spinning completely out of control, but he was helpless to prevent it from ricocheting off the wall and down the gently banked track into the oncoming cars.

Steve was swearing in a steady and entirely unconscious undertone as he watched them all, Taylor and
Rissoli and somebody else, Dan Hall, he thought it
was, come down the slope of the banked track toward
him like an avalanche. He tried to drive around them
all, low on the inside, but it was a futile effort; he
knew that even as the air around him was filled with
the shriek of twisting metal and the acrid smell of
burnt rubber.

The first impact was sharp, and he grunted as he
was thrown sideways, banging his ribs painfully. For
an instant he thought that might be the end of it, but
another car was sliding toward him, out of control,
and he watched with a sort of macabre resignation as
it struck his front end and lifted, one tire coming at his
head. He wrenched at the steering wheel, but he was
too tightly locked with the other cars to swerve away.

The tire swung toward him; he bent his head to the
steering wheel and felt a heavy impact followed by an
instant of searing pain and then nothing at all.

Opposite Kitty the crowd was on its feet, looking
toward the first turn, and she knew, somehow she
knew, what had happened. Steve had followed a pack
of other cars into that turn and something, somehow,
had gone horribly wrong.

"The yellow flag is out! The yellow flag is out!
There has been an accident coming out of turn one."
The P.A. speaker blared overhead as they waited
tensely for their hopes or fears to be confirmed.
". . . involved in the crash were . . . Watson . . .
Rissoli, Taylor . . ." The speaker crackled with static,
and Kitty held her breath, straining to hear.
". . . Hall and the leader, Steve Duncan. The race
will be finished under the yellow, and . . ."

Kitty turned blindly as a melee erupted around her, snatching the headset from her head and shoving it and her other equipment into Jack's hands. He shouted something at her, a command or a warning, but her brain didn't register the words as she pushed past him. There was only one thing that was important, and that was to reach Steve. The horrific visions of him lying unconscious in the mangled wreck of his car with those deadly, invisible, alcohol flames licking around him—the appalling images she had kept at bay all month could no longer be denied.

He might be hurt, he might need her, he might be . . . Her mind swerved away from the unthinkable. He might need her, and if he did she must be there.

For the first time she cursed her smallness as she fought her way frantically through the crowd, now streaming toward the pit area and Victory Lane, where the winner would be received and congratulated. It might have been Steve, but that was no longer important; the race and its winner no longer mattered in any way except that she had to struggle against this overwhelming tide of people.

If she were taller or stronger she could have seen over their shoulders, pushed her way through them, but as if in a nightmare come to life she was buffeted by the throng, her progress agonizingly slow, so that she was sobbing in frustration by the time she reached the open infield where she could run, dodging through the groups of spectators. The hospital wasn't close to the pits, it was a long distance to run, and she neared it sobbing and gasping for breath as two ambulances drew up to the rear entrance.

She ran along the fence toward the gate, looking over her shoulder as she ran to see who was in those ambulances. One man was lifted out on a stretcher; he was dark-haired, and she didn't recognize him. Then the other ambulance's doors swung open, and as the stretcher was rolled out she could see that the man lying on it was Steve.

"Steve!" she cried, then louder, "*Ste*—" Her shout was cut off abruptly as she tripped over a discarded blanket and fell headlong on the grass, the breath knocked out of her. She could only lie there for a moment, unable to breathe or even move, and when she struggled to her feet, assisted by a young couple who had seen her fall, Steve was being carried to the door.

"Miss, are you OK?" She heard the concerned question and nodded reassurance as she leaned against the chain-link fence, fighting for breath. They were waiting to carry Steve inside, and he was conscious; she could see him turn his head in response to something the attendant said to him and then turn back as someone shouted from the crowd at the gate.

Kitty followed his gaze and watched Irina run out of the crowd and across to the stretcher, bending her bright head to Steve's and then walking beside him into the hospital, holding his hand in hers. Numb, Kitty watched the door swing closed behind them, shutting them in, shutting her out.

"Miss?" the young man repeated, staring anxiously at her white, set face streaked with tears and dust. "Miss, are you all right?"

"What?" She blinked at him, then nodded jerkily. "Oh, yes. Yes, I'm all right. Thank you." She persuaded them that she was unhurt, that she needed no more help, and they walked slowly away, glancing back worriedly at her, a small, slight figure in a shiny scarlet jumpsuit.

She stood there at a loss, her reason for being at the hospital shown to be a hopeless fantasy, her job in the pits and at the garage at an end. There was no longer any reason at all for her to be at the Speedway. She turned away from the fence and began to trudge wearily along the service road, joining the fans streaming toward the exits. Moving with the crowd, she walked down through the tunnel and out the gates onto 16th Street and then hesitated, staring blankly around her.

It was odd that she hadn't noticed it before, but the predicted storm had apparently been building for some time and was now a mass of threatening black clouds moving rapidly out of the southwest. She shrugged; it didn't matter now, for behind her she could hear the P.A. announcer congratulating the winner. It was over now, everything was over, and Kitty herself had nowhere to go but home.

She began walking slowly along the street, unconcerned that home was miles away. It didn't matter how far it was or how long it took her to walk; there was no one waiting for her, after all.

She had been walking for more than half an hour when the first raindrops fell, hitting the sidewalk around her with loud plops, merging quickly into a steady, driving rain. She trudged on, uncaring that she was quickly soaked to the skin, her hair streaming in black ribbons across her face. Only the first flashes of lightning penetrated her wall of apathy.

She glanced up, squinting against the rain to watch as rolling black clouds were split by another jagged fork of lightning. Flinching at the sudden glare, she quickened her pace, wrinkling her nose at the metallic scent of ozone left in the air. A crack of thunder followed close on the lightning flash, and she sprinted

the last few strides to a bus shelter on the corner,
huddling back into its depths, grateful for even this
marginal protection from the storm's fury.

Kitty got off the bus at the stop nearest her house,
but she still had to cover several more blocks on foot
and was drenched and shivering again by the time she
turned her key in the lock and let herself in. Ignoring
the water streaming from her, she plodded to the
bathroom and opened the hot tap to its fullest,
sending a scalding torrent into the tub as she stripped
off her soaked and clinging clothes. She slid into the
steaming water, wincing as it tingled her chilled body
back to life, and lay back in the tub, staring at the
ceiling, her eyes dull and empty. Warm again, with
her hair washed and combed out, she wrapped herself
in a long, deep green, terry velour robe and spread
her clothes on the rod, moving mechanically, refusing
to think beyond these small tasks.

In the kitchen she put a kettle on to boil and
assembled coffeepot and filter, then stood at the
window, staring out at the wind-lashed trees until the
shrill whistle of the boiling teakettle called her back to
the stove. She placed the coffeepot and a mug on a
tray and turned toward the living room, only to set the
tray back on the kitchen table with an irritated bang as
her doorbell rang.

She had no idea who might be at her door, unless,
of course, it was Shelley, anxious to hear about the
race and the accident, and she hesitated in the kitchen
doorway, loath to see anyone. The bell rang again,
two short, angry jabs followed by a long peal, and she
moved forward with a sigh of resignation. The
deadbolt on the door was tight, the wood swollen with
dampness, and she had to lean her weight against the
door and pull with both hands to work the bolt free;
she muttered irritably as the metal squeaked in pro-

test. She gave it a last vicious jerk and it popped open unexpectedly, pinching her finger against the wood.

"Damn," she muttered and sucked her fingertip as she turned the knob, admitting a gust of wind and rain that caught her full in the face. Temporarily blinded, she blinked and dropped her head to wipe her eyes, then looked up again and froze, staring in shock at the man who stood facing her.

Chapter Thirteen

"What are you doing here?" she asked him curtly.

"Can I come in out of the rain before I tell you?" Steve replied, and after a moment of hesitation she stepped back, allowing him to follow her into the room. He turned to close the door on the storm, then stood on the small cotton rug by the door, water streaming off him, and met her hostile eyes calmly.

When she said nothing, didn't invite him to come farther in or sit down or have a drink, he asked tiredly, almost with a sigh, "Can I have a towel?" He looked down at himself and grimaced. "I'm kind of wet."

That was an understatement of heroic proportions. Kitty had no idea how long he'd been out in the rain, but he was absolutely drenched, his shirt and jeans clinging wetly to him, and she knew she couldn't let him just stand there and develop pneumonia. Silently she turned and walked quickly from the room, returning moments later with two thick bath sheets. He had slipped off his tennis shoes and his socks and was unbuttoning his shirt when she reappeared. Ignoring the breadth of bronze chest confronting her, she took the shirt from his hand when he had peeled it off and gathered up the shoes and socks.

"You might as well come in the kitchen," she said grudgingly. "You'll freeze to death out here." He followed her into the kitchen and took the chair she indicated, watching silently as she lit the oven and opened it, placing a chair in front of the open door and spreading his wet things out to dry in the heat.

With his eyes following her Kitty was suddenly acutely conscious of her nakedness beneath the soft fabric of her robe, and while her back was to him she surreptitiously tightened the belt. She could go and change, she thought, but that would be an admission that he made her uneasy, and she wouldn't give him that satisfaction.

Her mouth set stubbornly, she turned away from the stove, allowing her eyes to slide indifferently over Steve as she crossed the room to open a cupboard and take down another mug. She wouldn't let him see it—she would die rather than let him see it—but she was acutely aware of him seated at the table, toweling his chest and arms, his size making the room seem small. Deliberately ignoring the hand he extended, she banged the mug down beside the coffeepot, then reached for a different cupboard door. With her hand on it she hesitated, glancing back at Steve, who was pouring coffee. Her lips tightened, and she jerked it open, took out a bottle of brandy and set that on the table as well.

Steve raised an eyebrow at it but added a splash to

his coffee. He set the bottle on the table and reached for the cap to close it, but Kitty brushed his hand away, lifted the bottle and added a liberal measure to her own coffee. She capped the bottle herself and looked up to see a strange expression on Steve's face as though, like her, he was looking back in time. She held his gaze defiantly for a moment, then lifted her mug and drank deeply of her coffee, welcoming the warming effect of the brandy, which thawed the frozen numbness that gripped her.

She raised her eyes from her cup and studied him for a moment. "What happened in that accident?" she asked, breaking the lengthening silence.

He looked across the table at her, his eyes dark and impossible to read, but he took her question literally. "It was Watson again," he told her and shook his head ruefully. "He was in the middle of a pack of five or six cars, trying to pass on the inside, and he tapped Joe Taylor just out of turn one. Joe lost it and slid up to the outside wall, then hit Rissoli and Hall on the way back down. I tried to get around them on the inside, but Rissoli and Hall and somebody else all came down on me at once." He shrugged.

"Considering how many cars were involved, it's amazing it wasn't worse." He lifted one shoulder in an offhand shrug and winced, then raised his cup again. Kitty could only stare at him for a moment, the horror of what might have happened brought vividly to life by his laconic words.

"I—I thought you were hurt," she said in a shaky voice, and he shook his head.

"Nothing to worry about, just bruised ribs and a bump on the head." Her eyes went to his lean rib cage, and she could see the large, dark blotch on his right side. It looked painful, and he had winced when he shrugged; she seemed to feel his pain as her own

for an instant and wished fervently that she could ease
it somehow. He had followed her eyes and nodded as
she met his gaze again. "Nothing to worry about," he
repeated.

"But you were on a stretcher—"

His eyes narrowed at her, sharp and penetrating.
"They put me on it when they took me out of the car,"
he said, watching her closely.

"They took you out?" she whispered, unable to
conceal her reaction to his words. "Were you . . . ?"

"Knocked out?" He finished the question for her.
"Yes. Somebody's tire hit my helmet. Left a nice skid
mark on it and put me out, but not for long." He took
another sip of his coffee, watching Kitty's pale,
shocked face.

"How did you know I was on a stretcher?" he asked
very gently.

"What?" Her head came up in surprise, and she
realized that even if she hadn't given herself away
before, she had done so with that unguarded reaction.
"I . . . I was passing . . . just passing the hospital and
I . . . and they were taking you in . . . on a stretcher."

"Just passing by?" he said, still in that soft, gentle
voice.

"On my way home." She dropped her gaze to her
cup and kept it there.

"Why didn't you come in? I could have used the
moral support."

"You didn't need me; you already had moral support," she muttered.

"What are you talking about?"

Kitty's head came up with a jerk. "Oh, don't play
stupid, Steve!" she snapped, anger bubbling up to
swamp any other emotion. "You had Irina; you didn't
need me or anyone else!"

"How the hell would you know, when you didn't bother to come in and see?" he snarled.

"I didn't *need* to come in! I saw her walk inside holding your hand. And a very touching little scene it was, too."

"I'm glad you appreciated it," he said dryly. "But she was there to see Rissoli, not me."

Kitty had risen and crossed the room as he spoke, and now she froze, gripping the countertop.

"What . . . what did you say?" she asked softly, her face turned away from him.

"I said she was there to see Rissoli, not me," he growled, his voice low and husky with anger. "She's crazy about him. She's been eating her heart out for him for ages, not that I can understand why."

"You wouldn't," Kitty muttered, choking on a bubble of half-hysterical laughter. So Irina was in love with Marco after all, and he had found a way to tell her that he loved her, that he had changed. How wonderful for him; how wonderful for them both! She bowed her head, eyes closed, in a moment of happiness for Marco and poignant longing to know that kind of happiness herself.

"For God's sake!" Steve exploded behind her, seizing her arm and spinning her around to face him. "You didn't think he loved *you*, did you?" He glared down into her face, apparently mistaking the emotion he saw there for hurt at the knowledge that Marco loved Irina.

"I don't know what kind of life you lead," he said disgustedly, "but surely, if you had to have a man, you could have picked someone other than that Italian gigolo!"

Kitty's cheeks flamed at the insult, and she tried to jerk free of his hands. "He is *not* a gigolo," she snapped, unable to free herself from a grip that would leave bruises on her arms tomorrow. "And what would you suggest, anyway—if I *need* a man?" she asked with biting sarcasm. "That I call *you?* Well, let me tell you, Steve Duncan, you'd be the *last*—"

Her angry words were smothered beneath his lips as he jerked her against him, kissing her with furious savagery. There was no giving in that kiss, only anger and taking and punishment, and Kitty struggled to free herself, twisting within the iron band of his arms, pushing at his shoulders. She tried to turn her face away, but he caught her hair in his hand and forced her head back until she whimpered in pain beneath the assault of his mouth.

Her hands, pushing at his shoulders, slid ineffectually over his smooth, golden skin, and her twisting and wriggling only loosened her robe until she realized with a stab of panic that if she moved any more it would fall open. Defeated, she stopped struggling, went limp and still in his arms, slow tears sliding down her cheeks.

Perhaps he felt their wetness against his face, perhaps he simply tired of punishing her, but he released her and she stumbled away, supporting herself against the countertop as she fumbled her robe closed. When she turned to face him she was trembling with emotion and her voice was husky and shaking.

"Why are you doing this?" she cried through her tears. "Why? Haven't you punished me enough?" Her voice broke, and she covered her face with her hands. There was a shocked pause.

"Is that—" He touched her arm lightly and she flinched away. "Is that what you think I'm doing? Punishing you?" She lowered her hands from her face and looked up at him, distraught.

"Well, what else could it be? That's what you said

you were doing—making me pay for what I did. You never thought I might have paid for it over those seven years and maybe, in a way, you were right. I know that what I did was wrong, and I know you have a right to be angry, but how long must it go on?"

She shook her head as if to clear it and went on more quietly, wearily, "Go away. Can't you please just go away? I know you hate me, but haven't you done enough? Can't you just leave me alone?" She turned her back to him and bent her head to hide the tears that filled her eyes again.

"I can't leave you alone," he said very softly, and she shook her head in a quick negative, wanting the hurt to end. "I don't hate you, Kitten." He took her shoulders and turned her around to face him, taking her chin between thumb and fingers to tip her face up to his, and gently wiping the tears from her cheeks.

"Don't you know I'm in love with you, Kitten? I've loved you for years."

"No," she whispered in disbelief, and he nodded, his face grimly sober.

"Yes. I've loved you, and wanted you, since you were sixteen."

"But the things you said . . . the things you did. . . . You hated me . . . it was obvious."

"Isn't hate the dark side of love? There have been moments when I've been so insanely jealous that I hated you, but if I didn't love you I wouldn't have cared enough to be jealous."

"But you *didn't* care!" she cried angrily. "You left that night, and you know how angry you were with me. You never wrote or called or anything at all for seven years!"

"There was a reason for that," he said slowly, watching her face with a curious expression in his eyes. "John never told you any of it, did he?"

"Never told me any of what?" She frowned in confusion.

"He never told you about the agreement we made?"

"What agree—" She stopped herself and shook her head. "He never said anything about an agreement."

Steve was looking into her eyes with an almost hypnotic intensity, looking into her soul. "I promised John that I wouldn't contact you by letter, by telephone or in any way until you had graduated from college."

She stared at him in mounting astonishment. "You promised—" she whispered. "Then it wasn't . . . wasn't because you . . . were disgusted with me? With what I did?"

"Oh, Kitten." The name was an agonized groan as he pulled her, willingly this time, into his arms, kissing her with a starving intensity that shook her to the core. Eagerly she returned the kiss, her hands moving feverishly over his shoulders, his chest, delighting in the touch of him, the smooth, warm skin, the play of muscle as he braced himself against the counter and drew her between his thighs, lifting her slight weight against him until she was drawn onto her toes, her body arched against the strong curve of his.

Again and again he kissed her, quick, light kisses on her brow, her eyelids, her cheekbones, long, deep kisses to which her yielding lips parted willingly as he savored the sweetness of her mouth, and hot, tormenting kisses that fell on her neck, her shoulder and the curve of her breast as she shuddered with feverish pleasure. She tried to give back the delight he gave her, winding her arms around his waist and running her hands over the shifting muscles of his back, then slipping them around to slide up his chest, tangling in the thick, golden hair, glorying in the warmth and strength of him and in her power to inflame. She trailed her mouth along his shoulder, tasting the saltiness on his skin, feeling, rather than hearing, the deep growling sound he made in his throat as he lifted her face to his kiss.

When he tore his lips from hers and pressed her face into his shoulder she could feel the dampness of his skin, hear the heavy thud of his heartbeat and his ragged breathing.

"Steve?" she whispered, "What . . . ?"

"Shhh." He stroked a hand over her hair, massaged her neck for a few moments. Gradually their heartbeats slowed; gradually they breathed more easily.

"I want—" His voice was so husky she could hardly understand him. "I want, more than anything in the world, to make love to you." He brushed a strand of hair off her forehead with fingers that trembled ever so slightly. "But there are some things which have to be said first." Gently he steered her to the table and pushed her into a chair, seating himself across from her and pouring more coffee for them both.

The storm was bringing an early dusk with it, and he switched on the lamp above the table, then added a splash of brandy to each cup. Kitty waited, abstractedly wondering what he had to say, but too bemused by love to really care. Some of her warm glow began to dissipate when he hesitated uneasily, staring into his cup, and then drank deeply of the brandy-fortified coffee as though he needed it.

"Steve?" she whispered, suddenly frightened. "Is something wrong?"

"What?" He looked across at her, his eyes somber, then shook his head. "No, nothing's wrong. It's just . . . this isn't an easy story to tell. I'm not sure where to start."

"At the beginning?" she suggested in a weak attempt at humor, and he smiled wryly.

"Why not?" He shrugged. "The beginning of this story is the end of the one you already know. I was so disgusted and angry—no, furious—at myself for what I'd done that night that I took it out on you. I don't know if you can understand how I felt, knowing that I hadn't been able to keep away from you even though I was older and should have had more control, but I . . . I loathed myself for what I'd done to you.

"There was no excuse for what I'd done, just as there was no excuse for the things I said to you afterward."

"But, Steve, it was *my* fault!" she interrupted him in distress, unable to bear the pain in his eyes as he spoke.

"No." He shook his head. "I could see what you were doing, testing your wings as a woman, and I was old enough to know better, but you were so beautiful—"

Kitty felt her cheeks grow warm under his gaze and reached out to slip her hand into his, curling her fingers around his as his thumb gently caressed her palm.

"You were so beautiful," he repeated huskily, "that I let my better judgment go out the window and afterward took my own self-contempt out on you. When you ran out of the kitchen, I think I knew what was going to happen. I stayed where I was, pouring bourbon down my throat, and in a few minutes John slammed in, growled, 'You filthy bastard,' at me and broke my nose."

Kitty gasped and Steve's fingers tightened around hers as he continued. "He kept punching me, and I didn't hit back; I just tried to keep him from hitting

my face again and waited for the rage in him to spend
itself." He looked somberly into his cup. "I could
understand. . . I *can* understand how he felt, bitter,
angry, betrayed by both of us. I had no right to hit him
back, and when he finally stopped he just stood in the
middle of the kitchen, looking at me with eyes so full
of pain that it hurt to see them, and asked me why.
And I had to tell him.

"I had no excuse, and I told him that, told him I
knew it was wrong, but that I loved you."

"You loved—" Kitty gasped, and Steve's mouth
twisted.

"Oh, yes; I told you I've loved you for years." He
lifted her hand to his lips, pressing a kiss into her
palm, and Kitty could only gaze at him with her heart
in her eyes. "Anyway, I told John that I loved you,
and he was about as surprised as you, only it made
him furious all over again. He told me not to try to put
anything over on him." Steve paused for a long
moment, gazing soberly into her eyes. "I told him it
was true that I loved you and that I wanted to marry
you."

Kitty gaped at him, shaking her head slowly from
side to side. "Steve, I . . . I never knew," she whispered, stunned. "No one ever told me."

"You weren't supposed to know, Kitty. John was
surprised; no, he was thunderstruck. When he believed me, he said what I already knew, that you were
too young to be tied to a husband. I had to ask him,
what if you were pregnant? And he went for me
again." Steve shook his head. "He wanted to hurt me.
He wanted so much to tear me apart for what I'd done
to you that it nearly killed him to leave me in one
piece. As it was, I was trying to talk calmly to a man
who wanted to smash me, who had already broken my

nose. It wasn't easy; I was trying to reason with him, all the time holding a towel on my nose, which was bleeding all over the place.

"When he got a grip on himself, he said that if you were pregnant—he could barely get the word out—if you were, he'd get in touch with me. In the end we agreed, or rather John gave me no choice but to agree, that I would have no contact with you, in any way, until you were out of college. You deserved a chance to grow up, to finish your education, before you were tied to another person. Only if you were pregnant would John get in touch with me, and I would marry you.

"I kept in touch with John over the last seven years, and he gave me a few details of your life, though he wouldn't give me a picture of you, or tell me much more than 'Kitty went to the prom with so-and-so' or 'Kitty is dating so-and-so.' He knew how crazy that made me, and I know he did it deliberately, to punish me. It worked." He met her gaze, and she could see the remembered anguish in his eyes, in the lines cut deeply around his mouth.

"John and I kept in touch through the mail, but we were no longer friends. There was too much anger and hurt that hadn't died away.

"I had a couple of long talks with my mother while I was in Florida last week, and she seemed to understand, without my ever spelling it out, what was going on. Before I left Florida I called John in New York to see if he could come to Indianapolis for the race this year. I had some tickets, and I wanted to see him again, to clear the air."

Kitty shook her head in slowly dawning comprehension. "So that's why they didn't let me know they were coming." She frowned. "On Friday night . . . I in-

vited them all to dinner, but they had 'plans' that they
were kind of cagey about. Were they—"

"With me? Yes. John and I talked for a long time
about you and me and the way things had been this
month. I wasn't going to do anything about it until the
race was over, but last night I couldn't face that hotel
room and I couldn't face dinner in a restaurant with
reporters and autograph hunters. I was going to stay
away from you, but somehow I found myself on your
porch, begging for a meal. It was a fantastic meal, by
the way." He grinned.

"Thank you." She grinned back, then sobered.
"What I couldn't understand was why you kissed me
and . . . and everything, and then left. I thought you
were punishing me again."

"Oh, no, Kitten; don't think that. I had to go
because I knew if I didn't I'd carry you back to your
bedroom and make the same mistake I made seven
years ago."

She breathed something, maybe his name, but he
shook his head and went on.

"I don't know if you thought of me in all that time,
Kitten, but I couldn't get you out of my mind for very
long, no matter how I tried. I'd manage to forget you
for a day or two, and then a letter would come from
John, or I'd see a girl with hair like black satin, or eyes
the color of chocolate-brown velvet, and I'd be lost
again. I was crazy with jealousy, picturing you growing up, meeting men, dating them, learning about
love from someone else, and all the time knowing I
had no right to feel that way, no claim on you at all.

"In order to stay sane I had to persuade myself that
I didn't care about you, that the only reason I
remembered you at all was because John kept sending
me those damned, torturing letters, but I was lying to
myself. I've been lying to myself this month, too,

telling myself you mean nothing to me, even though every time I'm near you all I want is to make love to you." He smiled wryly. "It was my mother again, who seems to know a lot more about me than I do about myself, who said a few things which made me see and understand my own feelings and the way in which my jealousy had made me bitter and angry toward you."

Kitty gazed at him in amazed wonder, and he made a small grimace. "Don't look at me like that, Kitten; I don't deserve it. I took something from you seven years ago that I had no right to, and this last month I've let my jealousy rule me, treated you unforgivably. Just seeing you with Rissoli was making me crazy; I wanted to tear him apart."

He paused, then said, "Kitty?" She met his gaze with a query in her eyes. "I have no claim to your life these last seven years. The boys . . . the men you've known are no business of mine, and I'll never ask about them."

"Oh, Steve," she said gently, a small, sad smile lifting the corners of her mouth, "shall I tell you about the last seven years?"

"No!" he said harshly. "I don't want to know. I don't think I could stand knowing—"

She reached over and laid her fingers lightly against his lips, silencing him. "I want to tell you. You say you took something from me, but that's not true. You took something I gave you, something you never would have taken if I hadn't thrown myself at you. And you gave me so much more. .

"I loved you, Steve, as deeply as a woman loves a man, but I was too young to know how to handle it. I was shocked and hurt by your reaction, and John's, that night, but most of all by my own guilt. I learned a very important lesson that night; I learned that you can't just take what you want, that you can't compromise someone else's integrity without damaging your own. I tried to forget you, too, Steve."

"Is that what you were doing with Rissoli?" he asked, his voice rough-edged with pain. "Trying to *forget*? And why did it have to be with *him?*"

"Steve, stop it!" Kitty reached a pleading hand toward him, knowing that somehow she had to make him understand. "Marco is a *friend*, Steve, nothing more."

"Him?" His face was angry, his earlier resolve to ignore the men in her life completely forgotten. "I know what he's like, Kitty."

"No, you don't! Steve, he *loves* Irina. Oh, I know about the groupies and what happened between them; it changed him, it made him realize that he loved her. He doesn't love me, nor I him. We're friends, that's *all*." She met his level gaze with her own for a long moment. "Like you and Irina are. . . ."

He shrugged, aware that her statement had been in part a question. "I knew, I've always known, that she loved Rissoli, but he hurt her badly, and she needed a friend."

Kitty nodded. "I tried to forget you, Steve, but not that way. After all, it appeared that you had forgotten me. I pushed the memories down deep inside me and built a wall around them, but the wall also closed in my emotions. You don't need to be jealous, Steve. I didn't really understand it until I saw you again, but I could never let any other man get close to me because you were always there, in my heart, and there was no room for anyone else.

"I thought I was just protecting myself, but when I saw you again it hit me like—like an earthquake or something. I never reacted to anyone else, but you could make me tremble with just a look. I was fooling myself thinking that I'd gotten over you, and just the sight of you showed me how wrong I'd been." Her eyes were glowing as she gazed deep into his. "And now you tell me that you hadn't abandoned me, that you wanted to marry me."

"Still want to marry you," he corrected softly, drawing her around the table to stand between his knees, holding her there with his hands lightly on her waist. "If you want me, that is."

Kitty laid her hands along his face, brushing her fingertips through his thick, wheat-colored hair, her thumbs caressing his lean cheeks. "Oh, yes," she whispered. "I want you."

Slowly, very slowly, she bent to place her lips on his, kissing him softly; she was the one in control, moving her mouth on his, gently teasing until he could stand it no longer. His hands suddenly moved around her to crush her to him, and his lips took over the kiss, plundering her willing mouth.

She was shifted onto his lap, cradled against his chest, her hands moving restlessly over his skin, reveling in the warm, hard strength of him as she caressed the heavy planes of muscle and brushed her palms over the thick, golden hair. He shuddered beneath her touch, and his hand moved to push the robe off her shoulder and slip inside, caressing her throat, her shoulders, and moving lower to cup one small, round breast in his palm, teasing the nipple with his thumb. She shivered with pleasure, arching her body, moving sinuously against him as he caressed her ribs and waist, the curves of hip and thigh.

Her robe fell completely open, a deep green backdrop against which her body seemed to glow golden when he looked down at her in his lap, his eyes heavy-lidded and smoldering at the sight of her. He drew a rasping breath and bent slowly to press his lips to her throat, kissing the pulse that beat frantically there, then the hollow beneath her ear. Her head fell back as he took her earlobe in his teeth, tugging gently, then traced a path down to her shoulder, kissing and tasting, and lower still, as her breath came in shallow gasps and her slim body moved in instinctive invitation until he took her breasts, his mouth a sweet torment, fanning the fire he had lit within her.

She clung to him fiercely, whimpering in protest when he raised his head, slipping her hand around his neck to pull his lips down to her again. He resisted her, and her lids fluttered up.

"Steve?" she murmured uncertainly, and he shook his head, his mouth tight with strain, his eyes closed. Suddenly afraid, she touched his cheek. "Steve," she repeated, "is something wrong?"

He opened his eyes, hot flames in their depths as he gazed down at her. Carefully he folded her robe around her, then pulled her close again, nestled against his shoulder, his arms wrapped around her.

"What are you going to do, now that your job with Jack is finished?" he asked huskily. Kitty straightened within the curve of his arm and stared at him in surprise, startled by the change of subject.

"Well, I don't really know. Look for another job, I guess. Why?"

"Would you like a permanent job with a racing team, designing both Formula One and championship cars?"

"Of course, who wouldn't? But who—"

"You'd have to live in Europe most of the year and travel a great deal. Would you mind that?"

"No, I don't think so, but what job is this? Who would I be working for?"

"Me."

"You! Do you mean as a driver you'd be hiring—"

"No, as head of my racing team I'd be hiring you."

She stared at him for a long moment, then burst out laughing at the gleam of amusement in his eyes. "OK, tell me all about it, so I don't have to ask any more dumb questions."

"You never ask dumb questions." He bent to kiss her quickly, drawing back before she could respond. "I'm forming my own racing team. I already have a sponsor and two drivers, and we're preparing for next season's racing in Europe. No one knows it yet, but I'm retiring from driving. Today was my last race. After all," he teased, "I'll have to behave like a serious family man from now on, won't I?"

"But, Steve, I don't want you to give up racing on my account. You love it!" she protested, and he shook his head.

"I loved it," he corrected her. "I'm older than I was, and maybe a little wiser, and it's time for me to move on to something new, something that's more of a challenge. And I want you working with me."

"I want that, too," Kitty breathed.

For long seconds she gazed into his eyes, watching them widen and darken to a smoky gray. "I want that very much," she whispered and began sliding her hands up to link them behind his neck, turning her body so that her breasts pressed against his chest, only the soft fabric of her robe separating them. The skirt of her robe slid away as she turned, baring one slim, shapely leg, and Steve glanced down at her and groaned deeply in his throat.

"How soon can we be married?" Kitty asked softly, nibbling the angle of his jaw. "Tomorrow?" She traced the tip of her tongue around to his ear and nipped lightly at the lobe.

"No-o-o." The word was a groan. "Tomorrow's a holiday, remember?" He tried to evade her lips, which were nibbling delicately at the smooth, brown

skin of his shoulder, tried to turn her on his lap, but
his hand met the silken curve of her bare thigh and,
almost against his will, slid along it, then up to her
waist.

"Kitty, stop it," he groaned. "You don't know what
you're doing to me!"

"Mmm, yes I do," she murmured.

Her breath was light and warm on his face as she
nibbled his lower lip; he could feel her breasts straining against the supple fabric of her robe as her arms
tightened about his neck, and his hand moved involuntarily over the satin skin of her hip.

"If you know what you're doing," he muttered into
her hair, "then stop it."

"Hm-mm." She breathed the negative against his
skin, her lips exploring him, the robe falling off her
shoulder as she moved, clinging to the swell of her
breast.

"Kitty, no!" He lifted her chin so that he could see
her love-drugged face, his own strained with the effort
his control cost him. "We'll be married in three or
four days," he said with a sort of desperation. "We
can wait that long." Overhead the thunder rumbled
again, but neither of them paid it any mind.

Kitty smiled wickedly. "Maybe I don't want to
wait," she whispered, moistening her lips with a flick
of her tongue. Steve's eyes followed the gesture
helplessly.

"I've loved you for so long," he said, serious again.
"And I've waited for you for so long that I can wait a
little longer, until the time is right, to make love to
you again."

"Oh, Steve," she breathed, no longer teasing, "I've
waited all my life for you, and I didn't even know it.
And now you're here. . . ."

Their lips met and clung in a kiss of infinite tenderness; deep and timeless, it might have gone on forever but for a sudden brilliant flash of lightning overhead. Startled, they jerked apart, and the flash was followed immediately by a sharp crack of thunder and another lightning flash, whereupon the kitchen light blinked, brightened and then went out.

"Just a minute," Kitty said calmly and slid off Steve's lap, pulling her robe around her as she crossed the kitchen, sure-footed in the darkness. A hurricane lamp sat on the shelf above the sink, a book of matches beside it. She lifted it down, removed the chimney with a soft clink and touched a match to the wick. The small flame flickered, then grew and steadied, softly illuminating the room with its warm glow. She replaced the chimney and set the lamp on the table, then turned with a haunting sense of *déjà vu* to lift the curtain aside and peer out the window.

"Is it just us," Steve asked softly, "or did the whole neighborhood go?"

"The whole street, anyway." Kitty let the curtain fall back into place, turning to face him across the lamp flame. "It looks like we'll be in the dark for a while."

"That's OK."

The silence thickened around them, broken only by a hiss as the lamp flame danced. She raised her eyes to his and held them while tension grew between them like a thread pulling them toward each other. His skin gleamed bronze in the soft lamplight, the strong planes of his face thrown into sharp relief by light and shadow. In the dim light the two Steves, the Steve she had known seven years ago and the Steve she had been reunited with this month, merged together.

He was not two men, as she had thought; he was still the man she loved, older, presumably wiser, as was Kitty herself, but the same man. Her eyes were wide and shining with the love she felt for him, and he saw it and recognized it. His face changed as he gazed back at her, a flame of hunger in his eyes, and as she stood there she came to a decision.

She moved to the center of the kitchen, facing Steve, and her hands went to the sash of her robe. Steve came to his feet, saying something short under his breath, but he stopped a pace away to stand rigid before her, arms held stiffly at his sides.

The lamplight shimmered over her hair, glistened on her lower lip as she moistened it with the tip of her tongue, and Steve watched her with hungry eyes as she slowly untied her sash. As the ends dropped to her sides the lapels of the robe fell open, and Kitty slowly raised her crossed hands to ease it off her shoulders. She lowered her hands and with a soft swish the robe slipped to the floor.

Steve's breath caught audibly in his throat, but he held himself immobile, his eyes burning into hers.

"I think," she whispered, "that the time is right."

"Are . . . you sure?" His voice was thick in his throat. "Are you very sure?"

"More sure," she whispered, "than I have ever been of anything in my life." He still did not move, and she reached out with one hand to lightly touch his cheek. "Love me, Steve. I want you to love me."

His indrawn breath whistled between his teeth, and with a sudden fierce passion he caught her in his arms and swung her up against his shoulder to stride along the dark hallway to her bedroom.

Gently he laid her on her wide bed, gazing down at her as he stripped off his jeans. Lightning briefly illuminated the room, and Kitty couldn't suppress a soft gasp at the beauty of him, wide-shouldered and lean-hipped, strong and tall and totally male. She had known him as a lover, but that was so many years ago, and she had never seen him, not like this. She was no longer shy, as she had been as a girl; she was a woman with the man she loved, and she studied him with unashamed enjoyment as he crossed the room to pull the curtains closed, then came back to her, silhouetted by the frequent flashes of lightning.

He was more beautiful even than she had dreamed, moving with a strength and grace that were almost feline. He was powerfully muscled, but without an ounce of surplus flesh, and the light furring of golden hair on his arms and legs and chest caught the light in a way that made Kitty's mouth suddenly dry and her breathing shallow. The bed gave beneath his weight as he joined her, and Kitty let herself roll toward the depression he created in the mattress, reaching out to twine her arms around him as he gathered her against his body.

She marveled at how they fitted together as she arched her body into the curve of his, sliding one slim leg along his, the soft hair rasping against her smooth skin, bringing a low moan from Steve's throat. She reached up to pull his head down to her, but he resisted.

"My Kitten," he whispered, looking deep into her eyes. "I love you more than anyone or anything on this earth. Can you understand that?"

"It's the way I feel about you. There's no one else for me in all the world." She turned to press a kiss into his palm, which lay against her cheek, her tongue flicking out in an intimate caress.

"Kitty, stop it!" Steve whispered. "You're driving me crazy!"

"Mmm, I know." She nuzzled his neck, and he held her away from him, his face tight with the control he was exerting.

"Kitty, you have to understand," he said in a voice

that was almost a groan. "You have to understand
that if I take you again I won't let you go; I can't let
you go! You have to know that. If I make love to you
now, there's no way I will ever let you go."

"Even if I fall in love with someone else?" she
teased, and his hands on her shoulders tightened
painfully.

"No." His voice was low and harsh. "No, not even
then. You belong to me."

Kitty peered at him in surprise, barely able to make
out his face in the darkness and unable to read his
expression. He astonished her and almost frightened
her like this; the intensity of his voice, the iron grip of
his hands on her shoulders were those of a man who
was almost desperate. She shifted her shoulders,
seeking to ease the pressure of his fingers, and his grip
relaxed fractionally.

"That's not very liberated," she said lightly, and he
growled deep in his throat.

"No, I'm not. That's how you make me feel. I never
cared enough about any woman to care if she stayed
or not, to care who she slept with, but with you . . ."
He buried his face in the black hair spread across the
pillow and she felt him shudder. "With you the
thought that any other man might touch you is almost
more than I can stand. I won't let you go again, so if
you think you might ever want to, then go now."
There was a deep note of pain in his voice, and Kitty
took his face between her hands and gazed into his
eyes.

"I will never leave you, Steve. If you try to send me
away, I'll follow you. You belong to me."

He relaxed, some of the painful tension leaving his
body, leaving behind tension of a different sort. "Not
very liberated, are you?" he teased, and Kitty smiled
into the darkness and bit his shoulder lightly.

"No," she whispered, "I'm not. And if I see you looking at another woman, I just want you to know that I'll scratch her eyes out."

"My, my," Steve laughed softly, "we are a pair of unreconstructed primitives, aren't we?"

"No, we're not. We're just in love."

"Now and forever," he whispered into her hair, and began kissing her neck, her ear, tiny tantalizing kisses that sent warmth and a sweet lassitude through Kitty. "What can I give you?" he muttered. "How can I—"

"Love me, Steve." She reached up to kiss his mouth. "Just love me."

"Oh, I will," he murmured. "Yes, I will love you."

He levered himself half-above her, propped up on one elbow and smiling down into her eyes, heavy-lidded with passion, as his free hand lightly traced the line of neck and collarbone, moving lightly over her breast, teasing the nipple into a rosy pebble before stroking down her flank and farther. He traced the outline of her navel, caressed the slight, soft swell of her stomach and then moved lower, touching and teasing until she moaned low in her throat, her hands moving over his body, creating the same need in him that was burning in her.

He seemed to delight in tormenting her, creating a fiery need and withholding fulfillment until Kitty could wait no longer. "Steve, please," she whispered, sliding one thigh over his. "Please." He answered her plea, moving his body above hers as she reached to accept him, gasping with pleasure and then burying her face in his shoulder as the world slipped away and they soared together.

Kitty nestled against Steve as they came slowly back to reality together, safe and secure in the crook of his arm, in the one place in all the world where she belonged.

"Steve?"

"Hmm?" He lightly kissed the top of her head.

"If that accident hadn't happened today . . . would you have won?"

"What do you mean, would I have won? I *did* win!" Kitty sat up abruptly, propping herself on one arm to gaze down at him in amused confusion.

"You could you win?" she laughed. "By having the ambulance drivers take you around the track and park you in Victory Lane?"

"Oh, you mean would I have won the *race?*"

"What else? And stop teasing me!"

"I'm not teasing." He pulled her back down beside him and the amusement vanished from his voice, leaving it deep, vibrant, sincere. "What I won was something far more important than the race, and it will last forever." He turned on his side to smile down into her eyes.

"Oh." It was a tiny whisper of comprehension, and his smile widened.

"I claimed my prize," he said softly, "but I want to claim it again. Any objections?"

"None at all. You are the winner, aren't you?"

"We're winners together, now and always." He bent to kiss her again.

MORE ROMANCE FOR
A SPECIAL WAY TO RELAX
$1.95 each

2 ☐ Hastings	21 ☐ Hastings	41 ☐ Halston	60 ☐ Thorne
3 ☐ Dixon	22 ☐ Howard	42 ☐ Drummond	61 ☐ Beckman
4 ☐ Vitek	23 ☐ Charles	43 ☐ Shaw	62 ☐ Bright
5 ☐ Converse	24 ☐ Dixon	44 ☐ Eden	63 ☐ Wallace
6 ☐ Douglass	25 ☐ Hardy	45 ☐ Charles	64 ☐ Converse
7 ☐ Stanford	26 ☐ Scott	46 ☐ Howard	65 ☐ Cates
8 ☐ Halston	27 ☐ Wisdom	47 ☐ Stephens	66 ☐ Mikels
9 ☐ Baxter	28 ☐ Ripy	48 ☐ Ferrell	67 ☐ Shaw
10 ☐ Thiels	29 ☐ Bergen	49 ☐ Hastings	68 ☐ Sinclair
11 ☐ Thornton	30 ☐ Stephens	50 ☐ Browning	69 ☐ Dalton
12 ☐ Sinclair	31 ☐ Baxter	51 ☐ Trent	70 ☐ Clare
13 ☐ Beckman	32 ☐ Douglass	52 ☐ Sinclair	71 ☐ Skillern
14 ☐ Keene	33 ☐ Palmer	53 ☐ Thomas	72 ☐ Belmont
15 ☐ James	35 ☐ James	54 ☐ Hohl	73 ☐ Taylor
16 ☐ Carr	36 ☐ Dailey	55 ☐ Stanford	74 ☐ Wisdom
17 ☐ John	37 ☐ Stanford	56 ☐ Wallace	75 ☐ John
18 ☐ Hamilton	38 ☐ John	57 ☐ Thornton	76 ☐ Ripy
19 ☐ Shaw	39 ☐ Milan	58 ☐ Douglass	77 ☐ Bergen
20 ☐ Musgrave	40 ☐ Converse	59 ☐ Roberts	78 ☐ Gladstone

MORE ROMANCE FOR
A SPECIAL WAY TO RELAX

$2.25 each

79 ☐ Hastings	84 ☐ Stephens	89 ☐ Meriwether	94 ☐ Barrie
80 ☐ Douglass	85 ☐ Beckman	90 ☐ Justin	95 ☐ Doyle
81 ☐ Thornton	86 ☐ Halston	91 ☐ Stanford	96 ☐ Baxter
82 ☐ McKenna	87 ☐ Dixon	92 ☐ Hamilton	
83 ☐ Major	88 ☐ Saxon	93 ☐ Lacey	

*LOOK FOR WILD IS THE HEART BY ABRA TAYLOR
AVAILABLE IN JULY AND
THUNDER AT DAWN BY PATTI BECKMAN IN
AUGUST.*

SILHOUETTE SPECIAL EDITION, Department SE/2
1230 Avenue of the Americas
New York, NY 10020

Please send me the books I have checked above. I am enclosing $_____
(please add 50¢ to cover postage and handling. NYS and NYC residents
please add appropriate sales tax). Send check or money order—no cash or
C.O.D.'s please. Allow six weeks for delivery.

NAME _____

ADDRESS _____

CITY _____ STATE/ZIP _____

Silhouette Special Edition

Coming Next Month

Way Of The Willow by Linda Shaw

For Jennifer Howard there had been one trouble too many and now Everett Black, her childhood sweetheart, was back. Only this time she had no intention of letting their love slip away.

Touch Of Greatness by Ann Hurley

Two years had passed since the death of Torey's husband. Two years, and she was ready to love again, as Andrea Scarpi intended to prove to her with a gentleness that would heal all her wounds.

Quest For Paradise by Diana Dixon

Carol knew she could help Simon Forbes' young daughter, but who would help her? Simon's hands could turn inanimate clay into sculptures of stunning eroticism and his touch was no less potent on Carol's own silken skin.

Reflections by Nora Roberts

Lindsay Dunne thought she would have to give up her dance career to keep Seth Bannion—unless she could make him realize that her love for dancing would never compete with her love for him.

Golden Impulse by Fran Bergen

Clover didn't want to get involved with a man who always put his life on the line. But she knew a life without ranger Keith Sheridan wasn't worth living.

Dreams Lost, Dreams Found by Pamela Wallace

It was as though Brynne was reliving a Scottish legend with Ross Fleming—descendant of the Lord of the Isles. Only this time the legend would have a happy ending.

If you enjoyed this book...

...you will enjoy a Special Edition Book Club membership even more.

It will bring you each new title, as soon as it is published every month, delivered right to your door.

15-Day Free Trial Offer

We will send you 6 new Silhouette Special Editions to keep for 15 days absolutely free! If you decide not to keep them, send them back to us, you pay nothing. But if you enjoy them as much as we think you will, keep them and pay the invoice enclosed with your trial shipment. You will then automatically become a member of the Special Edition Book Club and receive 6 more romances every month. There is no minimum number of books to buy and you can cancel at any time.

Get the
Silhouette Books
Newsletter
every month
for a year.